Pebbles on the Beach

An Anthology

by

Bexhill Writers Group

Pebbles on the Beach

An Anthology

by

Bexhill Writers Group

The Bexhill Writers' Group

Bexhill-on-Sea

East Sussex

United Kingdom

Lineage Independent Publishing
Marriottsville, MD
https://lineage-indypub.com

ISBN (paperback): 9781958418260
First Printed in the United Kingdom

Publisher: Lineage Independent Publishing, Marriottsville, MD, USA

Maryland Sales and Use Tax Entity: Lineage Independent Publishing, Marriottsville, MD 21104

Contact: hurdmp@lineage-indypub.com

Website: https://lineage-indypub.com

To aspiring writers everywhere

Contents

Foreword

When Patricia Donoghue (a.k.a. author G. B. Carmichael) first approached me about the possibility of publishing this anthology, I was unsure of what might be in store for me as an editor and publisher. A few weeks later, I had a manuscript in hand, setting it on the back burner as I worked on getting two other novels out the door and into publication – with a promise that this manuscript would be ready for release in time for Christmas ordering.

When I did finally get around to "Pebbles on the Beach," I was absorbed into the creativity of the contributing authors. Everything from mystery to poetry, from unrequited love to unfathomable loss appear in these pages and I am honored (honoured, in the King's English) to be a part of it.

I do know that putting a compilation together such as this takes the patience of Job and the persistence of a seagull. In the end, though, the final product was worth the effort. I hope you will enjoy reading the stories and poetry herein.

Michael Paul Hurd
Author/Editor/Publisher
Lineage Independent Publishing

Barbara Beckett

27 Oct 1930 – 27 Feb 2019

Author Barbara Beckett onstage as a young actress
From her family's archives; used with permission

Barbara Beckett's Short Story, "Where the Heart Is" has been included posthumously. Sadly, Barbara passed away before this anthology could be compiled. Barbara was 88 years old.

Where the Heart Is

"Am I doing the right thing, Mum?" Anna fingered the rim of her empty teacup, her eyes seeking reassurance from the woman busy at the kitchen table.

Meg Thomas covered the bowl of dough and set it aside to prove before turning to look at her daughter's anxious face.

"You were never one to act in haste, Anna." Meg pushed a whisp of hair from her daughter's cheek, leaving a tell-tale smudge of flour. "You'll have given it careful thought."

"Besides," a brief sadness crossed her plump features, "now you know who she is, you won't rest till you've met her."

Anna had always known she was adopted. As a child it had never bothered her.

"I was chosen," she would tell her young school friends proudly, basking in their wide-eyed questioning. To the children at Cranleath Infants, this information raised her beyond the elite band of those selected for the Christmas Nativity play!

She had been a sunny child, surrounded as she was by the love of Meg and Brian Thomas, who had taken her into their home and their hearts when she was only four months old.

But as the years had passed and womanhood approached, she found herself wondering more and more about her background. Who were her real parents? Why had they rejected her? Resentment grew, like a storm cloud on the horizon, slowly gathering force, impossible to ignore.

She kept these thoughts to herself, knowing with a sensitive girl's intuition that they had the power to hurt Meg and Brian.

Anna owed them everything. She could only guess at the sacrifices they had made in order that she could have the clothes and books she needed; the replacement watch when she'd come home sobbing to tell them her own had been accidentally smashed beyond repair.

When the school had said Anna should go to university, Meg had willingly taken on extra work in the evenings, making pies and pate' for the local delicatessen.

It was not until she met and fell in love with Ken that Anna knew she had to discover the truth about herself. The old saying, 'What's bred in the bone...' kept nagging at her.

She needed to know; for the sake of the children she might one day have.

"Leave well alone, Anna," Ken warned her gently when she told him of her intentions.

He cupped her face in his hands, looking deeply into her troubled eyes. "You'll be a perfect mother and Brian and Meg will spoil them rotten. What more could any child want?"

They laughed together and went on to talk of their wedding plans, but secretly Anna had made up her mind.

As a journalist, much of her time was spent in ferreting out the truth. Once she had come to her decision, the rest was easy.

Claire Honeyfield! She still couldn't believe it. Her mother was Claire Honeyfield, the well-known writer of children's books.

How could anyone with such an insight into a child's mind have abandoned her own daughter?

Claire Honeyfield wrote books that got inside a child's imagination and sent it spinning off into a world of magic and make-believe. As a child, Anna had a collection of them on a shelf by her bedside. Now they were stored in the back of a cupboard, ready to be passed on to the next generation.

It had been Claire Honeyfield's work that had inspired Anna to follow a writing career. Too restless to opt for an author's solitary life, she had turned to journalism and was already establishing a reputation for herself.

Now it provided her with the perfect cover to meet her mother. What could be more natural than for a young journalist to seek an interview with one of the country's best-loved children's authors.

No-one would suspect the real reason behind the meeting – least of all, Claire Honeyfield!

A pleasant-voiced young woman took Anna's telephone call: "Yes, I'm sure Miss Honeyfield would be happy to give you an interview…" "Would Thursday, 4 p.m. be convenient?" "No, I'm sorry Miss Honeyfield couldn't see you any earlier; she works until lunch time, then takes a rest before further engagements."

Anna's mouth was dry and she kept seeing the look of loving concern on Brian and Meg's faces. Ken was right: she should have left well alone.

But she had come this far – she was determined to see it through. The rambling house stood on the side of a hill – the house that should have been her home. Its windows looked out over rolling countryside and along one side a terrace ran the full width of the house, its paving crammed with tubs ablaze with busy-lizzies and geraniums.

Their vibrant colours were in sharp contrast to the woman reclining on a chaise- longue. In a full-length white voile dress that matched the pallor of her skin, she lay like a lovely alabaster statue.

Was this the woman she had waited all her life to meet: a woman who transferred her responsibilities to someone else and now lived a carefree existence surrounded by luxury?

Anna was struck by a sense of injustice as she thought of Meg in her made-over clothes, her hands red and coarsened from work.

The woman turned and saw her standing uncertainly at the lynch-gate.

"You must be Anna Thomas," she called. Her voice was deep and musical. "So kind of you to come all this way." She beckoned Anna forward. It was too late for escape.

Slowly Anna mounted the steps to the terrace. *"Would there be a moment of mutual recognition: some pre-natal bond that would make itself instantly known to them?"*

Anna studied the face intently, searching for features that would confirm what she already knew. Silver-blonde hair was drawn back severely in a thick chignon that seemed too heavy for the slender neck.

Only the eyes, wide and grey, were identical to those Anna saw in her mirror each day. Otherwise, it was the face of a stranger. She was conscious of a disappointment as powerful as it was unexpected.

"It was good of you to see me," she managed, offering her hand.

Claire Honeyfield's touch was as light as a butterfly's, her hand almost translucent in its fragility.

"Pull up a chair, my dear. Theresa will bring us tea in a little while."

Anna settled herself in one of the white wrought iron chairs, her hands trembling as she took out her recorder and note-pad and laid them on the side table. The tools of her trade looked suddenly pretentious and alien.

Claire must have sensed her nervousness. With an easy charm she enquired after Anna's journey.

"You must do a lot of travelling," she added. "Far more exciting than an author's life,"

There was a hint of regret behind the accompanying smile. Anna began to detect an underlying sadness, a vulnerability that was at odds with her first impression.

She took a deep breath. "What made you choose to write for children, Miss Honeyfield?"

"Claire. Please call me Claire," she said with a disarming smile.

"I suppose - not having children of my own and loving them as I do, I felt that writing for them was the next best thing."

Anger rose up, almost choking Anna. "But I though – that that is – I understood you have a child."

The familiar eyes regarded her coldly, then a reluctant smile broke through the ice.

"I see you do your research, Anna. May I call you Anna?"

Dumbly, Anna nodded.

"There was a child once… She'd be about your age now."

Anna's heart stumbled.

"But that's a long story." Claire made a tiny dismissive gesture with her hand.

"Oh, no. Please." Anna stopped abruptly. The other woman was staring at her curiously.

For a long time, she sat, immersed in thought. Then, as if making up her mind, she gave a nod of her head, her eyes taking on a shadowy expression as they gazed off into the distance.

When she spoke, it was in a voice so low that Anna had to lean forward in order to hear.

"I'd been married six months. Rory worked on an oil rig. There was an accident." She paused, her eyelids fluttering with the pain of recollection. "I became a widow the same day I discovered I was pregnant."

Anna sat, hardly daring to breathe, afraid that the slightest movement would distract her... *mother.*

"That's when I started to write." Absently, Claire's fingers hovered above the flowers, dipping down to touch the blooms as she spoke of her escape into a child's world where death and heartbreak had no place.

"When my daughter was born, I began to come alive again. I had a future to plan for."

Her marble face softened as she talked about her joy at being a mother. For two months life had taken on a new meaning.

"Then suddenly... I became ill. Days of pain and exhaustion. No one could tell me what was wrong. I spent what little money I had on looking for a cure, but..."

Her voice trailed off helplessly and she turned anguished eyes on Anna. "But... what future could I offer a child?"

The question hung between them like a curtain of silence. A silence in which Anna's store of resentment and hurt dissolved into compassion. How she hated herself for coming and stirring up so much suffering.

But she could make amends! Impulsively she reached out to take her mother's hand, when footsteps sounded on the terrace, accompanied by the pleasant clink of china.

A young woman had come out of the house carrying a large silver salver tray laden with tea things. Anna thought she had never seen anyone so beautiful.

"This is Theresa," Claire said warmly.

There was an aura of serenity about the newcomer that acted as a soothing balm. Fascinated, Anna saw the haunted look fade from her mother's face. She became youthful and animated.

Theresa set down the tray. "Claire has been so looking forward to your visit, Miss Thomas." Anna recognised the voice on the phone.

She placed strong arms around the older woman, lifting her easily into an upright position.

Anna was shocked to see how helpless her mother was. The long dress had fallen aside to reveal a glimpse of legs that were thin and wasted.

"Theresa spoils me," Claire patted the girl's hand affectionately and added with a mischievous sparkle, "she also bullies me!"

Theresa gave her an unruffled smile and placed a cushion at her head. In all her actions Anna recognised a deep and comforting love – so like the love that bound herself to Meg.

For the first time Anna realised how much her secret had the power to change all their lives.

It was late when she arrived home. The smell of freshly baked bread lingered in the air and a jug of her favourite iced lemon had been placed in the fridge.

From the window she could see Meg and Brian in the gloaming. They were sitting beneath the old oak tree, each of them lost in thought, waiting for her return.

A deep sense of peace settled on Anna. Her secret was safe; there was no place for her in Claire and Theresa's world. And what did her family tree matter, anyway?

Her roots were here, in the home of her childhood. With the parents she loved.

Vicky Armstrong

Image credit: prettysleepy1
Pixabay

The Greater Goode

Sally reached for the last fairy cake. I kicked her under the table.

"It's for the Greater Goode," she whispered.

"You're only greater by two minutes," I hissed back.

"Stop arguing, you pair," said our mother wearily, "I'll cut it in half."

To a normal person, the resulting two pieces were more or less the same size – but we weren't normal, we were siblings at war. To our hyper-sharp eyes, one piece was definitely bigger than the other. Sally grabbed it, mouthing, "Greater Goode." I tried stabbing her with a teaspoon.

"That's enough," exploded Mother. "Tea's over. Go upstairs and do your homework." There was always homework to do in our house. It was the 1950s and we both went to the local girls' grammar.

At school, we were usually referred to as 'Sally Goode and her sister.' It was only occasionally that we were called 'the Goode twins.' Our twin-ship did not automatically come to people's minds because, although technically identical, we did not look completely alike. I was a smaller, paler version of Sally. She was tall, Junoesque and had a ravishingly pretty face. As if that wasn't enough, she also had sapphire-blue eyes and hair the colour of ripe corn. I was shorter by some inches; my eyes were a washed-out blue and the best thing that you could say about my hair was "fairish." As the Chemistry teacher said, "At least you got the brains."

Actually, we were both pretty bright. We passed the eleven plus a year ahead of normal, but while I found my pleasure in mathematics and the sciences, Sally excelled at sport. Over the years, she represented the school at everything on the physical curriculum: tennis, athletics, lacrosse, netball, swimming. You name it, she did it – superlatively well.

As for personality, suffice to say that when teams were picked, Sally was the first to be selected while I was always left till last, along with the girl in the wheelchair. This was even true when it was Sally picking the team. "I didn't want it to look as if I was favouring you," she would explain. Needless to say, she was appointed Head Girl as soon as we got into the sixth form.

Did I mind always being overshadowed? Of course, I did, but there was nothing I could do about it – it was just a fact of my life. However, there was one occasion when I reacted badly. I received a letter from Cambridge University to say I had been awarded an unconditional place to read Theoretical Physics. Mum and Dad had been very pleased. The next day I showed the letter to the Headmistress.

"Very good," she said, "I will announce it in Assembly tomorrow." At last, I was going to get the credit I deserved. People would applaud me and not Sally.

The next morning, for some weird reason (did the gods hate me that much?) the post arrived before we left for school. Usually, it came at about nine o'clock, well over an hour after our departure for the bus. There was a letter for Sally. It was from the British Olympic Committee inviting her to be part of the national squad to go to the forthcoming games. There was a second morning of rejoicing in the Goode household.

At the end of Assembly, the headmistress cleared her throat. "Girls, we have some very good news to celebrate."

I braced myself for my moment of glory.

"We have just learned that Sally Goode will be competing at the next Olympic Games."

The clapping and cheering were tumultuous. I turned to Sally, and she mouthed, "The Greater Goode." When we got home that afternoon, I put all her Cliff Richard records in the bath and turned on the tap.

After we left school, we went our separate ways. Cambridge was everything I hoped for. The work was engrossing, and I was valued for my mind to such an extent that I was asked to stay on after I had gotten my degree. Sally went into teaching – Physical Education, obviously – and was very good at it, again obviously.

We saw each other at family gatherings, Christmas, Easter and so on, when everyone wanted to know all about her life. It seemed they never knew what to say to me.

"Still a student, then?" was typical of the sort of question that came my way.

"Actually, I'm now a research fellow," I would reply – but by the time I finished speaking people had turned their attention back to Sally and her views on women's sport.

I made the mistake of taking my first boyfriend home with me for Christmas. After less than a day he was no longer mine. Instead, he was Sally's –and he wasn't her first by a long stretch.

I was awarded the Nobel Prize in Physics at an absurdly young age for my work on infinity quarks and the modular hypothesis. On the day the news was going to be made public, Sally once again stole my thunder. She managed to get herself killed. Typically, she didn't die in something ordinary like a road traffic accident, or because of an unintentional drug overdose, or as the result of a mugging gone wrong. No, she died saving children.

She had been coaching fifteen eleven-year-old girls in the finer points of throwing the javelin when a crazed protester had run onto the pitch waving a handgun and screaming that he wanted to save the world from nuclear oblivion (this was the 1960s). With great presence of mind, Sally told the girls to stand in a line behind her, so as to present less of a target. She then started to reason with the gun-brandishing madman.

Smiling at him and using a friendly, unexcited tone, she explained that injuring any of the children would be a pointless thing to do – it would detract from the very valuable message he was trying to propagate.

It almost worked. The man lowered the gun and appeared to be listening – but then the police arrived and arrived with a vengeance. Loud hailers, dogs, armed officers, black Marias, police vans – they all streamed onto the sports field, churning it up terribly.

"Put the gun DOWN!" bellowed someone through a loudhailer.

The would-be nuclear disarmer looked at my sister and said, "It's your fault." He raised the gun and fired at her before turning it on himself.

The resultant public enquiry into the conduct of the police decided that a new code for negotiating with terrorists and gunmen should be introduced – naturally, it would be known as the Sally Goode Code. It goes without saying that any mention of my Nobel Prize completely disappeared from the news bulletins.

Rather against my will, I accompanied my parents to Buckingham Palace for the award of Sally's posthumous George Cross. As I watched the Queen talk to my parents, I realised my sister would always be the greater Goode. There was no way in which I could ever beat her.

It also occurred to me that I had lost something valuable. Sally had been the spur that had driven me forward, the thorn in my side which had forced me to excel. She had been the piece of grit in my oyster, causing me to produce my pearls of brilliance. Furthermore, it was highly likely that without the stimulus of our sibling rivalry, I might never again achieve anything worthwhile. I promptly fainted.

When I recovered consciousness and looked around the gold and white room, I found everyone was bending over me – my parents, the equerries in their braided uniforms and even the Prince of Wales. For the first time in my life, I was the centre of attention.

I did not like it.

Image credit: Marilynreid,
Pixabay

The Painting

Piers Beauport-Bannatyne squinted at his laptop. His elegant sitting room was filled with afternoon sun, so it was hard to make out exactly what he was seeing. He changed the angle of the screen, cleaned his glasses, drew the curtains, but nothing helped. He sighed – some of the smaller auction houses really did skimp when photographing and uploading their catalogues. He realised he would have to go and look at lot 191 ("assorted 19th Century prints and drawings") for himself, something he hated doing. Such was his standing in the local antiques community that any interest on his part invariably alerted the competition to a possible find – and a subsequent hike in the price needed to secure it.

He looked at the calendar and sucked his teeth. Thanks to his long weekend in Florence overrunning, he had missed the public viewing day, which meant he would have to attend the actual sale – something else he hated doing. He much preferred the anonymity of online bidding.

Piers arrived early on the day of the sale. To avoid recognition, he was wearing a tweed coat with collar turned up and a cap with peak pulled down. Prior to leaving the house he had taken an envelope containing a sum of money from his wall safe and secreted it in one of the coat's many inner pockets. Experience had taught him that cash helped to oil the wheels of commerce and also avoided many of the government's more annoying taxes.

As he picked up a catalogue, he heard Frank, the auction house porter and general factotum, say, ""'Allo, Mr. Bannatyne."

"Damn," he thought, *"I've been spotted. Perhaps I should have worn the false moustache as well."*

"Beauport-Bannatyne," Piers automatically corrected.

"Interested in anything in particular?" continued Frank, ignoring the correction.

"Oh, err, Lot 161." He seized the numbers at random.

"Really? I wouldn't have thought assorted crockery was your thing at all, Mr B, but it's over there under lot fifty-three, the stuffed bear."

For a mere menial, thought Piers, grinding his teeth, Brian had a lot to say for himself. He made his way across to a decidedly moth-eaten grizzly rearing up on its hind legs. Conscious that Frank might be watching, he made a show of peering intently into the cardboard box that stood at the animal's feet. Lot 161 was pure tat: mismatched cups and saucers, chipped milk jugs, ugly ashtrays, and umpteen coronation mugs. Not for the first time, he felt depressed by the bad taste of ordinary people.

As soon as he was satisfied that Frank had moved away, he began to search among the other myriad objects that were due to go under the auctioneer's hammer: bicycles, a piano, assorted linens, vinyl records, old suitcases, glassware... and much more.

And then he saw it: Lot 191!

His heart thumping with excitement, he knelt down and began to riffle through the jumble of prints stuffed higgledy-piggledy into an old cardboard box.

Ignoring the many monochrome lithographs of dogs and shepherds and Biblical scenes, he at last found what he was looking for and what had been partially visible in the online catalogue: a small painting of a girl's face. This was no print; the colours were too vibrant and the expression of curiosity on the girl's face had been executed by a masterly hand. "

"Could it possibly be a Renoir? An early one, obviously, but – "

A male voice interrupted the moment. "A cap and a long coat, Piers? Are you auditioning for a part in Peaky Blinders?"

Piers whirled around. Blast! It was Max Bax, owner of Bax Collectibles and someone he loathed, but what on earth did the man mean?

"You don't know what I mean, do you, Piers? Popular culture isn't your thing, is it?"

"I ... err."

"It's where the money is these days, old bean – a ticket to a Beatles concert will get you more than a Ming vase."

"I ... err."

"Found anything interesting in that box?"

Piers came to his senses. Max Bax might be a Philistine, but he had an annoyingly good eye. He hastily stuffed the picture back into the box and stood up.

"No, just the usual rubbish."

"One man's rubbish is another man's collectible, old man."

"Yes, ha ha, very funny. Must get on. The sale starts any minute now and there's still a lot to look at."

As unobtrusively as possible, he gave the box a kick to slide it out of sight under a G-plan sideboard. He then turned away and walked, as casually as possible, down the length of the saleroom. Every now and then he stopped and pretended to be interested in something, all the time longing to go back and have another look at the painting. However, he was conscious that Max Bax was watching his every move. What's more, he knew that if he actually put in a bid for 191, Bax would bid, too – out of sheer devilment – and get his friends to do the same. He stared round the room. It had filled up and the auctioneer was making his way to his rostrum. The sale would start any minute. What should he do?

He felt a tap on his shoulder and heard a voice say, "Gosh, Piers. How smart you look in that coat."

He turned around to face an angular young woman in possibly her mid-thirties. She was wearing a strange kaftan-like garment in a range of autumnal colours and her long red hair fell about her shoulders.

His first thought was, *"I wish I had worn that moustache."* His second thought was, *"Oh, no. It's Araminta Trauttmansdorff."* His third thought was that perhaps here was the solution to his problem – as long as she had forgiven him for leaving her to pay the bill when he had taken her out for dinner last year. But, honestly, she had continually muddled Monet with Manet, so what was a chap supposed to do?

"Oh, err, hello, Araminta," he said, hesitantly. He was relieved to be rewarded with a beaming smile. She seemed to have forgiven him – perhaps she didn't even remember the incident.

"Actually, Araminta," he continued, "I wonder if you could do me a favour."

"Of course, Piers, what is it?"

"I want to bid for lot 191, but I have to get away smartish. My mother has been taken ill."

"Again? That was what you said when we went out for supper last year."

She obviously hadn't forgotten.

"It comes and goes, you know …"

"The poor thing, yes, of course, I'll bid for you. What number did you say?"

"Here, I'll write it down." He quickly scrawled the number on a scrap of paper.

"Thank you, I'll do my best not to let you down," said Araminta, "But do you have some money? I'm running a little short this month."

"Oh, err, yes, silly me," replied Piers. He burrowed into his coat and brought out the envelope. "Here, use this. Now I really must be off."

Back at home, Piers poured himself an extra-large gin and tonic. He wondered if he had done the right thing and quickly decided that he had. Araminta might be annoying, and she might get her impressionists mixed up, but she was pathetically eager to please, and especially eager to please him.

He felt a little unnerved when he opened his wall safe to put away his wallet and realised that in the rush that morning, he had picked up the envelope containing £3,000, rather than the one containing £300, but he comforted himself with the thought that Araminta was too honest to take advantage of his lapse. She would do the right thing.

At six o'clock, the doorbell rang. It was Araminta. She had the demeanour of a puppy desperate for approval. He stared at the cardboard box in her arms.

"That's lot 161 …"

"Yes, I couldn't remember what you said, and I couldn't work out which way up the figures were on your bit of paper, so I asked Frank. He said you were definitely interested in 161. Here, can you take it? It's a bit heavy."

"Oh, err, of course. What, what did you pay?"

"Well, I was quite surprised by how much was in the envelope and decided you must really want lot 161 – there must be something fantastically good included in it that no one else had noticed."

"What did you pay, Araminta?"

"Well, everything – I didn't want you to lose it."

He stared down into the box with its mismatched cups and saucers, chipped milk jugs, ugly ashtrays, and coronation mugs. He looked up.

"Did you, by any chance, see if anyone bid for lot 191?"

"Lot 191? The prints? Oh, I think Max got those, for a song. You know Max."

Piers closed his eyes and hoped it was all a bad dream.

Image Credit: OpenClipart-Vectors
Pixabay

The Phone Call

Muriel lay on the sitting room floor, surrounded by books. She knew she had broken something but didn't know what. If she stayed still, it was just about all right, but if she tried to move, the pain was excruciating. What made matters worse was that it was all her own fault. She really should not have tried to shift the bookcase without emptying it first. Actually, she should not have tried to shift the thing at all.

It had all started yesterday on her 75th birthday. It being a Sunday, her son, Ian, had turned up 'mob handed' as he put it. This only meant him, his wife, Araminta and the 13-year-old twins, Cordelia, and Perry, but he tended to talk like that these days – Muriel blamed Araminta.

Ian and his son were carrying a large and obviously very heavy cardboard box, which, with exclamations of relief, they put down in the middle of the sitting floor.

"What is it?" asked Muriel.

"Open it and see," said Ian.

This she did with some difficulty, having to get the large kitchen scissors to prise apart the industrial strength staples. When the box was finally open, she saw that it contained a television – a really big television.

"Happy birthday!" everyone shouted.

'But I've already got a television," said Muriel.

"Yes, but it's so old, I'm surprised it even gets colour," said Ian. "This, on the other hand, is a state of the art, smart television.'

"Oh."

"You'll be able to access all the streaming platforms – BBC I-Player, ITV Hub, Disney, Netflix – you name it you'll be able to get it."

It was all 'double Dutch' to Muriel.

"I don't actually watch much TV and I'm quite happy with my old one." She saw Araminta raise her eyebrows and realised she must sound ungrateful. "But thank you, it's a very nice thought. Perhaps you'll show me how it works?"

It took Ian and Perry the next three hours to set the thing up. Araminta rang and cancelled the lunch reservation at the *Pig in Clover* and Muriel said she'd better make some sandwiches: "Would salmon be alright with everyone?". Cordelia said that she was now a vegan and asked for a banana sandwich instead.

"Of course," Muriel answered.

"And I've gone gluten-free," said Araminta. "Do you have any rice cakes?"

"Erm, no, but the Co-op on the corner is open on a Sunday. They might have something like that."

"If you're going to a shop, Mum, could you get me some tofu," said Cordelia.

"And can I have some burgers?" asked Perry.

In the end the shopping list was so long that Cordelia volunteered to go with her mother, and Muriel felt she should pay – handing over a couple of twenty pound notes.

At last, the new television was up and running and Ian put the old one up in the loft. They then ate their improvised lunch watching Sir David Attenborough.

"Gross," Cordelia groaned as a zebra was mauled to death by a lion.

"Cool!"' said Perry.

Muriel produced the Victoria sponge she had baked for tea. Of course, Araminta and Cordelia weren't able to have any – they had to make do with rice cakes spread with Jam, which neither seemed to enjoy much. Ian and Perry, on the other hand, made short work of the cake.

'Why can't we have things like this at home?' asked Perry.

'Because I have too much to do,' said Araminta.

And then it was time for them all to go.

'Thank you very much for my lovely new television set,' said Muriel as everyone stood in the hall putting on their coats.

"I'm glad you liked it," said Ian. "We'll bring you a smart phone next."

"That's very nice of you, but please don't," said Muriel. "I'm really quite happy with my, err, landline." She congratulated herself on using such a modern word.

Ian said, "Mum, you're such a Luddite."

Cordelia, who had been feeling in her pockets, suddenly let out a wail.

"My phone! I've lost my phone!"

There was a mad scramble back into the sitting room, but no one could see it.

"I'll try ringing it on mine," said Perry.

"That's no good," sobbed his sister, "I turned it off because it was getting low."

"Dork," said Perry.

"I was going to recharge it in the car."

"Double dork."

"Be quiet, you two," Araminta commanded.

"Perhaps you left it in the Co-op," suggested Muriel.

"That's a good idea, Mum," said Ian, "we'll call in there on the way."

Alone once more, Muriel set about tidying up. When this was done, she sat down and turned on the vast new television. To be fair, the picture was much brighter and more distinct, but for some reason, she could only get BBC4. Try as she might she just couldn't change the channel; the new remote was just too complicated. She sat through a programme on modern art and then one on the Hapsburg Empire before giving up and going to bed. Perhaps she would be able to understand it better after a good night's sleep.

Of course, she couldn't, and to make matters worse, the next day she discovered that BBC4 doesn't start until seven in the evening. She felt thoroughly depressed and useless. To cheer herself up she decided to rearrange the furniture. Her old TV had fitted very neatly into the space between the

bookcase and the fireplace, the new one swamped it –
completely spoiling the dimensions of the room.

She started with the bookcase – pulling it and pushing it,
to no avail. She put her back against the side, braced her
legs and heaved. All at once, she felt it start to topple
forward, she turned, too quickly, caught her heel and fell
heavily, books cascading around her. Luckily for her, the
bookcase remained upright, although it teetered madly for
a good few moments.

After discovering she was unable to move, she wondered
what on earth she was going to do. There was no way she
could get to the phone in the hall and she wasn't due any
visitors that day. She really was a stupid old woman to have
ended up into such a situation.

From down on the floor, she was able to see under the
settee, and she noticed something small and flat – Cordelia's
phone! It must have been knocked there by all the
cardboard packaging that had strewn the floor.

After a lot of painful stretching and fumbling, she
managed to retrieve it and stared at it in despair. The screen
was blank. How on earth did it work? She felt hopelessness
wash over her: she really was a stupid old Luddite. She felt
like crying, but something stopped her. It might have been

pride or it might have been anger. Whatever it was, she told herself to stop snivelling and think.

How did Cordelia switch it on? She racked her brains. *Didn't the child press something at the side?* She ran her fingers up and down the plastic casing, pressing anything that protruded. At first nothing happened, but then suddenly and miraculously, the screen lit up and she found herself looking at a picture of Moggins, Cordelia's cat, which was all very well, but it was a phone, so where were the numbers? She tried stabbing at the screen. Nothing happened. Just as she was about to give up, she spotted a tiny picture of a telephone down at the bottom. She pressed it and – joy of joys – numbers appeared. Hardly daring to hope, she pressed 999 and held the phone to her ear. Within just a few seconds, a nice woman was asking her which emergency service she wanted, and then a nice man asked her what the trouble was. She explained and he said an ambulance would be with her in two shakes of a lamb's tail. Was there any way they could get into the house? She told him there was a spare key under the fishing gnome.

She lay back and prepared herself for the wait. Although still in great pain, she was jubilant. With that one phone call she felt that alone and unaided, she had dragged herself into the 21st Century. She was no longer a complete Luddite.

Image credit: jillWellington
Pixabay

In the Garden
© 2023 Vicky Armstrong

Marjorie knew that the other members of the art group laughed at her – and not always behind her back. They laughed at her for the flowered pinafore she wore to protect her twin set and tweed skirt from paint splatter. Also, for her blue-rinsed hair, and because she was so much older than the rest of them. But, above all, they laughed at her because of the sort of things she painted.

"Honestly, Marjorie, copying a postcard of a thatched cottage!" exclaimed Alun Oxenburg, barely disguised scorn in his voice. He turned away, the stud in his nose catching the light.

"Another kitten, Marjorie? Really?" queried Ellie Faversham, before she too turned away, her tie-dyed muslin smock billowing around her.

Nevertheless, in spite of everything, Marjorie persisted with the group for one good reason – it helped fill the time.

She had worked for nearly fifty years for a firm of local solicitors, having gone there straight from school. However, eighteen months previously, when she turned sixty-five, her employers called time on her career as a legal secretary. The senior partner said it was for her own good, but Marjorie knew it was because they wanted to go digital.

She had never married and her one sibling, an older brother, had died some years back. Consequently, she was at a complete loss as to how to fill the gap left by not going to the office each day. Pets weren't allowed in her block of flats, so getting a dog or cat was out of the question. Working in a charity shop didn't appeal, nor did joining the WI – after all, what did she know about jam-making?

Then one morning after several weeks of dithering, she noticed a poster on the community notice board in the library. It invited anyone interested in joining a local art group to "come and have a go." She suddenly recalled the pleasure that painting and drawing had given her at school. She even remembered tentatively suggesting to her parents that they let her go on to art college, but Mum and Dad had been simple folk. To them, the idea of anyone, let alone a girl, making a living from drawing pictures was completely alien.

"No," said her mother, "You need a proper job. You might not get married – you don't really have the looks."

Dad had patted her hand, "Come and help me prick out the sweet peas, lass." Gardening was his passion, and it did not occur to him that a teenage girl, even a moderately plain one, would not feel the same way. But that was all a long time ago.

For Marjorie, attending the art group soon became more than just a time-filling activity. She began to really enjoy it. She realised she was no great shakes as an artist, but that didn't matter – the process of trying to put stuff down on canvas or paper proved to be completely satisfying. And if the Aluns and Ellies of this world thought her work was rubbish, so what?

However, this pleasant state of affairs did not last for long; a new member joined the group: Selene Santamaria-Bradshaw.

"Selena?" queried Marjorie.

"No, Selene – my mother named me after the Goddess of the Moon," explained the newcomer. She was tall and thin and had a curtain of ash-blond hair hanging down her back. To Marjorie, she did indeed look a bit moon-ish.

Selene was ambitious for the group and for herself. She certainly talked the talk, using lots of words ending in -ism: futurism, deconstructionism, recessionism, neo-cubism. She said "zeitgeist" a lot, too. Marjorie wondered if she really understood what they all meant, but most of the other members appeared to be impressed by the flood of erudition. As a result, when the role of President became vacant, Selene promptly put herself forward and was unanimously elected. Marjorie thought of abstaining, but as it was a "show of hands" vote, her nerve failed her.

Selene's first act in the role was to scrap the group's annual art show, a rather low-key affair held in the church hall. Instead, she announced that they would have a *Concours d'excellence*.

"Cool," said Alun.

"Fantastic!" exclaimed Ellie.

"What does that mean?" asked Marjorie.

Selene sighed.

"It means that I will arrange for our work to be judged by a professional. I will also be hiring a venue worthy of the group, and I will be inviting the London press."

"Will we still be able to sell our pictures?" asked someone from the back.

"Of course, but I must warn you that I want us to appear both progressive and creative. I will only allow the very best examples of our output to be displayed. I'm afraid there won't be room for kittens and thatched cottages."

At the next meeting she announced that she had booked the Grand Ballroom at the Excelsior Hotel for the *concours* and that a lesser-known young British Artist had agreed to act as judge. The Treasurer sucked his teeth and said it all sounded rather expensive – they weren't made of money. Selene told him that it would put the group on the map and that new members would flood in – worthwhile members. Then she added, "Marjorie, you don't have to worry about submitting anything." Her meaning was condescendingly obvious.

Back at home that night, Marjorie felt sad. Perhaps it was time for her to leave the group – her style obviously didn't suit Selene, but she honestly didn't think she could change it. And anyway, what on earth could she paint that would be considered suitable? She went into the kitchen to make her bedtime cup of cocoa. When she came back, she was surprised to see that the small framed photo of her father that usually stood on the top shelf of the bookcase was now lying on the carpet. How had that happened? Had there been a gust of wind or had she slammed a door? She bent down and picked it up.

She took the photo years ago with her first camera, a Brownie 127. She had crept up on her father unobserved, so it was completely unposed. He was in the garden digging and looking totally happy. Everyone had liked it. She weighed it in her hands, an idea forming in her mind, but could she do it justice? Well, she ought to at least try. Cocoa forgotten, she set up her easel.

Three weeks later, she went to the Excelsior Hotel – it was hanging day.

"Hello, Marjorie," said Selene unenthusiastically. "Why are you here?"

"I would like to submit my picture."

"I'm sorry, but there's no room left. I wish you would have let me know sooner." She sounded totally insincere.

"I think there might be space near the fire exit," said the Treasurer. Selene shot him a furious look.

There was space, just, but not much light, and it was very out of the way. Undaunted, Marjorie said it would do nicely.

The Treasurer helped her hang the picture she had painted of her father.

"That's good," he said. "What's it called?"

"I hadn't thought of a name."

"How about 'In the Garden'?"

"Oh yes! I like that!" she exclaimed.

"Have you got anything else?" he asked.

"Only one of kittens playing outside a thatched cottage, and Selene wouldn't like it."

"I don't think we need to worry about that, give it here."

Marjorie attended judging day out of loyalty to the group, rather than with an expectation of winning anything, especially when she compared her paintings with the other works. Alun's entry, three crushed Coca-Cola cans mounted on a piece of hardboard, was called 'The End of Capitalism?.' Ellie's offering, 'Mother Love' comprised a collage of pictures of crying children torn very roughly from magazines. Selene, naturally, had painted a picture of the moon. It was huge and evidently had required a small forklift truck to bring it into the ballroom. Everything was just so "zeitgeisty," as Selene repeatedly proclaimed.

Selene, sporting a mauve kaftan made from some gauzy, shimmering material, led in the lesser known young British artist. Marjorie was surprised by how ordinary he looked – he was dressed in a three-piece suit and was wearing a tie.

He took the microphone from Selene and smiled.

"What a marvellous group of artists you are," he began before going on to say how hard it had been to pick a winner. "However," he said, "There is one painting that stands out for its humanity. It might not be the most skilfully painted, but it is the one that has managed, somehow, to capture what it is to be happy – that most elusive of states. I hereby nominate 'In the Garden' as the winner of your *concours d'excellence.*"

Marjorie didn't know where to look. Happily, by the time a representative from a greetings card company came up to ask for the rights to reproduce 'Cats Playing Outside a Thatched Cottage' she had recovered. Recovered enough, moreover, to be able to say she had plenty more where that came from, and to sign a surprisingly lucrative contract.

Ticketyboo

© 2023 Vicky Armstrong

"If only I could make the sea go back, then we could play on the sand," said six-year-old Nathan, leaning over the railings separating the promenade from the beach. There was disappointment in his voice as he stared at the wavelets lapping over the pebbles. It was a breezy, sunny afternoon early in the season and West Parade was busy with a mixture of pedestrians and cyclists enjoying its pleasant amenities, apart, that is, from any sand.

"You sound like King Canute," replied his grandfather. "Obviously not the playing-on-the-sand bit, but the bit about trying to turn the tide back."

"Who's King Canute?"

"He was a King of England, England, mark you, not Great Britain, a long time ago."

"When you were little?"

"A lot longer ago than that."

"Before iPads?" Nathan asked, watching a young woman walk by staring down and tapping at her device.

"Before iPads, before cars and planes, long before electricity, even."

Nathan nodded in satisfaction; this was one of the things he liked about Granddad Jim – the way he would always answer a question. He didn't tell you to shut up the way they did at home. Actually, it was his dad that did that. His mum never seemed to notice him. She just picked at her fingers. The thought of home made him feel strange. His mouth pulled itself into a funny shape and tears prickled his eyes. He reached for his grandfather's hand.

Granddad Jim said, "King Canute was King of England, Denmark and Norway early in the 11th Century – that's before the Battle of Hastings."

As Jim spoke, he felt the tremor that had been running through the small, frail body of his grandson gradually subside. He continued, "He's known these days as the king who tried to make the waves go backwards, but of course they wouldn't."

"He was silly."

"No, not really, he was just trying to prove to his people that there are some things that no one can control. I think he was quite a good king, and he's buried in Winchester, which is a big town to the west of here."

Jim had come to the end of all he knew about King Canute, and he and the boy walked on in silence. After a while he said, "What's happened to your glasses?"

The boy's hand went to the bridge of his spectacles that had been clumsily mended with sticky tape.

"I fell over in the playground."

"Did you fall or were you pushed?"

The boy raised and dropped his shoulders, then said, "When will I go back home?"

Jim closed his eyes. It was the question he had been dreading and one for which he had no answer.

"Well," he started, "What do you remember about the last time you saw Mummy?"

The boy's face became blank – it was as if someone had pulled a blind down across a window, and Jim wondered if he had gone too far. He was saved from having to say anything more by a Panama hat suddenly bowling past them, making them both jump. It had been blown from the head of an elderly man further along the promenade.

"Quick, pick that up!" He said to Nathan, pointing towards the hat. Nathan darted after it, catching it just before it blew over the railings and into the sea.

"Now give it to the gentleman."

The boy trotted up to the elderly man and handed him the hat. The man said, "Thank you very much, Sonny." He dug around in his pocket and brought out a coin, "Take this. Buy yourself an ice cream."

Nathan had never been given money before. At home, any money there was spent on stuff for his mum and dad. He showed the coin to Granddad Jim, and Jim said, "Well, we'd better do what the gentleman said." They went up to a small kiosk and bought two ice creams – a double raspberry ripple with a chocolate flake for Nathan and a small vanilla ice for Jim. Nathan noticed that Granddad had to give the woman some extra money out of his own pocket.

"Didn't you have enough money for a bigger ice cream, Granddad?"

"I'm old, Nathan, I can't manage big ice creams anymore. This size is just 'ticketyboo' for me."

"Ticketyboo, ticketyboo." As they sat on a bench and ate their treats, Nathan said the word to himself. He liked it.

After a while, Granddad Jim said, "What's the foster family like?"

"Alright," said Nathan. There was silence, then, "A bit strange."

"In what way?"

"They read the Bible a lot."

"That's not a bad thing."

"No, but they say I've been in a bad place, and I should try to forget my family."

"Well, they've let you spend the day with me."

"Only because the lady said so."

"Someone from Social Services?"

"S'pose so."

At that moment, a shadow fell over them and they looked up.

"Uncle Tom!" cried Nathan.

"Hello, Son," said Jim. Then, "Nathan, go and get your Uncle Tom an ice cream," and he handed the boy a £5 note. As soon as Nathan was out of earshot, he looked at Tom and asked, "Well, what was the result?"

"He was found guilty. He's been sent down for life."

"Thank God for that." Jim was silent for a moment then, "I just couldn't go to the Court today, in case he was found innocent. In case the Jury believed all those lies he made up about our Sandra."

"Well, they didn't. And he looked really sick when he heard the verdict and the sentence."

"Good. I hope he rots in Hell. She would never have started on the drugs without him."

"But we must talk about what happens to Nathan, Dad. Social Services say if he can't go to a suitable family member, he'll have to stay with the foster family. I'm single and I'm always away on active service, so they won't think I'm suitable. What about you? Are you up for it?"

"Me? I'm much too old." Jim stared into the distance. He had only just got over the death of his wife from cancer before his daughter had been murdered. For him, life was now just one day at a time. He kept himself busy with bowling, bridge, and charity work so that he didn't have time to think. Looking after a youngster, even if he were up to it, would put an end to his hard-won coping mechanisms.

"He's all we've got left of Mum and Sandra," said Tom.

They watched Nathan coming back from the kiosk, a double raspberry ripple ice cream with a chocolate flake in his hand. He was concentrating hard on not dropping it. His shabby anorak was too big for him and accentuated his skinniness. His trousers were too short. Every now and then he stopped to push his glasses back up his nose. He cut a pathetic little figure.

"You'd think the fosterers would sort his glasses out," said Tom.

"Too busy, I suppose," said Jim. He was silent for a moment then, with a sigh, "OK, see if Social Services think I'm suitable." Tom squeezed his shoulder and went over to Nathan to take the ice cream, laughing at its size.

After a few minutes, Jim said, "Look, Nathan, the tide has started to go out. We'll soon be able to play on the sand."

"Ticketyboo!" shouted Nathan.

When Worlds Collide

The engagement ring was much too big for Sharon's slim finger.

"Sorry, Shah, I didn't realise they came in different sizes," said Sebastian. "We'll go to a jewellers on Monday and get it made smaller. Now let's tell Ma and Pa the good news."

"Could I call my mother first and let her know."

"Afraid that will have to wait. It's nearly one o'clock."

Sebastian's parents, Lois and Godfrey Bailey-Pomfret were in the lounge – an impressively big room with wide picture windows looking out over the sea. Lois sat on a settee covered in ivory silk. She was leafing through a glossy magazine. Godfrey was fussing over an antique carriage clock on the mantelpiece. He looked up when the young couple came through the door.

"Oh, there you are. Thought the clock was losing time."

"We've been a bit busy," said Sebastian. "I've just asked Shah to marry me, and she has accepted."

"I thought it might be something like that," said his mother, laying aside the magazine. "I hope you realise you are a very lucky girl."

"Oh, er, yes, of course," replied Sharon.

"The ring's a bit big, though," said Sebastian.

"Yes," said Sharon, "but I love it." She stretched out her hand.

Sebastian's mother sniffed. "It was extremely expensive so make sure you don't lose it."

"Perhaps I could have a bit of Elastoplast?"

"Elastoplast?" queried Lois.

"Yes, to wrap round the ring to make it smaller."

"I don't think that would look very nice. No, just take care of it – I don't think that's asking too much."

"Let's go and eat, I'm starving," interrupted Sebastian's father.

Lunch, cooked and served by the Spanish housekeeper, was very good. They washed it down with several bottles of excellent champagne. More than once Godfrey said how pleased he was that Sebastian was "making an honest woman of Shannon."

"Pa, her name's Sharon," said Sebastian.

"What does your mother call you?" enquired Lois.

"Well, Sharon."

"How strange."

Afterwards, Sharon went upstairs to call her mother.

"Mum, guess what? Sebastian's asked me to marry him."

"What did you say to him?" replied her mother.

"'Yes,' of course. He's given me the most beautiful ring I've ever seen – a huge emerald surrounded by diamonds."

"Sharon, do you really love him?"

"Of course, Mum, what's not to love?"

"Money and good looks aren't everything."

"Mum, he's really nice."

"All right, my darling, enjoy the moment."

Sharon went back downstairs. Sebastian was standing in the hall.

"Let's walk off that big lunch," he said.

"That would be nice. I'll go and get my coat and gloves."

"You'll need a hat and scarf as well; it's pretty cold."

Sebastian was right: it was freezing. There was very little warmth in the weak winter sun and there was no escape from a bitter east wind. Arm in arm they hurried along the front. When they got to the remains of a Martello tower, they leant on some railing to look at the view. Sharon took the opportunity to burrow in her pocket for a hankie.

"I really can't understand," said Sebastian. "Why Ma and Pa come to the South Coast in January. What's wrong with the flat in Antibes or their place in the West Indies?"

"I think it's nice and the house is lovely, but, Sebastian, does your mother have a problem with me?"

"Ma? Don't worry about her, she's just not met anyone from Croydon before."

When they got back to the house, Sharon went up to her bedroom to take off her coat. When she removed her gloves, she realised that there was no ring on her left hand. She frantically shook the glove, but nothing fell out. She felt around in her coat pocket; there was still nothing. Had she actually worn it to go out? She looked in the little velvet box it had come in, but that too was empty. With mounting panic, she searched around on the floor – nothing.

She sank down on the bed and gnawed at her knuckles. Where had the ring gone? She went back over the sequence of events – lunch, the walk and then back here. But didn't they stop for a moment? And hadn't she taken her gloves off when she blew her nose? She must have lost it near the Martello tower. She jumped up and put her hat and coat back on.

"Where are you going, Shah?"

Sebastian was standing in the hall.

"I, er, I thought I would go and take a photograph of the old tower thing to send to my Mum."

"Why didn't you do it earlier?"

"I've only just thought about it and there's still a little sun left."

"I'll come with you."

"Honestly, Sebastian, there's no need."

"I insist."

Sebastian's mother came into the hall.

"What's going on?"

"Shah wants to take a photo to send to her mother."

"A photo?"

"Yes," said Sharon, "She said she wants to see what it's like round here."

"It all seems very odd to me," said Lois.

Sharon and Sebastian made their way back to the Martello tower, with Sharon looking down at the ground all the way. When they were at the tower, she peered over the railings down onto the shingle beach. Her heart sank. If it had rolled there, she would never find it.

"Aren't you going to take a photo then?" Asked Sebastian.

"Photo? Oh, yes, but, er, I forgot my phone."

"Shah, what's the matter with you? I'll take some and send them to your phone." There was a hint of exasperation his voice.

Back in the house and once more up in her bedroom, Sharon wondered what to do. There was a ping as Sebastian's photos came through. He was no photographer, and they made the Martello tower and railings look bleak in the extreme. As Sharon stared at the pictures, it occurred to her that she could stick some notices up in case someone came across the ring. It was a long shot but better than doing nothing. She needed paper. There were quite a few books on the bedside table – Lois was obviously a thoughtful hostess, or was it the Spanish housekeeper? She riffled through them and found, as she had hoped, a few blank pages at the front and back. These she carefully tore out. She then wrote "Lost ring – if found, contact 25 Cliff Top Drive". Now she needed sticky tape. What about the bureau in the hall? That was the sort of place one would find such things.

She stuffed the notices in her pocket and crept downstairs. No one was around. As silently as possible she opened the top drawer of the bureau – phone books. She opened the second – empty.

"Can I help you?" It was Lois. Her voice was icy.

"Oh, er, I was looking for Sellotape."

"Why?"

"I, um, want to stick something into my diary."

"Really?"

"Yes."

Lois shrugged her cashmere-clad shoulders.

"If it's so important, you had better ask Maria. She should be in the kitchen."

In the kitchen, Maria gave her a warm smile. "Seeel-o-tep? Of course." She took a reel out of a drawer and handed it to Sharon.

"Is there a way out of here without going back through the hall?"

"Yes, but you have no coat."

"I'll be alright."

It was icy outside – the sun had set and the wind had risen. Sharon's fingers turned numb, but she managed to put up three notices – one on a lamppost, one on the railings and one on the tower itself. She ran back to No. 25 and crept into the kitchen.

"Mr. Sebastian, he is searching for you," said Maria. "I say you have gone out for fresh air."

"Thank you, Maria."

"They are taking the tea in the big room."

Sharon ran upstairs, pulled a comb through her hair, and then went back down to join Sebastian and his parents.

"Where on earth have you been, Shah?" asked Sebastian, "Maria had some strange story about you needing fresh air."

"Yes, er, all that champagne at lunchtime made me feel a bit wasted."

"Wasted?" asked Lois.

"I think Shannon means 'squiffy'," interrupted Godfrey.

"Pa, it's Sharon," said Sebastian. "Help yourself to eats, Shah."

"I'll just have a bit of cake. It looks delicious."

"You're not wearing the ring," observed Lois.

"Oh, it's upstairs in its box, I wanted to keep it safe," said Sharon.

The next morning at nine o'clock, they re-assembled in the dining room for yet another large meal – dinner had quickly followed the sandwich-and-cake session the previous evening. After a sleepless night worrying about the ring, Sharon had little appetite.

"Still not wearing the ring, I see," said Lois.

"I thought I had better not in case it slipped off."

"Well, make sure you wear it when we go to Pomfret Manor – my mother will want to have a look at it."

"We've all been invited to Grandmama's for lunch," explained Sebastian.

Sharon's heart plummeted.

Just at that moment, the doorbell rang. Sharon's heart leapt back up.

"Should I go and see who it is?" she asked when it became apparent no one else was going to move.

"You?" said Godfrey.

"Maria will do it," said Lois.

"It's not your job," said Sebastian.

The bell rang a second time. They could hear the clack-clack of Maria's shoes as she crossed the hall. The front door opened. There was a murmur of voices and then the sound of Maria's footsteps again – this time coming towards the dining room. Unable to stand it any longer, Sharon jumped up, knocking her chair over and ran out into the hall.

"What in blazes is going on?" exclaimed Godfrey.

"Shah, have you gone mad?" said Sebastian.

"What else do you expect?" said Lois.

Ignoring them all, Sharon ran into the hall.

Seeing her, Maria said, "Man on doorstep wants reward."

"Tell him to wait just one moment."

She pelted upstairs, grabbed her bag, came back out onto the landing – and stopped. The scene unfolding below was surreal.

A man lay on the hall floor. Sebastian was kneeling on his chest, his hands around the stranger's throat. Godfrey was shouting into the phone.

"No, young woman, I do not want an ambulance or the Fire Brigade. I want the Police. Did you not understand what I said? A man has stolen a piece of our jewellery and is now trying to claim a reward for bringing it back. Send the Police – immediately!"

Lois was standing in the middle of the hall with something small and glittering in her hand – the ring. She was cackling, there was no other word for it.

At that moment, Sharon saw what life with the Bailey-Pomfrets would be like. She shuddered and ran.

Image Credit: Engin_Atyurt
Pixabay

Brian Langley

The Brook

Past mossy banks, through dappled shade the chuckling
brook flows by

With ripples glinting in the sun beneath a cloudless sky

And spinning on its surface, a twig, a leaf, rush past

Dancing mad mazurkas as they sweep along so fast.

Swirling eddies lap the banks where weeds sway in the
breeze.

While dragonflies and damsel flies fly patterns with such
ease

And then above the current, in a flash of brilliant hue

The kingfisher streaks past, electric red and blue

Beneath the busy surface another world is found

Where Sticklebacks, insect larvae, water nymphs abound.

And in the crystal water minnows darting to and fro

Mingle with the secret life existing down below.

And thus, aquatic life on the surface and below

Continues in the tinkling water with its merry flow.

But who would realise the treasures of the brook?

If they never take the trouble to take a closer look.

Questions

Did Wordsworth like those daffodils? I wondered in my
bed.

This and many other things keep going through my head:

Why do clouds float in the sky, and water fill the sea?

And why is air invisible? There's much to puzzle me.

When a door is partly open why is it called ajar?

When the sky is filled with suns why is each called a star?

If animals have hoof or paw why is it we have feet?

And when erasing words in prose why is it called delete?

How do microwaves cook food without a glowing flame?

Why is it that the innocent always get the blame?

When fed by only salt free streams why is the sea so salt?

And if a thing goes badly wrong why is it you at fault?

Why are we masters of a dog but servants for a cat?

How did they find the world is round instead of being flat?

When someone suffers from a cold why do they claim it's

flu?

And when we're told to wait in line why is it called a

queue?

If neighing is how horses speak then why do donkeys bray?

Why does a squirrel's nest sound like a brewers dray?

So many questions seeking answers they will never find.

Questions, questions, questions, messing with my mind...

Scandal
© 2023 Brian Langley

The scandal at the village hall had them all agog;

It centred round an aged lady and her soppy dog.

She had an easy lifestyle, was never short of cash,

But though she seemed quite wealthy, she didn't act too

flash

Some thought she'd been a lady, cast off by a knight.

When romance began to soar up to a dizzy height

But others said there was no way that that could ever be.

She didn't have the bearing; look how she drinks her tea.

Folk thought the hall might haunted be for sometimes in
the night.

Strange noises could be heard to cause the listener fright.

But every night she'd take a walk across the village green

While her dog produced more wee than ever had been
seen

And then she'd often go inside, spend time inside the hall.

And her dog would do more wee-wee up against the wall.

The structure of the building reacted badly to the wee:

It really didn't like it, as everyone could see.

And then one day, catastrophe, the floor at last gave way.

And in a secret cellar they found to their dismay

Counterfeit notes lay all around and buried in the mess.

The unfortunate aged lady beside her printing press.

The Soldier

She was one and he was two when they first met. Their parents lived next door to each other and were often in each other's houses. The children got on well together and when they were older the boy was given a set of lead toy soldiers. They spent hours playing with them and firing matchsticks at each other's army.

He was seven when he was sent away to boarding school. She was sad to see him go but he gave her one of the soldiers, a brightly coloured Hussar as a keepsake and she gave it pride of place on her dressing table. Despite the boy's frequent periods away at boarding school their friendship continued and grew. When he came home for the holidays, they took up together again, rode their bikes around the countryside and explored the woods. It was safe enough in those days for them to go out on their own and if they got into difficulties they could rely on any adult for help.

They were still like brother and sister as they entered their teens, but the relationship slowly changed, and they had their first kiss when she was fifteen. They had been to the cinema and were on their way home afterwards when the boy put his arm round her, pulled her to him and moved into a kiss. When they broke apart, she looked at him and dragged him back for another. The relationship developed and they became what in later times was referred to as an item.

She was twenty when he proposed. She said yes, and they were married a year later. He had a good job and before long they were able to buy a small cottage. Coming home from work he would call a cheery hallo as he strode up the path to the front door and she would run to meet and greet him with a kiss. She still had the toy soldier he had given her, and it now had pride of place on the mantlepiece.

They had many friends in the village and finally a baby son arrived to complete their family. She was very happy looking after him and there was no lack of babysitters when they wanted an evening out together. The baby grew into a lively toddler, putting her in mind of when they were small themselves, and she looked forward to a happy future.

Unfortunately, war was looming, and the day came when mobilisation papers arrived, instructing him to report for training and do his bit for the country. Holding her son close, she sobbed as he left. They had not been apart for as much as a day since their marriage and he came home on leave from time to time till the moment came when he was shipped abroad. She took her son with her to the docks to wave him off, shedding buckets of tears and returned home to eagerly await his letters. Then one day they ceased.

Finally, the dreaded black edged envelope dropped through her door. She was distraught. He had been her whole world and now he was gone and not even the end of the war eased her grief. As the years went by, she stayed in the cottage looking after her son. He grew into a good-looking boy and excelled at school. He went through a series of girlfriends before proposing to one and marrying her. Although he had moved out of the family home and the couple had their own home they lived nearby and visited frequently. She was now mainly on her own in the cottage but was delighted when they had a baby, and she was called on for advice and babysitting duties. She loved the time she spent with the baby but would often take the toy soldier down from the mantlepiece and hold it as the pain of her loss welled up inside her. Age crept up on her while the baby grew, and the years passed by.

The lead soldier still stood on the mantlepiece in the same place where he had stood for many years. His colours, after so long, were now somewhat muted from age and handling. The old lady gazed fondly at him, stretched out a hand but turned instead to the window to gaze out into the garden to where in days gone by she had run to meet her man as he strode up the path. Sadly, it had been many years since the last time she had heard his cheery call as he strode briskly to the front door.

Reaching once again for the toy soldier, she felt a great tiredness come over her. She slumped wearily back in her chair and clutched the soldier close as her head sagged to one side. Her breathing gently slowed then stopped as her unseeing eyes gazed through the window to where an attractive young girl ran eagerly to meet the soldier calling a cheery hallo as he strode up the path.

It's A Gift

Greg's favourite TV programmes were those about DIY and, despite encouragements by friends and family, he was forever attempting jobs far beyond his ability. Greg was totally incompetent at anything he did, and the result was sure to be a disaster. No matter how many of those disasters resulted from his efforts, he moved oblivious from one fiasco to the next, undaunted by his total ineptitude at anything involving tools.

He was showing off his latest effort to his friend, Andy.

"It's fantastic, don't you agree?" he asked, smiling broadly. "I made it myself."

"What is it?" asked Andy, eyeing the contraption warily as it shivered slightly in the soft breeze.

"You've seen them before," he pleaded. "You *must* know what it is."

"Not a clue. What is it?" asked Andy again. "It looks like a jumble of wood. You don't mean to say you made this... this... " He gave the crazy construction of badly fitting wooden pieces a shake. One of the pieces fell off.

"Hey, be careful!" cried Greg, carefully fitting it back into place.

"Looks like it's going to fall apart at any moment," said Andy. "I still don't know what it is."

"Look at it," said Greg. "It's obvious, isn't it?'"He gave the wheel a spin. It fell off.

"I forgot the locking pin," he said, carefully replacing the wheel and inserting a locking pin.

"Why don't you face it?" said Andy. "You don't have a clue about making anything/ You can't even make a cup of tea without getting it wrong."

"Don't be so down," Greg replied, "everyone can do DIY, be able to put up a shelf, slap on some paint, make a sledge for their kid. Don't you agree?"

"Yes, most can, but you're not among them. You just have a total lack of expertise. In fact, you're a disaster. Don't you agree?"

"I'm very good at DIY!" cried Greg, somewhat hurt. "What about all the things I've done?"

"Yes... The shelf that tilted and everything slid off before it fell off the wall. The table with the wonky leg that folded under it and sent dinner crashing to the floor. I could go on."

"You're worse than my wife," complained Greg. "She complains, too. It's not fair."

"So, what's this latest project?" asked Andy, changing the subject.

"I've made a spinning wheel," Greg said proudly. "' found all the details in Woodworking Magazine."

"Spinning wheel? I'm impressed by your optimism, but I've never seen one like that. I'm surprised you managed to... er... finish it, I know what you're like with a plane and a chisel." Andy was surprised. Normally these fads of Greg's rarely reached the end. This one was a shock.

"I agree it's more complex than putting up a shelf," said Greg, pointing to the one behind him. There was nothing on it, though there were plenty of things that could be put on it. Andy picked up a small vase and rested it on the shelf. It started to slide, and he grabbed it quick before it fell. Greg didn't notice.

"There's nothing complex about putting up a shelf but even that is beyond you," said Andy. "So, I don't understand how you managed to complete this... thing." He gestured at the jumble of wood Greg claimed was his newly constructed spinning wheel. "How did you make the bits so perfectly though the assembly is a mess?"

"You could buy a kit of parts from the magazine, so I decided to buy one. It saved trying to make them. I'm not very good on the lathe."

"Yes, I know," said Andy. "You had a week in hospital the last time you used that lathe."

"That was not my fault," said Greg. "I've got another project in mind now. I'm going to build a go-kart."

"It will fall apart before you ever get it to the start line. I shan't go anywhere near it." Andy gave the wheel a spin and another piece fell off. "Perhaps you should invest in some nails and glue," he suggested.

"You're always disparaging my projects. I'm very good at DIY. I just have a few teething problems when I start a project."

"Teething problems?" queried Andy with a laugh. "A way of life for you. Let me know when you've built your go-kart and I'll have a look at it... from a safe distance!"

"Don't be such a wimp. You can have a ride in it if you like," said Greg.

"Never!" cried Andy, "I want to live. Well, I'm away now. I'm off to the pub. Come along now, leave this... thing and buy me a pint." Pushing Greg ahead of him, he steered him out of the gate and down the road, while back at the house another piece of Greg's spinning wheel wobbled in the breeze before falling to the ground.

Despite the fiasco with the spinning wheel, Greg was as enthusiastic as ever and went about building his go-kart and still convinced of his expertise. A couple of weeks later he had a wheeled base complete with seat and engine while the motor mower languished in the back of the garage minus its engine. Greg looked it over with pride and invited Andy over again to view it.

"What do you think of it?" asked Greg. "I forgot to add brakes, but I'll do that in a minute."

"Do you really expect this to work?" asked Andy, gazing in awe at the construction.

"Of course," Greg asserted.

Andy was surprised. This had to be the first time Greg actually managed to make something that had a chance to work as intended.

"Look, I'll start it up for you, then you could have a go round the garden." As he tinkered with the engine, Andy stepped back a few feet. There was a sudden roar as the engine fired. The go-kart suddenly burst into flames and Greg rushed to find an extinguisher. The fire brigade was soon on the spot, having been called by Anne, his wife, who had been watching from a safe distance, but the garage was soon mostly a burnt shell.

Cleaned up but smelling faintly of the fire, Greg relaxed and sat in the lounge watching telly intently with Nick Knowles and the gang converting a loft space into a room. He got many of his ideas from such programmes and he thought this was a brilliant idea. He saw himself brilliantly converting his own loft space just like Nick and the gang converted theirs.

Anne, his despairing wife, could only wonder how he managed to avoid being part of his DIY and being carted off to hospital in bits. Now he had this idea of converting the loft into another room. Anne was very worried. Very worried.

She was sitting in the lounge reading a book while the noise of hammering and sawing came from above. From time to time, she glanced up nervously, wondering what form the crisis would take this time. It was not long coming.

There was a sudden loud crash and a shower of plaster fell on her as a leg appeared through the ceiling just above her chair, accompanied by a fit of swearing calculated to turn the air blue. This, she knew, was yet another project doomed to failure, and which would have an expensive outcome.

All her efforts to curb his enthusiasm for DIY came to nought and she had long since given up trying to dissuade him from doing any work round their home. Well used to the outcome of DIY by her husband, she sighed, shook the debris off her book and out of her hair and went to fetch the hoover as Greg appeared through the loft hatch. He clambered down the ladder muttering about stupid builders making ceilings out of nothing more than plasterboard nailed onto stupidly wide spaced lumps of wood.

"Are you all right?" he asked cheerfully, taking in her dust covered form. "I've scraped my leg; where's the Elastoplast? And how about a cup of tea for the workman?"

Anne stomped out of the room and went to the kitchen to slam the kettle on the stove. They once had a nice electric one but after Greg rewired it, the kettle had become a horrid black one. She now used a traditional one on the gas stove.

Anne wondered if they would ever have anything that Greg didn't destroy in his foolhardy swathe through their possessions. The car had ended up on jacks with the engine dangling below it when he tried to change the water pump, they had been reduced to candles in the front bedroom when he attempted to wire up an extra socket for bedside lights and a radio, and the boiler ceased to function after he had taken it apart to clean the flue.

The list was endless. He never seemed to be put out by the fact that nothing he touched worked afterwards, always having a good reason why they didn't, and he carried on with blind optimism. It was extremely fortunate they were wealthy enough for her to arrange to have things put right each time.

"Here's your tea," she said, banging the mug on the table.'

"Thanks, love," he said. "Gosh, it's dusty up there. Still, I'm on top of it now. Just have to wire the sockets back to the fuse box and nail the floorboards down."

"Are you sure it's safe up there?" she asked, expecting the next thing to happen would be for the ceiling to collapse completely. She had already had to call in Steve, the builder, to repair the roof after Greg had fitted a window in it.

"Of course, it is," he replied. "I've added some extra joists to support the floor. I'm going to move my den up there when it's finished. You can have my old one for a work room."

She sighed again and made a note to contact Steve in the morning. *"How much was it going to cost to fix things this time?"* she wondered.

Greg gulped his tea and returned to the loft. He fed a length of wire down to the fuse box and took off the lid. Seconds later there was a loud crack, and all the electrics went off.

"Damn," muttered Greg. "Have we got any fuse wire?"

"They are circuit breakers," said Anne, who had the electrics upgraded after his fiasco with the socket in the bedroom.

Greg looked at the row of switches. "They're all on," he said. "Blast. The main fuse must have blown. Wonder why?"

Anne disappeared into the kitchen and closed the door before loudly screaming "Aaaaaagh!"

Steve came round the next morning while Greg was at work. He climbed into the loft and his reaction made Anne wonder if he was having a heart attack and if she should call the doctor.

"Oh, my god," he muttered, white-faced and somewhat nervous when he reappeared. "He's really excelled himself this time. He's taken out most of the timbering that supports the roof. It could collapse at any moment. And his extra joists for the floor are only four by twos laid straight on the plasterboard with no other support instead of properly supported seven by fours. The lounge ceiling will collapse if he puts any weight up there. I'll have to call the lads off another job to secure the roof for you before it falls in. You'd best get in the kitchen right away for safety and stay there till I've got it fixed." He pulled his phone out of his pocket and made a call.

Finishing the call, Steve grinned. "You're keeping me in champagne and caviar letting him have his head where DIY is concerned – when he doesn't know his arse from his elbow where DIY is concerned."

"I know," she replied. "I've tried and tried to stop him, but he doesn't listen. I've got nowhere and I've given up. I'm just thankful that we have a high income and I can pay for all the repairs after he's finished."

A short while later, a van arrived with his men and a load of equipment and work began. Anne remained in the kitchen where she was kept busy with the kettle. It was afternoon when they finished.

"That was so dangerous, what he'd done up there, but it's all safe now," Steve told her. "We've sorted the wiring as well and the electric company is coming to replace their fuse. It would hit my business, but you really must stop Greg doing DIY before there's a major disaster. Sharpening a pencil is about the limit of his expertise."

"He'd probably make a mess of that too," she said resignedly.

"I think you're right," Steve chuckled. "Well, call me again when you need me. You're my best customer."

"With Greg for a husband, I have to be," she sighed. She was finding it hard to cope with his disasters and this one had proved to be not only horrendous but dangerous too. She decided that finally enough was enough: somehow, he had to be stopped. Fired up for a row, she tackled him when he came home from work.

"Steve the builder had a fit when he saw what you had done," she told him. "He's sorted it all out and the electric company replaced the main fuse."

"Oh, good," he replied., "I must have got a wire wrong somewhere."

"It wasn't just the wiring," she snapped viciously. "Steve said the roof was in danger of collapsing because you'd taken all the support away and he's had to put it back. You're an idiot. We could have been killed if the roof gave way and as you made such a stupid mess of the floor up there as well, the lounge ceiling would collapse if you put anything heavy up there."

"What does he know?" demanded Greg. "There was nothing wrong with my floor!"

"You always say that when anything goes wrong, which is every damned time you touch something. Steve is a builder. He knows what he's doing, but you don't have a clue. For God's sake, stop this nonsense. It costs a fortune to put everything right after you've messed with it, and you could have killed us with this latest effort."

"It's not my fault," he said, starting up the ladder. "There are no craftsmen any more; they're all cowboys these days with no idea how to do things properly.?

"And I suppose you do," she demanded angrily.

"Of course, I do," he said, grinning, not at all discomfited by her comments. "It's a gift."

He climbed back into the loft but reappeared a few moments later. "Hey, what's happened to all my tools? I can't get on with any work without them."

Anne smiled, thinking she, too, had a gift. "I told Steve to take them away and not let you have them back. Ever!"

A Ripple on the Water

It was a warm day in spring when she entered his life. The sun was shining, a soft breeze was blowing, and the hills faded into a pale distance while the valley below drowsed in the warmth of the sun. He was seated on a folding stool, his equipment about him, painting a watercolour of the scene before him. Concentrating on his work he didn't hear her approach.

"That's really good." Her sudden comment made him jump. "Oh, I'm sorry. I didn't mean to startle you." Her voice was warm and mellow.

Where had she come from? He turned to look at her and was instantly smitten. She stood before him, smiling, as his gaze travelled over her. Tanned and slender, with long nut-brown hair, wearing a T-shirt and denim shorts. She radiated warmth and laughter. A rucksack lay on the ground beside her.

"Hello, no, it's all right. No harm done." He paused, tongue tied, and wondered what on earth to say next. In just those few short moments she had made such a deep impression on him that he was desperate for a chance to get to know her and to avoid frightening her off with a clumsy approach. She solved the problem for him.

"Will you mind if I watch you paint?" she asked, settling herself on a convenient rock. "I won't put you off?"

"Not at all. I don't mind people watching."

"Do you paint a lot?"

"Yes, mostly landscapes. I have a selection at home. I paint portraits too, but I'm not so keen on them. I much prefer landscapes and outside subjects. I really enjoy painting, it's my favourite hobby."

"I'd like to see your paintings. If they're for sale I might buy one," she said, smiling.

He hugged himself. She was going to stay – and she wanted to look at his paintings too! Might even buy one. "Yes, they're all for sale, not that I manage to sell many. I'm not much good at selling. I'll show them to you in a mo. I live down there in the village, but I must finish this first before the light changes too much."

"That's all right. I have nothing special to do. I can wait.' The girl leaned forward to pull her rucksack nearer her feet.

"What's your name? Mine's Tony Roper."

"Isobel. Isobel Farr. Dreadful, isn't it? Belongs in the last century. I should be a Sharon or Judy or something, not Isobel Farr."

"No, it's nice. I like it." Tony said as he picked up his brushes and turned back to the canvas.

She sat watching him paint. "You really are good," she said after a while. "You've captured the scene beautifully. I wish I could paint as well as you."

Tony grunted as he continued to work. The girl reached into her bag and took out a pad and pencil. She looked at Tony briefly, taking in the easel, his palette, and his posture, then quickly drew on the pad. He turned and caught sight of what she was doing.

"Hey! Are you an artist too?" he asked, getting up and going over to her.

"No, not really," she replied, "I can draw but I'm no painter. I always end up with a total mess when I try to paint. I don't know why." She glanced at his equipment. "Anyway, all you need for drawing is a pad and a pencil, much easier to carry than all that stuff, and a bottle of water." She looked thoughtfully at her pad for a moment, then held it out to him. "What do you think?"

"Hey, that's fantastic! I could never draw like that," he exclaimed enthusiastically, taking the pad from her. The artist, sitting at his easel, lived on the page, depicted in an economy of line that captured the whole essence of her subject.

"May I?" he asked, lifting a page.

"Yes, go ahead," she replied.

He turned over the pages in wonder. People, birds, animals erupted from every page, each drawn in the same economic style, each almost alive in its rendition.

"These are marvellous," he breathed, "they are superb. I could never draw like this."

"Oh, they're really nothing special," she demurred, "just jottings to pass the time."

"They are nothing of the sort; they're brilliant!" he exclaimed. "*You're* brilliant. You put me to shame. I just splosh paint about."

"Nothing of the sort. It's your painting that's brilliant."

"It isn't. It's just a picture, but your drawings are alive on the page. They are amazing!"

"You're very kind but I've never thought of them as anything special. They're just doodles. I enjoy sketching but

I'd much rather see your paintings if they're all as good as this one."

Tony shook his head in wonder at her modesty as he continued to turn the pages, finding drawings also of churches, canal boats and river scenes. Regretfully he finally closed the pad before handing it back.

"I'll be finished in a minute, then we'll go and see them. My house is just down the hill." He settled on his stool again and added the finishing touches to his painting. "Right, done. I'll pack up and we'll go and look at my other daubs."

"Your other daubs, indeed," Isobel thought as she shook her head in wonder. She recognised his talent and wondered why he didn't. But then she didn't recognise her own, it seemed, so that made them a right pair of fools.

Tony gathered up his equipment and she helped him carry it as they walked together down the hill to a small cottage on the edge of the village. Opening the door, he showed her into the living room. A few of his paintings hung on the walls and she went over to look at them while he put his gear away.

"These pictures are wonderful!" she exclaimed. "Why can't you see how good you are?"

"I'm no better than lots of artists and most are probably better than me," he said modestly. "These are just a few I especially like. The others are upstairs in my studio."

He led the way upstairs and into a large room. A number of paintings were stacked along one wall, and three paintings hanging on another depicted the scene he had been painting as it changed through the year.

"My morgue," Tony said, waving round the room as he added his latest picture to the collection. "This is the last of the set; I was going to sell them that way. I sell a few paintings to the tourists when they come but I don't sell many. As I said, I'm not much good as a salesman."

"Morgue, indeed!" she exclaimed as she studied them then shuffled through the other paintings in wonder.

"Look, Tony, you obviously don't know your own worth. I have a friend who owns an art gallery. He'll be happy to show your paintings. Sell them too. I'll have a word with him. Do you have a telephone?"

"Yes, it's downstairs in the kitchen. I use it very little; it's not my favourite instrument."

He showed her where it was and she dialled a number. After a while she put the receiver back. "No reply," she said, "I'll have to try again later."

"Would you like a cup of tea?" he asked, lifting the kettle.

"I'd love one," she replied as he filled the kettle and put it on the stove.

They sat around the kitchen chatting while sipping their tea and nibbling biscuits. Tony, his eyes drinking in her beauty, could hardly believe his luck at having such a lovely girl in his house drinking tea with hm. She suddenly reached for her bag, took out her pad and began to sketch rapidly.

"What are you drawing?" he asked, "can I see?"

"Uh, uh, not till I've finished," she replied, her pencil flying over the page.

"Go on, don't be a spoilsport, let me see." He edged round to see what she was drawing.

"No you don't,' she teased, holding the pad to her chest. "Wait till I've finished and maybe, just maybe, I'll show it to you then."

"All right," he accepted, "but your drawings are all so good I can't wait to see it."

"I'm not sure if you'll like this one," she said, smiling playfully. Making a few last strokes of the pencil, she hugged the pad to her chest. She looked at him for a moment, then held out the pad. He took it, looked at the drawing, looked at her, and then at the drawing again.

"Well?" she said, laughter in her voice.

He looked up again and burst into hoots of laughter. "You're wicked," he gasped, waving the pad. "I've been sussed."

"Only what you deserve," she said, grinning widely. {You've been goggling at me since we met and I couldn't resist a tease."

Tony looked at the drawing again: he was seated at his kitchen table, a cup of tea wobbling in his hand and his eyes standing out like organ stops as he gazed at an attractive girl sitting opposite him.

"OK, I deserve that, but you really are a lovely girl."

She grinned and tucked the pad back in her bag. "Teasing over. I'll try that number again."

She picked up the phone and this time got an answer. After a short chat, she put the phone down and smiled broadly at Tony. "He was impressed with what I told him, and he said he'll be able to come to see your work in a couple of days' time. I know he'll love your paintings and I'll stay till he arrives and introduce you. In fact, I'll stay to help you get sorted."

"Thanks. That will be appreciated. Do you need somewhere to stay?"

"I usually book into a motel or find a barn or something when I'm travelling around. I do that quite a lot."

"I can offer you my spare room if you like," he said.

Isobel smiled. "That's kind of you. I'll accept your offer with thanks. Much better than a mucky old barn."

"You haven't seen my spare room," said Tony.

He showed her the room and despite some art items tucked in a corner it was nothing like he had led her to believe, being bright, clean, and tidy. Dumping her bag on the bed she followed him downstairs to clatter about in the kitchen organising tea. She proved to be an inventive cook, producing an appetising meal from the few bits and pieces he had in the larder.

The next day, at her suggestion, they looked through his paintings and arranged them into some sort of order. They were mostly landscapes showing a variety of scenes from a general view to individual trees drooping by a lake, but other subjects were included. She put a small one aside saying she liked this one and would like to buy it.

"No, please. Just take it," he said.

When Richard, Isobel's friend and gallery owner arrived, he was at once struck by the paintings. He studied the downstairs display for a while before being persuaded upstairs to view the other paintings. He found them just as fascinating.

"It's been a long time since I saw a quantity of such quality in one place and from one artist," he said. "There's a range of subjects, all good, and I can't wait to take a selection back to my gallery. I assume you want to sell them?"

Before Tony could answer, Isobel spoke. "Of course he does, but he's clueless about selling. That's why he has so many stacked up here."

"I'll sell them with no trouble. They'll go like hot cakes. He's got the knack of picking and portraying subjects that appeal strongly to others," said Richard, 'I'll price them too. Tony should do very well out of it."

"That's brilliant!' exclaimed Tony. "I really ought to have some sort of clear out. I keep painting but don't sell many, so they pile up."

"They'll all sell," said Richard. "I'm confident of that but we mustn't offer too many too soon. I don't understand why you haven't sold a lot already; trippers are often good customers of local talent."

"I'm a hopeless salesman," said Tony, "I'd struggle to sell food to a starving man."

"Well, at least you're a good painter. Have you done anything in oils? Watercolours are nice but oils are popular, too."

"I prefer watercolour," said Tony. 'I've been thinking I ought to have a go with oils, but I haven't got round to it yet."

"Get him to try it, Isobel," said Richard. "If he can paint in oils as well as he does in watercolour I'll show those too, like a shot. Now, which of these should I take for my gallery? They are so good it's hard to choose but I can't take more than about six. I don't have the space."

After the selection was made, they returned downstairs and sat in the kitchen chatting over tea and biscuits for a while till Richard stood up and prepared to go.

"Well, I'd best be off. I'll send a van to pick up the painting," Richard said before walking out the door.

The van arrived a couple of days later and the paintings were taken away to the gallery. Tony, standing with Isobel, watched them go.

"I know they have to go and I can always use the money, but that's part of my life disappearing off in that van," he said sadly.

She gave him a hug. "They're no use gathering dust up in that room," she said, "much better to get a cash benefit from your work.'

"I suppose you're right," he sighed. "Richard wanted the set of four but I decided to hang onto them for the time being. They're of my favourite view. I might let them go later."

Several days later they had a phone call inviting them to view the display in the gallery. When they arrived, Tony was surprised to see that several had already been marked as sold.

"I never expected this," he said, "it's amazing."

"Only what I expected," said Isobel. "You are a brilliant painter."

"You said that before," Tony noted, "but you're an amazing artist and deserve recognition, too. Your drawings should be on show as well, like my pictures, but don't you dare show that cartoon anywhere. I think you should give it to me for safe keeping."

She turned and aimed a secret smile at him. "Hmmm. Maybe," she murmured.

The success of the sale meant Richard had more space on his walls. Isobel, busy helping with Richard's paperwork, suggested Tony should pop back home to collect a few more pieces to fill the empty spaces. He did so, borrowing the van and stayed overnight before returning with another selection of his paintings.

"That will be plenty for now," said Richard, pleased with how popular Tony's paintings had been. "I'll be putting just a couple of these up now and then. We mustn't flood the market. Best to leave it for a while, maybe even a year or so to whet the appetite before showing a number together again."

"I think he should do something different, like you suggested, having a go with oils," said Isobel.

"Encourage him," said Richard.

Before returning to their village, they bought materials for Tony to try his hand at oils and a book on oil painting techniques. His first efforts with still life in his studio were not particularly good but with Isobel's encouragement he was soon producing creditable results. When he felt competent enough, they went out into the countryside to find a wider range of subject material as he preferred country subjects to studio ones.

Isobel accompanied him on his outings and sketched anything that took her interest while Tony worked at his paintings. They enjoyed each other's company and found they had a number of interests in common in addition to art and over the weeks they became very close.

Blissfully happy that Isobel had stayed with him, Tony was fired with enthusiasm and worked hard to master the new medium. His efforts paid off and he eventually turned out a couple of excellent pictures. Surreptitiously, Isobel rang Richard to tell him about the oils; he asked her to bring them and Tony along for him to see. Tony hadn't thought them good enough and was a little put out she had told Richard about them.

"They're not very good," he said grumpily to her. "You shouldn't have raised Richard's expectations. It will be a wasted journey."

Somewhat indignant, Isobel replied, "Well I think they are good enough and Richard will love them."

Tony sniffed but found some packaging to wrap them for the journey. Richard was pleased with the pictures and said he would like to put them on show straightaway, and that he would be happy to take more when they were ready.

Tony returned home in a happier mood and busied himself painting more pictures in oils. He was making more money from his paintings than he thought possible. Isobel was pleased with his good fortune and the recognition he was gaining.

However, he was becoming absorbed with his painting and when she suggested they had a relaxing day out, he brushed her away, saying he had to get on with the painting. She felt a bit upset and said she thought it was taking him over to the exclusion of everything else, including their previously blossoming relationship. After a while she only went out on the hillside with him to help him set up before wandering off on her own.

Concentrating on his painting, he was now paying little notice to other matters and Isobel began to feel superfluous. The first rows occurred and it was brought home to him soon after how their relationship was falling apart when he returned home from a shopping trip and found to his dismay she was no longer there. When he checked her room, he found all her things had gone so it was clear she had left. No one in the village had noticed her leave and no one had any idea where she had gone but there was a large envelope waiting for him on the kitchen table.

Sitting miserably at the table, he opened it and found the cartoon, a drawing of a canal scene and a photo of a canal boat showing the name 'Isobel'.

Tony's mind raced: *"What did it mean, where had she gone? Why had she gone? Did she live on a canal boat? Why these pictures, were they clues? Did they mean she had left now she had helped him become established as a painter of note, or had he driven her away with thoughtless neglect? Did she want him to find her, were they supposed to help him if he really wanted to see her again?"*

These questions and more filled his head and he wanted answers. She had become very special to him: he had been intending to ask her to marry him but suddenly realised how much his obsession with painting had damaged their relationship. Whether or not the drawings were intended as clues, he desperately hoped they would somehow help him to solve the puzzle and bring her back into his life.

Thinking about the photo of the canal boat, he suddenly remembered there had been several canal-based drawings in her pad – so clearly she liked canals. Tony could see they provided great possibilities for pictures and would also make a starting point for his search.

He wished he could remember the drawings better. There had been boats moored along a towpath, canal-side buildings, and other structures but names were unrecognisable in her drawings. However, he felt he should be able to recognise places from memory once he found them. He knew nothing about canals; with nothing beyond the drawing and the photo to help him, he would need to do a lot of research into the hidden world of canals. Realising the work ahead of him, Tony sighed and put the papers to one side for another go tomorrow.

The next day, he went to the library to research the canals but all they had to help was one book. Nevertheless, it was a mine of information, and he was amazed to discover just how many canals there were and how they ran all over the country. His hopes rose: he had his starting point but didn't expect the puzzle to be solved very easily.

It seemed that Birmingham was at the centre of the network with a maze of canals threading through the town so he thought it would be a good place to start his search. He decided to try to get more information off the internet; after all, everyone did so why couldn't he?

There was a snag, though: he didn't have a computer, didn't know how to work one, and hadn't a clue how to access the 'net. Fortunately, the library had computers for public use, so he approached one of the staff and persuaded her to show him how to operate it.

Once he got the hang of things he spent some time familiarising himself with the technology. When he typed 'canals' into his computer, he couldn't believe how many sites were listed. There was so much information available that he struggled to pick out material he felt would help him in his search for Isobel. Returning to the library over several days, he printed off a lot of data in the hope that somewhere in it he would discover the vital fact to set him on course to find her.

After reading through his printouts, he set off on his hunt, starting with the canal basin in Birmingham. Since the narrow boat in her photo was called 'Isobel', he was sure it was a connection to her. For several days he travelled to villages on different canals seeking information on the movements of the narrow boat 'Isobel' without success.

Given possible sightings, he went on many fruitless trips till at last his perseverance paid off and he struck lucky. Someone mentioned they had seen the boat a few days ago near Braunston on the Grand Union canal and his hopes rose. He had had such tips before that had resulted in fruitless journeys. It was by no means certain that Isobel would be on the boat with her name, but the photo clue suggested a strong connection.

However, Tony realised that after a couple of days the boat could be anywhere. He studied his printouts and recognised that there were several routes it could have taken from there. As it had been heading southward, there was a good possibility it was still headed that way as there wasn't much chance for it to branch off or turn round like one could in a car.

Full of hope, he took off for Braunston. Enquiries there proving no use, he begged a lift on a boat going south and learned they would shortly pass through Blisworth Tunnel, a long creepy burrow through a hillside. He was told that in the past, before engines and when boats were towed by a horse, a plank was laid across the boat so two men could lie on it and walk the boat through the tunnel, a process called legging, while the horse walked over the hill. Tony shuddered at the thought and was relieved it no longer happened; he didn't fancy being volunteered for the task.

Thankful to reach Stoke Bruerne safely at the other end of the tunnel, he left the boat and started asking if anyone had seen the 'Isobel'. He struck lucky again. A man said he knew the boat and its people well and that it had stopped there the previous day but had moved on by the evening. Tony thought that if he had stayed on his boat he might have caught up with the 'Isobel', but the man then said that when it came here it always moored up a short way along the towpath for a few days away from the bustle around the pub and the museum.

"How far would they have gone?" Tony wondered. The man assured him he would probably find them if he walked a short way along the towpath. The boats didn't travel very fast and usually stopped for a day or so to stock up with shopping from the village store, so they would most likely be within walking distance.

Tony decided to try and was relieved to find the boat after just half a mile or so of urgent walking. A man was standing in the cabin hatch smoking a pipe while he watched the water.

Tony called to him, "Excuse me, do you know a girl called Isobel? I'm trying to find her and I think she is connected with this boat in some way."

"Yes, I know her," replied the man, turning round and looking at him. "What did you want with her, I'm Mr. Farr, her father. Call me Reg."

"Oh, how do you... I... er... she – " he stammered.

Reg interrupted, "Well don't stand there! Come aboard, lad." The man turned as a head poked out of the cabin. "This is my wife, Kathleen. Meet Mr. Roper,darling."

"Hello. Nice to meet you at last, Mr. Roper. I'll make us some tea. Won't be a mo." She smiled at him and disappeared again.

"How do you know my name?" Tony asked as he clambered awkwardly aboard.

"Isobel told us all about you and there is such a pile of her sketch books below it's a wonder we don't sink under the weight. She seems to sketch anything that ever existed and there are lots of drawings of you in one of them so it was easy to recognise you. She seems to have taken quite a shine to you."

"Really? We were very close... I was going to ask her to marry me but she disappeared. I've been looking for her ever since to find out why she left so suddenly. Is she here?"

"No, she left the boat just after the tunnel, but she'll be along before long," Reg explained.

Kathleen bobbed up from the cabin again and handed out mugs of tea. "Here you are; drink it while it's hot." She leaned against the tiller rail and sipped her tea. "So you really want to find Isobel." It was more a statement than a question. "We know why she left but it's up to her to explain, not us."

"Yes. I must find her. I love her," said Tony, gulping tea. "I must dash back to find her before she disappears. I couldn't bear to lose her again."

"Don't worry, there's plenty of time. She'll be coming back to the boat tonight," said Reg with an understanding smile. "If you can't bear to wait that long you'll probably find her at the Boat Inn in a while. How did you track her down?"

"She left me a cartoon and a couple of pictures when she left. I wondered if they were meant to help me find her," said Tony, on the verge of becoming emotional.

"They were," said Kathleen. "She hoped you would realise they were clues to help you search for her if that were what you wanted. I'm so pleased that you did."

After they chatted for a while, Tony was surprised to feel at home with the couple; it was hardly the usual way one met prospective in-laws. At last, Kathleen suggested Tony should make his way back to the village since Isobel would be sure to be at the Inn by now, and he set off full of hope.

Reaching the Boat Inn, he paused in the doorway and happiness welled up inside him. She was there, sitting on her own with her back to him, idly doodling in her sketch pad. Moving quietly towards her he reached round and placed the cartoon on the pad., She started and turned to face him, jumping up with a cry of joy.

"You found me!" she said with a smile, "I was so hoping you would." Her eyes were moist with happy tears.

"I had to," he answered simply. "I am in love with you. Why did you leave?"

"When you started concentrating so much on your painting, I began to wonder if I had been just a path to fame for you and no longer needed – rather than being the long-term girlfriend I hoped I had become."

"I don't want fame," he replied, hugging her tight as she came back into his life once more, hopefully this time to stay. "What I want is *you!*"

Edna Akam

Image credit: GDJ
Pixabay

Coming Up Roses
© 2023 Edna Akam

I am still bewildered whenever I think about that garden and how I went on far too long without pursuing the questions that constantly came to mind, ignoring the signs that now seem so obvious.

I retired from teaching the cello six months earlier and felt at a loose end. Bill, my husband, was still working at the local library, so much of my time was spent on my own. It's very difficult to adjust, I discovered, when your life has been so full and busy. I really enjoyed teaching and missed the stimulation, the social life.

Now I have various hobbies that I never had time for whilst working. Water colour painting is perhaps my favourite pastime, although my friend Anita, an art teacher, wasn't impressed by my efforts! Still, I enjoy it. It's very therapeutic and once I begin to paint it's difficult to get me to stop, I become so involved. Now I'd have more time to indulge in painting. I'd really like to join an art club, I thought. Plenty of people with a similar interest and an opportunity to develop any talent I might have. Anita said she was delighted that I was at last finding time to relax, and suggested I went along to her class.

Gardening is another thing I love. I have transformed two or three gardens over the years. My current one is very pretty. It was quite wild when we moved here and I remember when we laid the lawn, Bill and I danced over the area to be seeded to try to level it. We had such fun! I don't like straight lines very much, so all my flower beds are curvy. I've filled them with herbaceous plants mostly, although I occasionally have a spending spree and buy lots of annuals that I dot about in empty patches.

We have a pond too. We dug it out one Sunday when Bill wasn't feeling too well. I got bored and started digging. Bill felt compelled to join in and four hours later we had a kidney-shaped hole that we then lined and filled with water. The hard bit was waiting a few weeks for the water to build up beneficial bacteria before we could put fish in it. Now, it is a mature pond, and we have fish, frogs, toads, newts and quite a lot of visiting dragonflies and birds.

Anyway, our garden was at last fairly easy to manage, and I began to feel the need for a new garden project. As luck would have it, I discovered someone not too far from home who needed some help. I saw a card on the front gate of a house on which was written the offer of a part time job.

The house was a modestly sized Edwardian end of terrace with, as far as I could see, a fair-sized garden at the back. I had not been to this part of the town before, but since retiring I had walked along quite a few previously unknown streets. I do like looking at other people's homes. You can get some good ideas from their front gardens to use yourself. I made up my mind there and then to ask if I could have the job and went straight up the front path and rang the doorbell, which was set in one of those large wooden disks mounted on the wall. The top half of the door was panelled in beautiful stained glass in the Art Nouveau style. Bold purple irises with long narrow leaves. Whist I waited for someone to open the door I glanced around at the front garden. It certainly was overgrown but had obviously been lovingly cared for at some point. Some quite unusual perennials were growing there, some of which suggested a level of interest and knowledge not found in the average garden.

The door opened and revealed a very old lady whose bent, twisted body was clearly the reason why she needed help in the garden. She was delighted to discover that I was as keen on gardening as she was, so as you can imagine we had a long chat.

"It's a bit overgrown," Mrs. Conmore told me, "and there are one or two changes you might need to make to the borders. Just do whatever you like, Mrs. Eldrich, because I can't get out there myself nowadays. I have such awful arthritis that I find it too painful to dig or weed the beds. If you could do what you can over the next six months or so, that would really help. As many hours as you can spare. After that, we'll discuss what to do next."

I was pleased to have been given such a free hand and began planning at once. I made a sketch of the garden with approximate dimensions then went home to jot down one or two ideas that were already careering around my mind. Autumn is a good time to revamp a garden if the weather is reasonable and that year was quite dry and bright. Mrs. Conmore said that I was to come and go as I wished and had given me keys to the side gate and shed so there was no need to trouble her every time I visited. As far as payment for my work was concerned, she was more than generous, agreeing to a weekly sum that would cover as many hours as I felt necessary. I asked her if she would mind saving it up for me as Bill and I had decided to donate the money to a charity.

The week after our initial chat, I arranged to spend the afternoon in her garden. There were plenty of useful tools I could use so I grabbed a spade and some secateurs and made a start in the far right-hand corner. After an hour or so of some pretty strenuous digging I decided to sit down for a bit. Sipping the fruit juice that I'd remembered to bring with me, I looked around to take stock of the situation.

If I carried on sorting out this border I thought, it would give me a reasonably good idea of the dimensions of the whole garden. Although I had some plans in mind, I always find I'm clearer as to what is entailed in the task once I've made a start. It would be a bit of a marathon I decided. The border I was currently sorting out was pretty wide although there were some magnificent shrubs and perennials there so I supposed it would look glorious at the height of the summer. Perhaps once I'd cleared the debris, I'd find room for a few spring bulbs in the front of the border along the curve of the lawn.

I finished my juice and returned to my task. Another hour and then I'd better get back home, I thought, or Bill would be wondering where I'd got to. There were no mobile phones then, and I didn't want to bother the old lady. I really enjoyed the work, strenuous though it was. I managed to complete quite a large area – cutting off all the dead twigs and flower heads, turning over the soil. I thought I might change the shape of the bed later on so that it would fit in with my overall plan. That would have to wait though, until I'd dealt with a few more areas of chaos!

I was just finishing off the last section of the border when something caught my eye as it twinkled in the fading light. I bent down to see what it was and realized with astonishment that it was a pretty bracelet that looked like gold. Little diamonds were embedded all along its length, alternating with sapphires. I hurriedly tidied up my tools and made my way round to the front of the house. I rang the doorbell, hoping I wasn't disturbing Mrs. C. during her afternoon nap. She opened the door and looked enquiringly at me. When I showed her what I had dug up she was thrilled.

"How wonderful, Mrs. Edrich!" she cried, "I lost that some years ago when I was stupidly wearing it whilst gardening. You must have it. I feel you are meant to have it."

I protested but she cut me short. "No, no, don't argue, I insist. I am so happy it's been found."

As you can imagine, I was extremely embarrassed as I walked home. I decided to put my beautiful bracelet in a little box in my dressing table for safekeeping in case Mrs. Conmore changed her mind.

The following weekend Bill had to visit an old schoolfriend who was emigrating to Australia soon. I took the opportunity to get back to the garden. I was already feeling rather proprietorial about it. Saturday afternoon was fine, so off I went.

I was rather disappointed when I saw how little I seemed to have achieved. It had appeared so much larger a few days ago. I shrugged and comforted myself with the thought that fishermen always think that the fish they nearly catch is absolutely huge, when it is probably only a tiddler. However, I set to and turned my mind to another length of border on the other side of the garden where some delicate young saplings were resplendent in their autumn attire of red, gold, and various shades of yellow. Beneath them grew two or three types of sedum, some with dark red flower heads and others were pink with crinkly edged leaves. Dotted about amongst the trees and sedum some spiky leaved plants stood proudly waving in the autumn breeze. I couldn't remember their name, but that's not unusual. I have an appalling memory for plant names.

I ended up with a wheelbarrow piled high with compostable stuff, which I took over to the existing heap behind the shed. I'd had enough for now; perhaps I'd do a bit more tomorrow, I thought. After tidying up the tools and wheelbarrow, I wandered over to the gate. Glancing back to survey my handywork, I was startled to see how meagre my efforts looked. Shaking off a feeling of despondency, I walked back home determined to get rid of this mood. "*It's often the way with a big project like this,*" I told myself, "*I expect too much too soon.*" I was also missing Bill.

I was unable to return to the garden until the following Wednesday as the weather decided to break, and we had one or two downpours. However, by Tuesday the sun shone boldly once more so the ground was wet but workable when I resumed my labours the next day.

Off I trotted after an early lunch full of the joys of autumn. I was agreeably surprised when I let myself in by the side gate. I had been so downhearted the previous week that I was a bit apprehensive as to how to continue my work, but my plan of action was obvious as I inspected the garden, although the whole plot did seem to be much less extensive than my original impression. I thought I'd begin with the central bed. It was rather overgrown so some pruning back and deadheading would be the best way forward.

I collected the tools I needed and began with the dead flowers. There was a mass of foliage to wade through; tall Michaelmas Daisies, a couple of clumps of Esther Reeds, and rather a lot of roses to try to avoid. After an hour or so (I tend to lose track of time when I'm gardening, and I'd left my watch at home), I straightened up and looked around me.

There was still a lot of clearing up to be done before I could start reshaping the beds, but I needed to have an idea of how it was beginning to appear in its current layout, as I'd never seen how it had looked before it had been so neglected. I don't think I'd ever make a reliable witness in a courtroom! The dimensions of the garden were smaller than I remembered. Still, considering I had only been in it a few times I suppose that was understandable.

I had a drink from my flask as I walked around trying to decide where to pounce next. I decided to tackle the rockery; at least that's what I supposed the pile of overgrown stones was. There was an abundance of very unruly rock plants that must have looked beautiful in the summer. In my opinion a well-stocked rockery with a mass of colour takes some beating, but that lot would have to wait until the middle flower bed was finished.

By four o'clock, I'd more or less completed all I needed to do. The light was fading, so I packed away my tools, sorted out the compost material and bagged up some rubbish which I stacked up against the gate. I thought I'd bring the car the next day and run it all up to the tip.

As it happened, I couldn't do any more for a week or so as family commitments prevented me from doing anything other than babysitting, visiting a sick friend and generally 'being there' for everyone. Retirement certainly reminds people how useful you are. I was really happy to see more of my grandchildren, though, and spent some pleasant days taking them to different places of interest.

Eventually I was able to get along to Mrs. Conmore's garden on a Saturday afternoon. There didn't seem to be any sign of her through the windows overlooking the garden. She had told me she would not interfere with my work but would be interested to see the changes I had made. Anyway, there were quite thick net curtains at the windows, so I probably wouldn't see much through them.

I stood at the back of the house and glanced over the garden. I thought it needed something clever done to make it less narrow. Perhaps I could shorten the long side borders and maybe put a shrub or two across the lawn to give the impression of more width. My memory must surely be seriously at fault as my original impression of the size of the area had been considerably bigger. In the end, I decided to bring the side borders into the lawn at more or less the middle so as to break up the length a bit. It took some effort, I can tell you, to dig out the area of lawn to create the wider beds. I carefully put the squares of turf in a pile by the bottom fence as I might need them later on.

After a longer session than usual, I downed tools with a sigh of relief. Looking around me I felt pleased with my efforts. It was beginning to take shape. I decided to visit the local garden centre to buy a few extra bits and pieces for the borders and rockery. I love buying new plants. The trouble is that nowadays there is so much to choose from...

Eventually, the car was crammed full with bags of shrubs, bulbs, and rockery plants. I drove back to Mrs. Conmore's where I unloaded everything. Then I remembered the rubbish bags I'd intended for the tip. I loaded them into the boot and then went round to the front door to ring the doorbell to see if Mrs. Conmore was available. She came to the door after some delay, and smiled happily as she complimented me on my efforts so far.

"What a pleasure it is to see how well you are getting on Mrs. Eldrich!" she cried. "I'm delighted with the progress. I've been watching with great interest and am thrilled with the reshaping of the borders."

I told her about the plants I had bought and that I intended returning on Monday to bed them in.

"I shall add the amount you have spent on the plants to your wages if that's acceptable, Mrs. Eldrich. If you need to buy any more don't hesitate to do so."

She was almost childlike in her enthusiasm. I said I'd see how it went and let her know during the week.

On Monday I got down to arranging all the plants where I had pictured them. Strangely, there seemed to be far too many although I thought I'd been quite careful not to overspend. I managed to find room for everything in the end and once again tidied up all the tools and equipment I'd used.

After sweeping the patio clean, I did my usual critical survey of the work. It was all beginning to look a lot better and had a much more interesting shape than before I'd started. Amazing how different a garden can look with a little bit of tender loving care. The trees and shrubs seemed to be turning their faces towards me nodding their approval.

I could hardly wait for Spring to arrive so that I could revel in the beauty of the transformed garden. I enjoyed working for someone else for a change. I had been more careful and yet at the same time more ruthless with this project than with our own garden.

That evening, we had some sad news: Bill's sister, who had lived in New Zealand with her husband and two children for the last twenty years, had died suddenly after a heart attack. Simon, her husband, was so distraught when he phoned. He asked us if there was any chance of us going over there. Bill immediately made arrangements to be away from the library for at least a month. He had quite a lot of time owed to him as he had been going in on his days off to help with some reorganization-something to do with videos.

The next day we made arrangements at the local travel agent and I popped into Mrs. Conmore's later on to explain I'd be away for a while. By Wednesday, we were off. I couldn't help feeling excited about the prospect of going so far away, even with the sad reason for our trip. Helen was only fifty-eight and had been so healthy all her life. It would be nice to see our niece and nephew, though, as we'd only seen them as small children. Now they were both adults and had small children of their own. Christmas was also soon to be upon us, and I had never experienced this time of year in a hot climate. So it was with very mixed feelings that we made our long journey to the other side of the world. Needless to say, I didn't think about gardening at all.

On returning four and a half weeks later, we felt exhausted, sad, confused and a bit disorientated. Bill was still reeling from the shock of Helen's untimely death, and I was rather loathe to do anything at all. Jet lag, I suppose. Well, it was some days later when Bill went back to work that I turned my thoughts to Mrs. C's garden. I didn't feel like gardening, but I decided to wander round there to see how things were coming along and have a chat with the old lady.

Imagine my astonishment when I walked through the side gate into the garden to discover that it was looking absolutely beautiful, with early bulbs in full bloom, flowering shrubs resplendent in vibrant colour and trees full of leaf. Everything was out at once. After my initial surprise and pleasure, I looked around again and felt claustrophobic. Too much, it was all wrong. I stood still and stared. No progression from bulbs to Dianthus to Sweet Williams to roses, as I had planned. The effect was frankly crude and so wrong.

The weirdness of it all began to worry me. What on earth had happened? Something in the soil? Something I'd messed up? I hurried round to the front of the house and rang the doorbell. Mrs. Conmore opened the door quite quickly to my surprise and seemed pleased to see me.

"Oh, Mrs. Eldrich," she cried, "I am so pleased to see you! The garden has really taken shape since you went away, and I have been enjoying it immensely."

"But everything is out together, Mrs. Conmore; that's not what I had in mind at all. It's all gone wrong. I don't understand." I handed her the keys, which she took and shoved in the pocket of her floral print overall.

"Mrs. Eldrich, it is splendid," the old lady interrupted, "I could not rest until I had seen it once more in all its glory. You see I was taken ill and for months I worried about all the tasks that were being neglected here. You have made me very happy."

Puzzled at her lack of comment on the extreme growth of all the foliage and blooms I asked what she would like me to do next.

"Oh, nothing at all! You have carried out your part of our arrangement admirably," she replied, "there is nothing more to do."

"But what about the weekly maintenance and trying to fathom out why all the plants and flowers have blossomed at the same time, and – "

"There is no need for any further work to be done in my garden, Mrs. Eldrich. It is complete."

With that, she closed the door and I was left standing talking to myself, feeling hurt and confused. Still, it was her choice. I had to accept that working for other people gave them the right to make their own decisions regarding what should be done, especially in their own home. She hadn't paid me, either. I'd have to go back again when I was not so upset. It was for charity, after all.

Still a little confused by what had just happened, I wandered round to the library to see Bill. Fortunately, he was having a spot of lunch, so I went up to the staff room. He was surprised to see me as I rarely intruded into his workplace, other than to choose books, of course. When I told him what had happened, he was very sympathetic and comforted me by suggesting I searched around for another project.

"Go and look in the newsagent's window. You might find someone else who needs a helping green finger or two," he said.

I left him feeling a bit more cheerful, but I couldn't get completely out of my mind the disappointment over the rejection I had experienced. It was also very weird how rapidly everything had grown and matured at the same time. I decided to take one more look at my handywork and made my way back to the house. At least I tried to. I could not find the street however hard I searched.

"This is ridiculous," I thought, *"I must be going senile. How can you lose a whole street? I was only there an hour ago."*

I searched in vain for some time and then saw a lady digging in her own front garden.

"Excuse me," I called, "can you direct me to Gloucester Street, please? It seems silly, but I've lost my way, although I know it's round here somewhere."

"Well, you must have been away a long time." The lady chuckled as she straightened up, brushed a wisp of curly blonde hair from her eyes with the back of her hand, and came over to the fence.

"Gloucester Street was bombed in the war and all the houses demolished. A new estate was built on the original site about thirty years ago."

"But that can't be," I said, frustrated and puzzled. "I was there only a short while back. Today, in fact."

"You can't have been," was the rather exasperated reply, "perhaps you've got the name wrong."

The lady began to turn back to her digging, obviously thinking she was talking to an idiot.

"Oh, no!" 'I persisted, "that's the right street name. A Mrs. Conmore lives there. I've been doing her garden for her."

The lady turned back, her face pale. After a few moments, she broke the silence.

"That 'Mrs. Conmore' was my grandmother. She lived in Gloucester Street until she became too ill to be on her own. Just before the war, she was taken to hospital very much against her will and she died soon afterwards. She loved that garden and worried so much about its upkeep. Are you sure that's the right name and address?"

My face paled, too, as I nodded, apologized for bothering her, and turned to make my way slowly home, leaving a very puzzled lady who I was too upset to enlighten about something I didn't understand, either.

When I arrived home, I sat for some time trying to think of a logical explanation for all that had happened. I had certainly been somewhere over the past few months, working hard in a garden I had come to be so proud of. Much as I hate to think in terms of ghosts, I was beginning to believe I had been very much taken in by one. I wasn't so much scared as bewildered.

Where had I been? I still had a few traces of scratch marks from being attacked by brambles and other thorny things. I'd definitely been somewhere. It was all very real, so what – oh – my memory took me back a few months to the beginning of my exploits; all the times I had puzzled over the diminishing flowerbeds, the frustrating feeling of not achieving as much as I'd thought.

I realized the garden had been gradually shrinking and by the time Bill and I went to New Zealand, it was about half its original size. On our return, the spectacle of glorious colour and growth had blinded me to the fact that it was even smaller than before we went. Evidently, the whole garden had now vanished completely.

I pulled myself together and went upstairs to look at the bracelet I had found. Was that a reality? That would prove I'd been to Gloucester Street, and the talk of a ghost was nonsense. I certainly had never owned a bracelet like the one I had found. Far too expensive. There it was; as pretty as ever with its sparkling jewels; proof that my hard work was a reality. Mrs. Conmore had achieved her goal. Her garden had had its makeover and the bracelet – well that could be sold, and our charity would get its donation. We'd never be able to convince anybody, but Bill and I knew it had happened and perhaps I'd help lay a troubled spirit to rest.

Anguish

We sat quietly on the overstuffed chairs that were arranged almost carelessly around the ornately decorated room.

My friends admired the heavy brocade curtains, so richly draped over the tall windows; rich, predominately deep red, with a complicated pattern in green and gold. The walls were wood panelled and supported a number of well-painted portraits of past members of the family. Not by well-known artists, but 'of the school of' various eminent painters.

One portrait in particular caught their eyes. The most beautiful girl imaginable stared down in an almost mocking way. What had she been thinking whilst the artist enjoyed his work?

She must have been about eighteen then. Her light brown hair was caught up in a glorious swirl with a midnight blue satin bow. Her skin, fair and unblemished, enhanced finely chiselled features that seemed in need of no makeup. Indeed, her lips had a natural pink glow, and her eyelashes were long, curling with no help at all.

She reclined on a dark green chaise-longue, leaning on the high upholstered end, with her pale blue gown draped effectively along the length of the seat.

My friends shook me away cruelly from my contemplations.

"We must be still and allow nothing to ruin our chances of seeing her." Robert, ever the leader, was reminding us how delicately handled the whole process had to be.

There were three of us, friends of longstanding, same college, about the same ages – in our thirties – and all with no family commitments to hinder our mission.

"It's a perfect evening, John," Simon said quietly to me, "Autumn, dry and calm after a sunny day; cold enough though, for a fire to be roaring in this huge stone fireplace." He shivered, as there was no fire on this occasion.

I thought about the last time I came here. It too had been such an evening. I had been reading things about the property which I knew already. The long wait had been, it seemed, forever, but at last she had come. Softly, gently, through the door that led to the adjoining library.

"Hello, Michael." She had breathed the words so quietly that I could hardly hear them. "I have longed for this moment. My heart was broken when you left me. Oh, I know your conscience compelled you to go, and I admired you for that, but war seemed so far away, and our life together so real and important. Do you remember our last meeting together? You never knew of the child I bore who so resembled you. Such utter joy, but such abject misery. I was rejected by my family and our son was brought up in poverty, but I loved him dearly."

She had stood serenely in her blue gown and spoken with dignity but also with an element of reproach.

I could hardly bear to listen to her but stayed, miserably aware that I needed to know more about what I had read and try to verify other bits of information I had gleaned. Now it seemed she was confirming what I had suspected. She truly believed I was the Michael she had loved.

I requested the help of my friends after my first visit to the house. My family had lived in the area for many years, and some branches of it could be traced back for centuries in that county. Having read History at college, I turned my attention to my own family tree, which proved quite a difficult task to accomplish.

The house in which my friends and I were now sitting had once been owned by a wealthy farmer, a cousin of one of my ancestors. I discovered the inevitable scandal these families always tried (but rarely were able) to suppress. In an effort to learn more, I had managed to gain access to the house, which was now unoccupied, having been abandoned by the present owner who now lived in France. He was desperately trying to sell, but evidently there was little interest from buyers, partly due to its size I guessed.

It had been a traumatic experience for me. Merely wishing to 'get a feel for the place' I had been sitting in this same chair staring in admiration at the portrait of the girl, when she had walked into the room and greeted me as I have described.

Now, after more research, and discovering my namesake had been her lover, I needed to know more. Why did I feel this affinity to her? Why had I always had this feeling of guilt about something undefined?

My father told me a little about our family. Much information was missing but evidently there had been two parallel branches, one very rich, one decidedly poor. I descended from the latter branch.

As I read further, the Michael she had loved became more familiar to me and was by all accounts very like me in character and looks.

Now I had returned with my friends to see if we could reconstruct what I had experienced some months ago.

"Look!" whispered Robert, "The library door is opening."

We stared at the door, our eyes wide and mouths open as we waited to see what would happen. Slowly a woman appeared, but she was nothing like the beautiful girl. She was old, very old, with gnarled fingers reaching out towards us. Her face was a mass of wrinkles beneath a head of white wispy hair.

Still dignified though, and still reproachful, she turned towards me.

"Michael, I knew you would return. Our son must know his father. I will not rest until he meets you. Come with me," she commanded.

Her voice was deeper than when I had first met her and I could see brown teeth and ugly gaps in her mouth, which had been so pretty and tempting before.

She reached out her thin bony arms towards me as if to lead me – who knew where?

I recoiled from her as she advanced towards me.

"No, I am not your Michael! Leave me alone. Go, go, please go away," I pleaded.

I was terrified. Why had I returned? Why delve into the past? What had happened to her son? Why had she been so beautiful the last time I saw her? Perhaps to ensure I'd return?

I felt the tug of my friends' hands at my sleeve as they tried to drag me away and out of the house. She came closer, still reaching for me, still walking slowly, menacingly.

As we reached the door to the hall, she began to fade. We did not wait to experience her final departure but saw, as we scrambled awkwardly out and ventured a last look back, her face on one side had become young and beautiful again, full of yearning, the other remained wizened and full of hate.

A Fantasy
© 2023 Edna Akam

I stared at the screen. It was always like this when I started a new story. No inspiration. Where should I start? It was worse when there was no given title or subject. Always too much choice. I remembered when my English teacher at school gave us a so-called treat.

"Now girls," she'd bark from her desk, "you're all being given carte blanche this Easter." She loved to show off her knowledge of other languages. In fact, she only knew the rather obvious phrases. "An essay on any subject you like. Five hundred words by the first day of term."

I would sit on our old leather settee at home in front of a blank piece of paper, flicking my biro between my fingers without a jot of an idea. It took me ages to think of a subject before even contemplating building a story around it.

Now it was just as difficult. Write a fantasy, we were told at the writers' circle. "*Hey, ho! So here I am again,*" I thought as I twirled my grey curls round my fingers, back at school and with about the same attitude, but with a computer, not a pen and paper.

I sipped my coffee and kicked off my slippers to be more comfortable. I live alone since my husband died, so I had no commitments other than my own pursuits. Retirement can make you a bit lazy, but I do belong to a few groups, including pottery and painting.

"Damn! The screen keeps blanking as I'm not doing anything. It'll stop altogether in a minute and give up the ghost," I shouted.

"Ha ha, that's funny!"

What the hell was that?

"Give up the ghost. I haven't heard that one for many a long year."

Who's speaking? Who are you?

"I'm a writer; like you."

"What do you mean? 'I'm no writer. I try, but I'm not very good yet.' *Anyway,* I thought, *what the heck am I talking to myself for, or is there someone in the kitchen? Did I leave the back door open?*

"ome on Jamie, stop mucking about."

I got up and peered round the door into my tiny galley to see if my neighbour had dropped by, but there was nobody there.

"I'm here. Do come back. I want to help."

I turned back towards the computer and saw it was not a blank screen anymore but showing a picture of a man grinning his head off. It really was off, too. His body was neatly seated on a chair by the table. The head was quite unconcerned on a separate chair, as the left hand attached to the body gently tidied a stray quiff out of his piercing blue eyes and smoothed it back over the rest of his dark brown locks. I suppose he must have been in his thirties, although his hairstyle wasn't very trendy for a man of that age. He had a finely chiselled beard and wavy moustache.

This was bizarre, but I wasn't frightened, just curious. The internet is such a mystery to most of us. We use it, and as long as nothing goes wrong – great. At the least provocation it seems, the screen can go blank, or your work doesn't save, or worst of all you get scammed. Really, we've been pushed into this technology with only a veneer of knowledge. Like icebergs, most of it is hidden from sight, and we are at the mercy of experts – or the neighbour's teenage son.

"Who are you?" I asked again, aloud.

"I'm Jacob. I used to write stories to amuse people. You'd be surprised how bored people got, back in the day. I made quite a hit with the ladies. They liked my short pithy tales of love and lust. Men preferred the derring-do type of yarn. I could do it all. Turn my hand to anything. Now, how can I help?"

I'm no computer genius, but I was pretty sure pop-ups weren't supposed to be like this. Skype I can understand, but surely you have to dial first, and accept a call?

"How did you manage to get on---er---*into*, my computer? I don't know you." Now I was talking to the machine as if it were another human being.

"Of course, you don't know me, silly! I know you, though. I know all the would-be writers trying to create a masterpiece. 'There's a book in everyone,' they say — what a load of rubbish. Takes talent to write. I was very successful, though I say it myself." He preened himself and smirked irritatingly.

"I didn't become very famous, or make much money more's the pity, but people craved for my next shortie. I had them produced as weekly broadsheets and sold in town centres all over Sussex. Unfortunately, I got a bit carried away and, so it was claimed, I got a bit raunchy with the lust and love. Had a bit of a barney with some of the husbands, and they came at me one night, using, I might tell you, all the tricks of the trade they'd learned from the tales I wrote for them – and chopped off my head. I was livid. I still had a full-length novel in me, so that was a bit of a drawback. Anyway, after the initial shock and my lifeblood had finished oozing out, I lay there for a while, contemplating my next move.

"It took a while before I got my bearings and realised I was hovering above the two separated parts of my body. Of course, the lynch mob had scarpered, so there I was, just lying there. I tried to work out which bit of me was looking down on the other bit. I came to the conclusion I was dead. Pretty obvious, I suppose, but it takes some getting used to. How exciting! You see, I was immediately wanting to turn all this into a story! Writers are born; you can't learn genius."

I was beginning to think this headless wonder was rather big-headed, but looking at him with more compassion, I thought that was an inconsiderate assumption. Poor bloke hadn't got a head, well, on his body anyway.

"So, given what you've told me is true, and I'm not saying I believe you, what would you suggest I write for this fantasy?" Was I still really talking to this – talking head? I was sure Alan Bennett didn't have this scenario in mind when he produced his own successful 'Talking Heads' series for television.

"Well, you could tell them about me for a start. They'll never believe it, but I bet they'll all rush home to their computers to see if they can find me. They won't, of course. I'm very selective about whom I choose to converse with. There was a nice chap I helped back in 2000. He was stuck like you, and I was able to give him a few pointers. You know, I had to resort to different ways of communicating before the computer age. Back in the early 1830s, for instance, I noticed a promising young writer called Charles who was having a spot of bother. I liked him, because he was keen on publishing in magazines at first, rather like me, but just had so little inspiration, although boy, could he write! Anyway, I managed to sort of 'appear' to him one day, had a chat, gave him a bit of encouragement, a few ideas, and the result was a work about a bloke called Pickwick. I wasn't happy about the name, but it seemed to take off in 1836, as he became quite famous. I'm pretty sure I'd have become that famous if I hadn't had my head chopped off."

I stared at the screen. This bloke was so full of himself.

"This is ridiculous! You can't be real, and I'm going to switch off the computer and get it checked out at PC World.

I'll write my own fantasy thanks. I don't need a headless wonder to help me." I didn't want to bother my neighbour, as he probably wouldn't believe me.

I shut down, but not before I saw the look of disappointment on the man's face. His body just sat there, motionless. I hadn't found out anything about him; where he had lived, and when. Now I'd never know. Too late, the screen went blank.

After I've been to PC World, I'll start my story again. Maybe he had helped though. Perhaps I'll write about him.

The Clock is Ticking
© 2023 Edna Akam

It doesn't tick, it's digital,
It's really lost the plot,
Efficient, smart, it looks the part,
But Timex it is not.

My Timex lasted ages,
I had new straps times ten;
But progress meant some changes;
Life seemed so simple then.

But now the darned thing's let me down,
I'm later than I thought;
I didn't see the battery
Had died and gone to pot.

I've resurrected Timex
The winder functions still.
It's down to me, and as you see,
My Timex fits the bill.

Unexpected

"I can't stand them!" shouted Molly from the top of the stairs. "Why do they always have to come every year?"

"Stop being so silly," Harriet replied, "you know they are very generous and give you lovely presents. Not that you deserve them."

Harriet wiped her floury hands on a cloth and reached for the kettle. Time for a cuppa before getting on with the cake. She'd finished the mince pies and was keen to get the cake in the oven. They do make Molly and Ben go through hoops at Christmas, Harriet thought. True, as she had said to Molly, they were generous. Always gave them all money and a useful present.

A couple of years ago year she and Ben had been able to have a complete makeover in the kitchen with the money they'd been given. Molly and Saul had new bikes, which gave them both a bit more freedom. As teenagers living in the country, they'd had to rely on busses, which were very infrequent, or persuading mum or dad to take and collect them from their friends or a club. They were taken by bus on the half hour journey to school every day, so that wasn't a problem. The bikes were much used in their free time, and really the twins were grateful, but it was always at such a cost.

Last year, Saul had been made to cycle over to Grandpa's allotment to dig over the plot for new vegetables and then was expected to go at least twice a week after school to weed, water and fight off the bugs and birds.

Molly had her tasks too. Grandma didn't want to waste money on a cleaner, so Molly cleaned the house twice a week and did bits of shopping.

"That's not much to ask, and it keeps you both occupied," said Harriet.

"Yes, but we have homework and our own things to do," said Saul.

"Stop the moaning," Ben called out from the sitting room, "I'm sick of hearing your voices. Yak-yak-yakking all the time."

Harriet said nothing. She sort of agreed that Ben's parents asked too much of her children. A certain amount of help for the oldies was okay but she thought they pushed their luck a bit. On the odd occasion when Saul or Molly had argued with them, they had threatened not to give them presents again. The twins were not strong enough to say, "Okay, you do that!"'

Harriet didn't blame them. She and Ben couldn't afford all the little luxuries that his parents showered them with, but it did seem a bit like blackmail, or at least a way of keeping the family under their control.

She didn't even like them very much, because Ben had told her that his childhood had been very restricted, and his friends very carefully vetted. His parents would often visit the school to complain about his lack of homework or some rule or other they didn't agree with. Ben suffered a lot of embarrassment then. As the only child of older parents, they were both in their late forties when he was born, and he didn't really feel free until he left school to start an apprenticeship with an electrical firm. He did very well, and enjoyed his work, but it was never going to make him rich.

His parents, however, had done well for themselves. They had owned a string of hardware shops and now, having sold them and made a pretty good return, lived in comparative luxury. Ben didn't get any help, though. His dad would tell him, "You've got to make your own way in life, son. You can't expect handouts from us all the time. Your mother and I got where we are today by sheer hard work."

The family home was indeed substantial. A late 19th century detached property in a good area with wide roads and tree lined verges, it had a walled garden with an orchard, a pond with loads of goldfish in it, and flowering shrubs that were strategically placed artistically by a landscape gardener.

Ben loved the house more than he did his parents. He often said he felt guilty about his lack of love for them. How could you love someone who brought you up so strictly and with no warmth; no cuddles or treats? No praise or encouragement? They had been busy with the shops of course and had to keep an eye on all their employees who they never really trusted to run the businesses efficiently.

Well, it was Christmas again, and they would be arriving soon to demand being waited on hand and foot. They never hosted Christmas themselves. Always came in, plonked themselves down in the two most comfortable armchairs and waited impatiently for their dry sherry. They got up only for dinner, tea, and their trips to the lavatory. Always leaving at 9 o'clock, that was the time Ben, Harriet, Molly, and Saul heaved a family sigh of relief and opened their own presents. This included ones from the oldies.

This year would be exactly the same. Harriet felt guilty as she dreamed of their demise. Still, they were getting on now, well into their eighties, and with luck the family's patience would be well rewarded sooner or later.

There was a knock on the door.

"Mr. Geeson?" asked the policeman.

"Yes, what is it?" Ben replied. Already on his second beer to fortify himself against the intrusion of his parents, he stared at the visitor questioningly.

"I'm sorry to say, sir, that there's been an accident. May I come in?"

Ben stepped aside to let the constable in. Harriet came out of the kitchen looking anxious and hot.

Evidently an out-of-control car had ploughed straight into his parents' car. Drunk already at midday, the young man was dead, and so were Ben's parents.

The family's feelings were a mixture of horror, guilt, grief relief, then guilt again. A week later Ben and Harriet were contacted by his parent's solicitor. He had their will, which left all their money and the house to Ben as he had expected.

"Whoopee!" shouted the twins. Their parents glared at them.

"However," continued the solicitor solemnly, "unfortunately the will was written ten years ago. Since then, your parents have been spending beyond their means and there is no money, and the house is near to being sold to pay further debts. I'm so sorry."

Ben had no idea his parents were such spendthrifts. So, they were going off on expensive holidays and living it up whilst he and Harriet slaved away trying to make ends meet. How mean of them. He discounted the gifts, which he considered were due payment for his family being at their beck and call.

After the funerals, that Ben had to pay for as there was no money from the parents to deal with it, the family went home still reeling from this unexpected turn of events. After debts were paid there was the princely sum of five hundred and sixty-seven pounds. Thirty-six pounds left for Ben, who had seen his childhood home sold to become a nursing home. They got on with their lives, and the twins started to pay more attention to their studies. GCSEs were looming.

The young man who had caused the fatal crash and also died left truly grieving parents. However, they contacted Ben and Harriet some months later.

'We are so sorry for your loss. Our son, our only child, was very precious to us. We understand you, too. were the only son of Mr. and Mrs. Geeson. We cannot bring them back to you but want to make a difference to your own family."

Molly and Saul finished their education at an exclusive sixth form college and had their university fees paid for. They and their parents felt rather ashamed that they weren't really sorry the oldies had gone, but managed to keep up the pretence as they enjoyed their gift from the wealthy parents of the reckless driver.

An Unwelcome Gift

© 2023 Edna Akam

I love it to bits, it's just what I need.
The colour's so me, I've always liked tweed.
I hope you like your one -I searched every shop.
And eventually found it right there on the top!

(I hate it, how could she? She knows I hate green.
I never wear woollens; I think she's so mean.)
(Right there at the top is right where it should stay.
Who'd wear a hat like it? It's so not 'today.')

I'm so glad you like it! I get in a pickle
When people I buy for are awkward and fickle.
You're so very clever - I'll wear it next weekend.
(I'm off to a meeting; why should I pretend?)

It's awful, I hate it. You have such bad taste.
I don't like yours either – you bought it in haste.
Let's go back together and choose something new.
I know what I want, and I'm sure you do too.

Let all who will: go digital
We Luddites just don't care.
We'll muddle through in our own way;
Just stop us if you dare.

The Wedding
© 2023 Edna Akam

I like a wedding, love to dress in different clothes and shoes;

A chance to meet the family too and find out all the news.

'I meant to write' - 'and so did I' - 'I'm sorry for your loss.'

'Oh, that's ok, he was quite old, and now we have a horse.'

'Ah, there's Aunt Jane, she's looking well, I wonder if she's

noticed

That Herbert and his husband Sam are now at last united.'

'A shame about poor Vivienne. she lost her seat you know;

She came a sorry fourth in fact, to Lib Dems – such a blow!'

'Oh look, the bride's arrived with all her children looking smart

In little suits and dresses pink embroidered with love hearts.'

The Vicar's nice, with long red hair all tied back with a bow.

It matches all the pink love hearts but picked out in a row.

The ceremony's over and the guests all leave the Nave
To join the bride and groom for snaps; they do a special wave

And all say 'cheese,' make sure they're seen, they jostle for a
place
To stand, but not behind Doreen – she's always in your face.

She's very large and very tall but always has to be
Right in the front, which isn't kind for someone rather wee.

The food was good, the band was loud, but everyone had fun
Except the Vicar - skin got burned, exposed to too much sun.

So off they went to sunny Spain – a week for Honeymoon,
Then back to work and children – that will happen far too
soon

Patricia Reilly

Image Credit: Iconbark
Pixabay

I Made Them Myself
© 2023 Patricia Reilly

Margo opened the door with a flourish. "Come in, darlings," she gushed, "come in and welcome. Please excuse the mess, I am just beginning my Christmas cards. So many to send, the list just gets longer and longer each year. Do make yourselves comfortable while I get the coffee."

"Do you need any help?" June ventured to ask, knowing full well what the answer would be.

"No thank you, darling, it's all organized; won't be a tick." The four friends looked at each other and winced as Margo swept out of the room leaving them to bathe in the aroma of her heavily applied Chanel No. 5.

When they could hear the percolator bubbling away in the kitchen, they sneaked a look at some of Margo's Christmas cards.

"Crikey!" said Pauline, "these are a bit weird. They remind me of those the children made last year in kindergarten. The glue's still wet on this one." As she spoke, she lifted a small card with a fat robin stuck on the front to show them – the robin promptly fell off and fluttered to the carpet.

"Now you've done it," said Carol, "Quick, pick it up and stick it back on, she will be back in a minute."

The girls sat themselves down on Margo's chintz sofa and matching chairs and waited for their hostess. She seemed to be quite a long time. While they waited, they chatted idly, and Pauline fished a wipe out of her bag to try to get the glue off her fingers.

Margo appeared eventually, looking somewhat flustered.

"Sorry to have been so long, I had a slight malfunction in the kitchen." She went on to explain that the mince pies she had been cooking as a treat to have with their coffee had been a little overdone.

"Do you mean burnt, darling?" Jessie asked with a grin, "you should have just bought a box from Waitrose and warmed them through. We would never have known the difference."

"Nonsense," said Margo, "I always make my own mince pies and Christmas puddings and Christmas cake. Harold wouldn't have it any other way. He says he can't eat that shop-bought muck."

"Well, he tucked into the mince pies at our house last year and they were 'Tesco's Finest,' and he didn't seem to notice," Jessie offered.

"Well, he would have been too polite to say anything dear." said Margo. "Anyway, let's have coffee and there's plenty of homemade shortbread and muffins, so tuck in and enjoy."

While they sipped the somewhat bitter coffee and nibbled at the shortbread and the rather dry muffins, they chatted about their plans for Christmas and New Year. June and her family were going on a cruise over Christmas, so she had no preparation of food to worry about, though they would have open house over the New Year's Day. Pauline was having her family over and was doing the full roast turkey and trimmings, and had them all laughing when she described one Christmas spent with a friend in America, when the turkey was so big they had to cut its legs off to get it in the oven. Jess had bought a Sainsbury pudding, brandy butter and rum custard, and double cream.

"Hush," Carol urged, "think of your cholesterol levels... All that fat!"

"Oh, well," laughed Jess, "a little of what you fancy does you good, and I'm no great shakes as a cook, really. But I do know what we like, and after all, it is Christmas."

So the morning wore on, and the friends made their excuses to leave.

"Let's help you clear up first, Margo," said Pauline, piling the plates and cups and saucers onto a tray; before Margo could stop her she made her way to the kitchen. On entering, she nearly dropped the tray she was so surprised by the scene before her eyes. Margo's expensive worktops were littered with boxes that had held mince pies and shortbread, and there were plastic trays that had held muffins. By the sink, there was a baking tray with the charred remains of what might have been mince pies.

Margo *had* tried to serve up her own mince pies, but as she had truthfully admitted, they had burned. She must have nipped out of the back door while they were chatting and rushed down to the Tesco Express at the end of the road and bought some readymade ones. To say nothing of the shortbread and muffins. Pauline decided that she would also say nothing. She had enjoyed Margo's friendship for several years now and had no wish to make her friend look a fool in front of the others. So, she hastily put the tray down and went straight back to the lounge. Margo was helping June into her coat; avoiding Margo's eyes, Pauline just picked up her own coat and put it on.

"Thank you so much for this morning, Margo," Pauline said, "it's been lovely having the time to chat together. You must all come to me next week and we can toast June before she goes off on her cruise. We can exchange cards then, too, save on a bit of postage, eh?' They all agreed and got ready to leave.

Oh," said Margo, "I wanted to show you my Christmas cards. Do have a quick look, darlings: I made them myself."

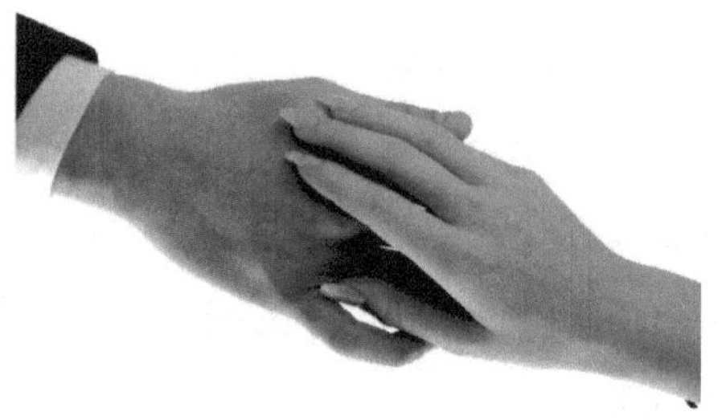

Image Credit: Bru-No
Pixabay

Perfect Partners - Perhaps
© 2023 Patricia Reilly

"Pay the papers while you are up town, Joe," Pauline croaked from the bedroom. Stricken with an unspeakable flu virus, she knew she would have to rely on Joe to cope with all the weekend chores. A perpetual fear of debt had dogged her since she had to witness her parents' bankruptcy and subsequent suicide when she was a teenager. The recurrent nightmares of receivers claiming her hard earned and treasured possessions had led her to settle household bills regularly. The minute Joe put his rent alongside her pay-packet on a Friday, Pauline totted up who was owed what, ready to settle up next day.

She was lucky in her relationship with Joe, who agreed with her fetish to keep solvent at all times, knowing that would help to keep her fears at bay.

Joe Baxter had come along with a gang of tarmac layers when the M1 was being constructed and had taken lodgings with her and her sister. When the latter had run off with the over-amorous postman, Joe had stayed on, ostensibly to help Pauline keep a roof over her head. Deep down, he felt genuinely sorry for her but unbeknown to Pauline, Joe had some dark secrets, and it suited him to appear to live a quiet, almost boring existence in the small rural backwater. He liked to think the neighbours saw him and Pauline as being a devoted pair although marriage had never been mooted.

This was just as well. Over the years, working away for months at a time, Joe had played the field – not just one marriage under his belt, but three – and no records of any divorce!

In blissful ignorance of his devious character, Pauline went about her business in the village generally with Joe when he was home. The locals called them 'The Odd Couple' behind their backs; Joe being tall and wiry, while she had a fat, round little body. He was a huddle of shapeless garments when he left early mornings to join the gang on motorway maintenance, but he presented a very different figure in a well-cut jacket and flannels on the weekends.

She, however, always looked a frump. With parents in penury and a selfish sister, no one had offered her guidance in the fashion stakes. A canteen cook for years, her lumpy figure, (an obvious legacy of her trade), was shrouded in a large overall. On her days off, sweatpants and trainers sufficed. She showed little femininity, which was probably why Joe felt so comfortable living with her as her lodger: there were no physical complications in his relationship with Pauline. He had spent more nights under her roof than with any of his three wives, and the fact that she was totally unaware of the games he had been playing for nearly twenty years meant that he felt more at home with her than anywhere else.

There was, however, always a fear in the back of his mind that his lurid past would catch up with him one day. Although he felt that he had covered his tracks each time, and that Pauline didn't have a clue, he had got a fright when he found her in his room the week before. She said she'd been looking for any dirty washing. His guilty conscience was working overtime, and he was beginning to think perhaps he ought to move on, but he knew there would be talk if he did. Perhaps now was the time to take one last chance.

That Saturday he paid the papers and Pauline's other outstanding bills, making sure all his own personal debts were clear too, and then he got the weekend shopping. On his return he heated a bowl of chicken soup and took it into Pauline.

"Drink this up, love. 'Cures all ills,' my mum used to say,"
he said with a grin.

"Did you pay the bills?" she asked.

"Yes, yes. Don't worry. All settled."

"The insurance as well?" she queried.

"Oh yes. Most definitely. Wouldn't do to fall behind with
that one. I'm glad you took my advice. it's a good policy, and
the company will pay up promptly on death."

"You're a cheerful beggar," she snapped, feeling hot and
feverish as she choked down the soup. Did she imagine it,
or did it have a bitter taste? Perhaps it was just the tin.

Joe laughed. "Don't you fret, girl. Finish that up and have
a sleep. I'm going out to finish off preparing the base for
your new patio. The concrete's coming on Monday." With
that, he donned work clothes and set to in the garden.

He worked all afternoon, filling, and levelling as though
he was on one of his road jobs, but all the while he was
preoccupied with the past. Working at different locations
had made it so easy to fool his wives.

His first wife, Mona, who he had met while working in
Leeds, had lived up to her name, and her constant nagging
had later sent him into the arms of Beth in Nottingham.

Alone in the world, she had been grateful for his gentle loving, and they had married. On returning 'home' to Leeds, Mona confronted him with the receipt for Beth's ring that he had so foolishly left in a jacket. He had had to silence her, and a flashback of her falling from the lonely bridge sent shudders through him. Her mental health had been fragile, and the coroner's verdict of suicide was accepted by her family.

Shortly afterwards, Beth had announced she was pregnant. This didn't bother him much, but she was sickly right from the start. When she miscarried, she became cold and distant and reliant on antidepressants, leading him to seek solace with a blonde in Rigby called Penelope. Things moved along so fast with her he was soon walking up the aisle yet again. When he next returned to Beth she was poorly and had begged him not to leave her. That night, he mixed a quantity of her pills into some hot milk. Once she was asleep, he washed the glass and left. On returning the next week, she was still in bed – and very dead. Again, the same verdict from the coroner saved him.

Penny had been different. He had really loved her, until he had caught her *in flagrante delicto* with an old boyfriend. After he sent him packing, he totally lost it with Penny, shaking her senseless then pushing her down the stairs. On the way down, she hit her head and never regained consciousness. Again, he was saved by the coroner, this time with a verdict of accidental death.

At last, he was free from his life of philandering, without a stain on his character, but his conscience was wearing him down – and now he had struck again, simply out of an inherent fear of his crimes being found out.

He put away his tools and went to see Pauline. He crept up the stairs and quietly opened her bedroom door; there was no sound from the bed. Pauline was lying on her back, eyes staring. It was obvious she was dead. A small globule of soup glistened on her chin. Joe quickly wiped it away with a tissue which he stuffed into his pocket. He leant across and gently closed her eyes; she was still warm, and for the very first time he kissed her lightly on the forehead.

"Sorry, old girl, but you were getting too close to me. I couldn't have you finding me out and spoiling it all."

He took the tray with the soup bowl down to the kitchen where he carefully washed the bowl and spoon, rinsing them well. Then he cleaned the sink and let the water run for some time.

"*Now,*" he thought, "*time to call the paramedics.*"

They were there within minutes, responding to his frantic call that his partner was ill and that he couldn't wake her. They could only confirm that she was dead, and that it was probably due to respiratory problems brought on by the flu virus. This was later confirmed by her doctor who, having seen her the previous week, did not consider a postmortem was necessary. Joe appeared suitably devastated and accepted condolences from the locals with the expected sad demeanour.

The funeral was a very quiet affair. No one knew where her sister had gone to, and they had had no close friends, so after the cremation service Joe went home alone.

Pauline had told Joe a while back that she had made a will. The contents were known only to her solicitor, who was named as executor. After Pauline's death Joe had had to contact him, and to produce a death certificate and other documents, including the life insurance policy. He was anxious when he was later summoned to the solicitor's office. He need not have worried. Pauline had left him everything: the house and all her money, including the sum coming from the insurance. Something in the solicitor's attitude concerned him, though. Could it be that he harboured some suspicions? If so, he kept them to himself. They shook hands, but only Baxter was smiling!

Photo by Patricia Donoghue
With permission

Wartime Bride, Longtime Widow

As the coach pulled away, the sun broke through the mist shrouding the sleepy seaside town, bringing smiles to the faces of the elderly passengers who were all hoping for good weather for the long day ahead.

Nelly settled back in her seat and relaxed. It was early, only 8 a.m., an unusual time for her to be out and about. Today was a special day, though. She had risen at six o'clock, dressed with care and had a bite of breakfast. A neighbour had kindly driven her down to the pickup point for the coach. There were folk in the queue that she knew from the day centre and from the Legion, but she chose to sit on her own, rapt in thought. Memories of over sixty years ago were still fresh: a mix of early joyful months, so soon to be overtaken by the misery of war. And the eventual necessity to pick herself up and get on with life.

There had been some good years; her Mum and dad had seen to that. When little Joe had been born, a few months after her husband Fred's unit had been sent to France, it had been her dad who saw to it that the little chap wanted for nothing, though times had been hard for everyone then.

They had lived near the docks in London and watched friends and neighbours lose everything in the bombing raids. Some had even lost their lives.

Somehow, Nelly and her family had been spared, though, and with regular letters from Fred, she had coped, always looking forward to the end of hostilities and Fred's return. However, that was not to be, and the dreaded telegram had arrived one morning to say that Fred had been killed on the 6th of June 1944 during the invasion of the Normandy beaches. He was never to see his son. For Nelly this was the most poignant memory of all.

Again, it was her dad who supported them, played footie with Joe, took them on bus trips. They had even managed a seaside holiday once: it was then that she had decided that one day she would make her home by the sea. Joe had grown into a bright, caring lad and it had broken her heart when he chose to marry an Aussie girl and went to live over there. He did phone regularly and sent photos and letters, though. Two lovely grandchildren she had, twin girls, but she had never met them.

The coach was slowing down now, and Nelly was jerked out of her reverie by a voice on the mike saying, "Please have your passports ready. We are about to queue for our slot at the Channel Tunnel." Nelly fingered the slim red passport book – the first passport she had ever had. Joe encouraged her to go, to go to where it happened. To where her young husband had lost his life and was buried. He lay in a British War Cemetery not far from Bayeaux. 2004 marked the 60th anniversary of the D-Day landings in Normandy, and the British government were offering to pay for elderly veterans and war widows to visit the beaches and war graves. Now there was only the English Channel between her and the miles of straight French roads that would take her to her dear Fred's last resting place.

It was a day of firsts for Nelly, beginning with the wobbly but not unpleasant ride on the train through the tunnel. They had stayed on the coach, all too old to be scared, and they laughed when the driver said they only needed to worry if he suddenly put the wipers on! Once through and on their way again after a stop for coffee and sandwiches, something bothered Nelly, but it took a while for her to realise just what it was. Nothing seemed to be overtaking them, then of course it dawned on her, they were driving on the righthand side of the road!

The driver knew the route well and took time to point out all the places on the way that he knew would be of interest to his very special passengers, especially the old soldiers. It was a long journey. They crossed the Somme at Abbeville, then drove on through the French countryside to the cathedral town of Rouen. They then left the major road and, crossing over the Seine, made their way to the picturesque city of Honfleur. Lunch had been arranged in a pleasant hotel overlooking the harbour, and they enjoyed a good meal and rest before setting off again for their final destination.

They were joined by a French woman who was to be their guide as they drove alongside the famous beaches, and in perfect English she revived memories of the battles, the landings, the dreadful losses, and the final victories. They visited Pegasus Bridge and the famous *Café Gondrée*, the latter just as it was all those years ago.

As for the bridge, it had been widened to cope with the extra traffic of the day, both on the water and the road. The original bridge structure was preserved in the garden of the nearby museum. Nelly had read a lot about the bridge over the years and was fascinated to actually visit the spot.

On again to Ouistreham where the Normandy landing beaches began, the guide pointing to where the strategic places had been all along the coastline and explaining the names that had been given to each during Operation

Overlord: Sword, Juno, Gold, Omaha, and Utah. Then on to Arromanches, stopping on a cliff overlooking the sea to view the remains of the manmade mulberry harbour, so cleverly designed, and put in place by the British.

By this time, Nelly and her fellow passengers were looking for a cuppa and a comfort stop. After this, they were on the last lap of the journey, to the place that Nelly and the other widows on this emotional pilgrimage were most anxious to see. It was not long before they were parked in a lay-by in front of the British War Graves Cemetery at Bayeaux. They all sat transfixed for a few minutes, quite overcome by the beauty of the place. The rows and rows of creamy white marble headstones, the perfect symmetry of their ranks, surely reminiscent of the servicemen they covered, standing to attention.

The guide led them off the coach, ladies first, and explained the layout of the cemetery. Then she told them that all the flowers and shrubs, so lovingly maintained, were all British plants, carefully chosen for their stability in all weathers, and offering some all-year-round colour. Some of the headstones were carved with regimental insignia of the departed, together with their name, rank, and date of death, sometimes with a verse or a line from scriptures.

Many others were only identified by their regiment, and listed 'Known to God,' on the lower part of the stone.

Emotions ran high, some of the sternest old soldiers shed a tear for comrades whose names they recognised. Nelly just stood and stared – she was quite overcome. There were two marble shelters with the names of all the known servicemen and where their graves were situated. One of the younger helpers offered to go and look for Fred's details, but a familiar voice from behind Nelly spoke up.

"That's very kind of you, but I will take care of her."

Nelly felt her spine tingle. She slowly turned around and found herself looking up into the smiling face of her son, her dear, dear Joe.

"Couldn't let you go through this important moment on your own, Mum," he said taking the now crying old lady in his arms. They stood for a while, till she was more composed, and he pointed to three women standing nearby.

"Look Mum, we're all here, Liz and the girls too. If you're ready, we'll go and pay our respects to Dad. He's been waiting a long, long time.

The Secrets

There he was, standing in the shade of an olive tree, scuffing his cheap Bata shoes in the sandy soil, while the smoke from his ever-present cigarette hung about him in the still, hot air. A year had passed since their last meeting, but he had not changed. His black hair, still tight curled and unruly, framed the familiar Arab face. His olive skin darkened by the fierce heat of the sun during the midsummer months.

His deep smouldering eyes lit up as he saw her coming towards him, and he smiled. She felt the beat of her heart quicken; after all that had happened, he could still raise the flames of passion deep in her soul. She wondered if she would ever be really free of this man who had hurt her so much. Why had she come? He would only take and take again, lie, and lie again, and then wave her away, only to follow up with the usual, inevitable, begging letters, tugging once more at her heart.

She took a deep breath – this time would be different. She had to distance herself from his emotional blackmail, especially now, now she had decided to reveal everything that had gone on during the last year. Whilst she had befriended this man after the traumatic accident and got to know his family, it had been a while before she realised she was being duped. Now she was here to let him know she was aware of his secret. It would frighten him to learn this and to know that his generous benefactor would not be returning. She was aware that she would have to be very strong when the time came to leave, for when she revealed her own secret, she would be the one to know fear.

During her last visit, after the first night of delirious lovemaking, she had suddenly noticed the telltale mark on the finger of his left hand, where the sun had burned around what could only be a wedding band. Apparently, he slipped it off whenever she was around. Instead of challenging him there and then, and his family who were obviously covering for him, she had searched his pockets one night and found the light rough circle of Arab gold and taken it. A trophy? Perhaps, but it would never match the value of the money and gifts she had showered on him when she felt there was a future for them together. What a fool she had been, trapped by lust and the dubious prestige of having a handsome young Arab husband. She had suddenly realised he would have bled her dry if she had not awoken to his wiles.

Now, watching his lithe body approaching, she felt a mixture of pain and pity, but managed to greet him with affection, saving the inevitable bitter confrontation for the privacy of her hotel room. She hoped above all that he would not become violent. In all the years she had known him, he had been gentle at all times, always the peace maker. This was foremost in her mind when she raised her hand for a waiting taxi and gave the address.

As he got in beside her, she sensed his unease. They had always gone straight from the airport to his sister's house, but this time she needed to be in control, without the pressures of his family. She had booked her return flight for later that evening, so time was precious. There was so much she wanted to say on what was to be her very last journey to this desert land.

In the past, she had longed to be with him deep in the Sahara, sharing a Berber tent and all the traditions and hardships that went with the nomadic life of his people. That had been a fanciful dream, and on reflection she thought it less likely than seeing the moon turn blue! It was a dream that had now become a nightmare, a *cauchemar*, to use the French she had had to learn again after so many years in order to communicate with this man.

The hotel was cool, and a maid brought mint tea and a tray of sweetmeats. She had paid in advance, so she had the sanctuary and privacy of this room, where now she had to steel herself to face the future alone. As he began to query why they were there, and not already making love in the tiny bedroom at his sisters, she ignored his words and simply asked how his wife was.

His shock was tangible, and the fact that he obviously intended to carry on as before, as though his wedding had never taken place, gave her the confidence she needed to pour out all the misery she had been holding back since leaving the airport. When he finally managed to calm her and ask how long she had known, he seemed surprised that she had made the journey at all. Why had she not telephoned and finished with him at once? Why wait a year, still writing and sending money?

She just looked at him, all her emotions dried up and under control now. The thought that he might have ever loved her had obviously been as fanciful as her dreams of wedded bliss. So, why *had* she come? Oh, there was a good reason, a very good reason. She rose to her feet, collected her small bag, and reaching into it, took out an envelope. She handed it to him without a word and left the room. Alone he opened it, and drew out a photograph, smiling up at him was the face of a beautiful baby boy, with dark eyes and tight curling hair.

On the back was written in French, *"This is our son. I called him Mohammed, after your Prophet. He will be brought up in the Moslem faith. Allah he will come to know, but never you, his earthly father. I moved house before I came out this time. You will never find us, so don't try."*

I'd Rather Be Knitting
© 2023 Patricia Reilly

The dust in my house is appalling

I'm ashamed when people come calling.

But I'd rather be sitting,

And doing my knitting,

Cos housework I find is quite galling

A Last Goodbye
(To someone I knew well)
© 2023 Patricia Reilly

Arrayed in black of mourning

With roses red they stand.

Watching their guests arriving

Wife and daughters, hand in hand.

All Godly needs discounted

The humanist pastor read.

A history of the departed

From his birth, till he was dead.

So many steps along the way

Their love, their children, work, and play.

They showed his best side here today.

Forgotten, all his flaws and woes

The drinking bouts, the jokes, the pain.

The promises, the gift of pearls

To gild the times she took the strain.

So paint him large, true blue and bold,

Fly high his flag and praise his life,

And then give strength ten thousand fold

For the future, to his weary wife.

The Bottom Line
© 2023 Patricia Reilly

It was a warm, balmy evening, with a slight breeze coming off the Potomac River. The girls drove along I Street, Washington, DC, enroute for The Bottom Line bar. This had become a favourite dive since they had both come to work in DC, and happy hour at the Bottom Line was legend. The drinks were cheap, and the snacks and hot food on the menu were tasty and reasonably priced. The only downside was the size of the place- a very small cellar bar, that if you were not there before six p.m. there was little chance of getting a seat. Also, there was only one toilet for women and one for men which regularly caused long queues in the narrow corridor. However, after a long day sitting in the office, the girls didn't really mind standing for a while. There was a small dance floor in the centre of the room, where couples smooched to the constant music. It was a very popular place.

On this particular night, there had been a ball game at the local stadium, and the place was crammed. The bouncers were outside the main doors, chests puffed, shades on, checking everyone's ID with a pen torch, and physically turning people they considered undesirable away.

After finding a place to park, Danielle and Inez took their place in the queue, ID cards at the ready. No-one under twenty-one was allowed in at all. Once inside, Inez looked around to see if there was a chance of a seat while Danielle pushed her way to the bar in search of much needed drinks. They were still in time for happy hour, so, armed with four cocktails balanced precariously on a tray she made her way towards Inez who was standing on a bench across the room, waving like mad – and proving that she had indeed found somewhere for them to sit.

"Coming through!" bawled Danielle in her husky southern voice. Being almost six foot tall and very well built, a path cleared miraculously in front of her. To her delight, she saw that two other work colleagues were already in, and had managed to save a booth for them all to sit in. "Well done, y'all," she drawled, "lets down these margaritas and get us some more before happy hour is over." No sooner said than done, it was Inez's turn to push her way to the bar, though Edwin and Joey both chipped in some dollars towards the cost of the drinks.

The evening wore on, the music got louder, the dancing more frenetic, and the laughter at their table bordered on hysteria. The whole place was heaving. "Good job this is a cellar," yelled Edwin, trying to make himself heard, "or the floor would be caving in at the weight of all these bodies charging around." More laughter, and then the lights suddenly went out. With no power, the music abruptly stopped as well.

For a few seconds, it was silent, then all hell let loose as those who had been dancing tried to get to the stairs to the exit. Women screamed as they lost their partners in the dark, and several men just shoved and pushed others aside as they tried to make their way out. It was sheer pandemonium: some had taken a wrong turn in disorientated panic, desperate to find the exit and safety.

Danielle went to stand up, only to be pushed back into her seat in the booth by Joey. A company lawyer, he was always the thinker, and he yelled at her to stay put. "Just stay where you are, we are safer here than risking getting trampled on by the masses. They must have some emergency lighting down here. If we just stay calm and wait, we will be okay."

True to Joey's prediction, things did seem to quieten down a bit, and most of the booths seemed to have remained occupied, though it was hard to tell as it was still pitch dark. Some customers were shouting for the management to tell them what was happening, but the already sparse number of staff failed to answer. It would seem they had all disappeared.

Suddenly there was a loud bang, "Oh, Mama," groaned Danielle, "I've been shot! I've been shot!" She gave a gurgle and slumped over the table sending empty glasses flying to smash into pieces on the now empty dance floor. Inez and Edwin slid out from their side of the table and helped Joey pull her upright.

Danielle's whole body was shaking. Inez tried to comfort her but did mention the warm blood running down Danielle's right arm.

"We have to get some light, for God's sake," Inez roared. "Where are the bouncers? Why doesn't someone call the police? Something is wrong here."

Almost on cue, someone with a torch came hurrying across the room, shoes crunching on the broken glass.

"Was that a gunshot we heard? I'm the manager. Someone turned off the main power and they broke the switch, so we can't turn it back on. Where are the bar staff?"

"How the hell should we know?" said Joey. "Our friend has just been shot. Find your phone and get an ambulance, pronto. Why haven't you called the police already if you know the electrics have been sabotaged?"

The manager made his way to the end of the bar. "The phone is over here by the till – oh, my God. The till, it's empty. Not a dime left in it, and the phone wire's been cut. We've been robbed!"

"Stop waving that bloody torch about and go and get some help," Joey yelled, heaving himself over the back of the booth. Between them, Edwin and Joey managed to lie Danielle down along the bench and tried to make her comfortable. Inez groped her way across the floor towards where she thought the stairway should be.

"Good job we come here often," she thought as she fumbled for the handrail, and finding it, ran up the stairs and into the street.

There was no sign of the bouncers, but several customers, some of them much the worse for drink, were leaning against the wall of the building, either too scared or incapable of going back inside to find their belongings.

"Has anyone got a mobile phone?' yelled Inez, "we need the police and an ambulance. Someone has been shot and the bar has been robbed... Come on, one of you must have a phone!"

She heaved a huge sigh of relief as a lanky youth sporting a t-shirt and scarf for the Washington Redskins pushed himself away from the wall and tottered towards her brandishing a phone in his hand. Hastily she grabbed it, thanking him as she dialled 911, and was quickly connected to police, ambulance, and fire services. Within what seemed just minutes, sirens could be heard approaching along Connecticut Avenue, help was at last at hand.

The fire crew quickly rigged up some lighting, and paramedics were able to see to Danielle. Happily, the bullet had only grazed her arm, and she was soon bandaged and fortified with a brandy from the manager. Whilst Danielle had been lucky, the same couldn't be said for the body that had just been discovered lying behind the bar.

It looked as though one of the barmen had tried to stop the robber from stealing the money and had caught a bullet for his trouble. Danielle's injury appeared to have come from the same bullet that had gone clean through him. They were all shaken; what had been a fun evening up to then had turned into a nightmare. Statements were taken, though it was hard to describe what had happened with the whole room in total darkness.

When they were allowed to go home, Inez decided they should leave the car in the downtown car park and take a cab instead. The girls lived in apartments in the same block in Adams Morgan, so Inez could easily go up to Danielle if she were needed.

The boys lived at Foggy Bottom, so after putting the girls into the cab, they headed off for the metro. As they strolled along, they tried to make sense of what had happened: *why had the bouncers not been there to help the bar staff when the robbery took place? Where had the manager been all evening? Why hadn't he been around when the screaming and stampede to get out was going on?*

There were many questions that would have to be answered, but at least Danielle had only been slightly injured, and the four of them were alive. They wondered how the awful happenings would affect the owner of the Bottom Line, and whether it would ever reopen after such a tragedy.

Next day, the events of the previous night were splashed across the front page of the Washington Post:

"Violent robbery at the Bottom Line; bartender shot dead. Managers and bouncers held on charges of theft and murder."

The Pilgrimage
© 2007 Patricia Reilly

To the Kingdom of Jordan we travelled,

Christian Pilgrims, inspired long ago

By the Biblical stories of Moses, and

The land that his people would know.

In Amman, the historic and modern,

An eclectic mix built side by side.

Where Palestinian refugee camps

Sprawl on hillsides far and wide.

To Bethany and the Jordan river,

Where we washed our feet and prayed.

On leaving we all felt a shiver,

As a white dove flew out of the shade.

On top of Mount Nebo, we gathered,

The most revered holy site in the land.

We took mass in Moses Memorial Church

And stood for peace, hand in hand.

We spent a whole day in Petra

The rose red city, a sight to behold.

Our eloquent guide spun legends and tales

That made the history unfold.

In Saint Catherine's monastery at Sinai,
We viewed icons and relics and robes.
The charnel House of the long, long dead,
And the monks in their stark black clothes.

The "Burning Bush" in the courtyard
Caused some sceptics to raise a brow!
Could this really be the Moses tree?
Still green and still growing now.

Up Mount Sinai at dawn on a camel,
Proved quite a painful pursuit.
Once again in the footsteps of Moses,
Did he find it an arduous route?

Whilst our tours were steeped in History,
The current day terrors prevail.
The tourist police watched our progress
From armed checkpoints along every trail.

A guard rode with us in Egypt,
A thick jacket concealed his huge gun.,
He sat alone silent and brooding,
Does he sigh with relief when we're gone?

We have walked on the banks of the Jordan,

Where we know that Jesus Christ trod.

We're so thankful we made that great journey,

Which brought us nearer to God.

(written after the author's pilgrimage in 2007)

Photo credit: beautyjm0103
Pixabay

Love What You Have
© 2023 Patricia Reilly

Here I am, standing with a laden tray, looking around the crowded station buffet, searching for somewhere to sit. There seemed to be only one seat available, at a table where an elderly woman is sitting. I hope she won't mind sharing with a bloke. As I approach, she is hunched over a plate and seems to be making heavy weather of cutting a toasted teacake.

"Do you mind if I join you?" I ask. She gives a little start, as if I had made her jump.

"No, of course not. Sorry, I was miles away. Please sit down," she says, hastily trying to rearrange her plate, cup, and saucer to make room for me.

"Thanks. It's so busy in here today. Must be the weather; the icy wind blowing along the platform is enough to cut you in two." She nods and returns to her fast-cooling teacake.

I pour my tea and slowly take the first few sips, enjoying the warmth of the hot liquid. I'm starting to feel more comfortable, more relaxed. It's been a hectic day in the store – so many bargain hunters – and more than usual not intending to pay! Working in store security is not a very safe job these days, too many hardened types stealing. Fists and sometimes knives at the ready when I manage to catch them.

The Police help out, but it's not that easy to uphold our "prosecute all thieves" policy unless we can really make it stick and prove intent to steal. Still, I've done well today and saved a lot of merchandise. The manager was well pleased. All I want to do now is get on the train home. I'm exhausted.

Above the general din in the room, an announcement comes over the public address system: the 18:15 to Redhill has been cancelled. I don't believe it. There's not another till 18:45, and that will be standing room only by then with a double trainload clambering to get on, all pushing and shoving, and picking a pocket or two I shouldn't wonder. Means I'll miss Eastenders, too, and my dinner will be all dried up again!

The wife never thinks to turn the oven off if the train is late. Insult to bloody injury. Her cooking's an unappetising mess even before it's languished in the oven for ages.

My table mate is looking at me. I suppose I must be glowering into my cup. She says something to me, but I can't hear her whispered words over the noisy chatter. I manage a slight smile as an attempt to show interest, but she looks away. She has butter running through the hairs on her chin, and the hand holding the teacup is shaking. If she's not careful she'll be wearing the tea, too!

There's still nearly twenty minutes to wait. How I hate just hanging about. Travel in the UK is definitely getting worse. Why? If they can send people into outer space, land on the moon, even, you'd think they could run a train schedule to time. Perhaps there's been a jumper somewhere up the line, some poor sod desperate to escape from life's problems, so damned inconsiderate. Why do they always do it in the rush hour when everybody wants to get home?

Now the tables are vibrating and the Gatwick Express whizzes through. All those lucky people heading for sunnier climes, no doubt. What wouldn't I give to be jetting off somewhere! That would be my escape route!

The old lady looks quite shaken. I give her a reassuring smile, but she doesn't respond. She just grips her now empty cup harder. How I wish she would wipe her chin. Poor old thing: can't be much fun out on your own at her age. I reckon she must be pushing eighty, even eighty-five. She ought to be at home in the warm. Her coat seems good quality, but it's not very clean. Her hair is frizzy, over-permed (like the wife's mother's used to look before Joyce took her in hand.) Damn, I've dropped my paper under the table and made the poor girl jump again. I'll just reach for it. Blimey, she's wearing bed socks and slippers, and the skirt peeking out below the coat looks more like the cloth nighties are made from. I really can't make her out. The crowd is thinning now; their trains must be running, lucky people! I'll try and ask the old soul where she's going.

"Excuse me, dear, when is your train due? Have you got your ticket? Where are you going"? I ask.

She looks at me, nodding. "Home," she says, "I'm going home."

"Where is home?" I'm asking her, but she doesn't seem to understand. It is almost time for my train now, but I don't like to leave her. Suppose she gets on the wrong one or slips off the platform? I don't know what to do, I've got to catch that train, or I'll never get home tonight. Then the dinner will be in the dog, poor brute!

Ah, the tarty looking girl behind the counter is waving at me, she's coming over.

"Don't you worry about Doris," she says, "I've phoned the old folks' home where she lives. They'll be along to collect her soon. She managed to escape again, and she always comes here. I just give her a cup of tea and a bun and keep an eye on her till they come. She can't seem to settle there. She just wants to go back home. You could cry for her, couldn't you, really?".

I've just said good-bye to Doris. I honestly do feel sad. What might the future hold for me? Good job we can't see round corners! Anyway, I'd best get on the platform, the train is coming in. Suddenly going home to Joyce seems very much more appealing, whatever her lack of culinary skills. Who was it said, *"If you can't have what you love, you have to love what you have"*?

I'll give her a call on the way, she'll like that – and I'll ask her to turn the oven off till I get in.

Beryl Doig

Image credit: dongsik.yoon
From Pixabay

The Daughter In Between

A, B, C: Archie, Bernie, and Charles. That's me in the middle - the in-between. I was always that; I didn't become my own person until an adult. I yearned to be Bernie the beloved sister, but Archie wore that crown from early on.

Our childhood was relatively comfortable. Our parents gave us a safe, secure, home. Archie, the first-born son, was their pride and joy. He grew strong and learned quickly how to please. After seven years I came along - a longed-for, perfect daughter. Except that I wasn't. With health issues needing medical attention and hospital, I soon became the "sickly child." By the time I was four, my mother decided she needed a 'reliable nanny' to take over. At twenty-one, Emily came to us as fully trained, and this was her first inhouse appointment. It was nice to have a constant companion; someone I could relate to, so I felt lucky. We became friends as we developed together.

My parents, both professional lawyers, continued their careers and busy social lives. Emily, as the live-in, came in for all the baby-sitting and extracurricular duties. She never complained, was always on hand and became a diplomat at diffusing situations I experienced with my parents.

I liked Emily from the start. Later I loved her as a sister. She had my back time and again. We became a duo, working and experiencing together. I discovered that Emily hadn't always had it easy, either. Her childhood had been disrupted by the early death of her mother. Her father decided she would be better off at boarding school amongst young people, so she was despatched by the age of nine. She learned to hide her emotions to survive bullies and was quick to protect herself throughout her years there.

By seventeen, Emily knew what she wanted to do. It was time to stand up for the underdog and to enhance another person's world. She would train to become a nanny and was accepted at a well-known college where she gave her all. It was a perfect fit. She liked being in control and she embraced the strict regimes, absorbing all the learning.

My mother, with her connections, had been anxious to employ a reliable person able to look after her poorly child. She had neither the time nor the inclination to continue the regular appointments and physiotherapy sessions. So that was how we were matched.

Four years after Emily joined us, mother gave birth to her third child. Another son, named Charles. I liked helping Emily with her additional duties in his early years. Like her, I learned fast and enjoyed being a little surrogate mummy. Charlie was a lovely smiley baby who enjoyed our spoiling.

By the time I entered my teens, my system had strengthened, and I no longer needed medical assistance. By now, Emily and I were devoted, while she became embedded in our family. She taught me not to waste an opportunity. Her mantra was to 'learn day by day to deal with what is in front of you, to gain knowledge and abilities all the time.' She always wanted me to see possibilities.

Together, we talked about what I wanted to achieve. My strengths were showing themselves. I had abilities, but little confidence. I pulled out some impressive exam results, much to Father's surprise. He had always backed his sons to be the best at everything. Now here was his only daughter showing she had flair and ability.

My strengths were in languages and in composition. Emily and I had read many books together and I always longed for more. With her encouragement, I researched different University English Literature courses. For the first time in years, we might be separated if I was accepted somewhere away from home. The time had come to talk to my parents. They listened quietly. Supportive of my quest, they secretly doubted me. I was to prove them wrong.

I was accepted at Warwick University for a three-year degree course. My world was opening up and with Emily's support I found the strength to go forward. She promised always to stay in touch and to visit often. I was spreading my wings at last.

Elder brother Archie, now a military officer, was away at Sandhurst on another course. Still seen as the shining light, I thought he was trying to please all and sundry. I worried about him sometimes and felt thankful I had been left under Emily's wing rather than parents' critical eyes.

Young Charlie, now ready for senior school, was the bright spark with a lovely smile and great sense of humour. I think Emily's influence on him was the reason for that.

It was a time of sadness when I said my farewells. My first foray outside the confines, but I was ready to embrace this new beginning. My parents insisted on a farewell family dinner the night before I left. Everyone behaved as expected and really it was a memory to treasure.

Father stood to make a toast, wishing me well. He hoped I would benefit from the extended learning, as it marked the beginning of my adult life. He also thanked Emily for her longstanding dedication to the family. Emily, as ever the diplomat, thanked my parents for giving her a precious home with siblings to love. Charlie endorsed all she said and promised to keep her occupied so that she always stayed.

Mother, who had come to completely rely on Emily, reiterated, saying she would always have a place at the heart of our home. I thought that was a lovely comment to make and entirely justified after so long. Emily had made my life worth living. I couldn't imagine being without her company or her wisdom.

My life opened up completely in the following three years. I loved the course and its challenges. Emily kept her promises, and we kept in constant touch by texts and Face Time. She became the conveyor of updates, both ways. I learned that Archie had a fiancée and was headed for a glittering military career. Probably suit him, I thought, after such a controlled childhood.

My parents left Emily in charge of the homestead while they travelled on an extended jamboree abroad. With Charlie studying for school exams, she had more time for herself these days. I know how much he enjoyed having her to himself at last. Now in her late thirties, sometimes I wondered if she would like to leave us all behind to make a life for herself. Questioning her one day, she vehemently denied needing more - but as I said, she would make such a lovely parent.

I graduated with a First at the end of my three years. Should I stay on another year for a master's degree? Pleasantly surprised, both parents gave their blessing. Emily had decided on a long well-earned break away from the UK. Everyone agreed it was just what she needed and helped her find a little cottage in the Greek islands for the summer months. I was invited to join her if I wanted. Of course, I wanted!

We had such fun that year in the baking sun, relaxing, walking in beautiful surroundings day after day. We practised speaking in the local Greek dialect while I regained both French and Italian, so we were accepted wherever we went. We both cooked the local dishes and drank local wines. It was heaven. I was no longer the in-between. I was just me in my own time and space. Bless Emily forever.

Life blossomed for us both. Emily became attracted to an 'oh, so attentive' single guy who was staying nearby. I think it was her first big romance. Mine had been back at Uni. I wished her all the luck in the world. We just went with the flow. It was a summer we both fondly remembered.

Time moved on. In later years, we shared a flat together in London. By then I was a professor of English running courses based in Kensington, a long way from my in-between beginning. Emily left behind her nanny days and enjoyed being a researcher for a company tracing lost relatives. It suited her perfectly. We enjoyed a good social life, and both had interesting male companions.

The brothers went their own ways as adults while the parents retired to a home in the country, quietly winding down with advancing age. At last, I had been accepted as a valued daughter. More importantly I was now my own person.

Image credit: NoName_13
From Pixabay

Lady In Red

Who was she, this lady in red? A solitary figure who, mid-morning, walks across the bridge and into the local cafe. MacKenzie, an undercover policeman, on the look-out for suspected gun runners, had watched her now for several days. Today, he intended to get a closer look than from his covert position at a second-floor apartment window.

He gathered his jacket, ran downstairs and out the front door. A quick sprint across the square and he was at the cafe. Inside, it was buzzing as usual, with the welcome smell of coffee and warm pastry. It was popular locally and MacKenzie enjoyed the excuse to revisit.

Yes, there she was: seated alone at one of the small corner tables. He guessed she was in her middle years, immaculate in a red wool suit, a silk scarf covering her neck. Her hair was swept up into a chignon, her long legs elegantly displaying good shoes. She had the daily newspaper open and appeared to be concentrating on inside articles. But who was she: was this her cover?

MacKenzie took a seat at the opposite end of the room. He ordered coffee and pastries to give himself time and opportunity. The lady in red had made a similar order. She raised her head only to acknowledge the arrival of her selection. With barely a smile and eyes focused, she slowly began to eat.

MacKenzie found it strange that she neither looked around nor made eye contact with anyone. No-one approached or acknowledged her. Elsewhere, other customers met and greeted one another, like old friends. Was anyone watching her? What was this about? Had there been a silent message from the owner who seemed familiar with everyone?

With iPhone in hand, he surreptitiously took a shot of the scene, ensuring she was in the picture. If only she would raise her head, he thought; I need to get a mug short. MacKenzie, on finishing his repast walked to the desk to pay. The flamboyant Maurie De Balker, flourishing the receipt, thanked his customer and hoped to see him again soon. MacKenzie, seizing the opportunity, enquired how long this popular cafe had been running. The owner proudly declared it was one of the family's businesses, running many years. MacKenzie turned to leave; then noticed the lady in red, listening intently.

He tried to catch her eye: she was definitely aware of his presence, but she evaded contact. He turned away and left.

Outside, he walked slowly across the square and over to the bridge. Tourists everywhere, busy photographing the picturesque scene. He casually leaned over, looking down at his reflection in the water.

Phone at the ready, he wanted to wait for her to leave. It took another half-hour before, out of the corner of his eye, he saw a glimpse of red. She was returning the way she had come. His back still towards her, he watched her walk as she made her way back across the bridge. He let her almost disappear before he swiftly followed. Intrigued, he needed to know more.

Keeping her just within sight, he walked with long strides on the opposite side of the street. Surprisingly, she turned into the revolving door of an upmarket hotel.

Within minutes, he was there. He knew this place and the staff who ran it. Walking in, he quietly greeted the receptionist. They knew each other from previous undercover work and he was a respected official.

"The lady in red who has just returned: can you give me any info, Georgio?"

"Well my friend, Frau Meyer comes and goes every few months. She always stays with us, but never converses or meets with anyone. She is polite, always settles her bill, but divulges nothing I think."

MacKenzie's instinct was alerted. "Know for sure German from her passport?"

"Yes, because the booking form asks for origin. Is there a problem here?"

"I can't be sure, but it doesn't sit well with my investigation. Can I ask you please to keep me informed of anything unusual about her or anyone she meets."

"Of course, my friend. We always want to stay on the side of good law, as you know".

MacKenzie smiled and left with thanks to this man who could be relied on to cooperate.

Back at the police HQ, MacKenzie posted his latest findings online. The gang they were onto had links across Europe; they were suspected of transacting gun supplies for terrorist activity. On top of that, he had received word that within Bruges traders were being pressed for protection money to keep them safe and away from targeting. Of course, no-one admitted to being listed, but the police knew it to be true.

Sharing information between countries was beginning to pay off. Interpol were nearing their deadline to strike before the next arms delivery was made. MacKenzie received the response he anticipated within days. German police had been alerted to Frau Meyer's trips to Bruges. Underground sources claimed she was the likely overseer putting pressure on small enterprises to keep paying protection money. Her visits were seen as 'silent' threats, ignored at the cost of safety.

MacKenzie wanted to bring her in for questioning but was warned not to act — just to keep watch. Those on the front line were ready to pounce on addresses in France and Germany, where the gang members were holed up. He waited to receive his next instructions.

News had been kept from all media for security reasons. Everyone involved was on tenterhooks. Within forty-eight hours, heavily armed teams were sent to different addresses, storming through at dawn each time. They had under arrest a number of individuals involved in arms dealing, together with all the background contacts needed to prosecute. It revealed that vast sums of protection money had been used to secure the deals. This must have been going on a long time, it was stated.

MacKenzie received an online instruction to arrest Frau Meyer if she was still in Bruges. If not, to report back immediately.

MacKenzie immediately telephoned the hotel to enquire. He instructed them to keep her there on any excuse, till he arrived. Fully kitted out in a bullet-proof vest, he exited HQ in an unmarked car, accompanied by a woman police officer. She had been told the outline plan only but was ready for resistance.

Frau Alina Meyer was ready to leave that morning, having visited various businesses on her list. She made her way to reception to settle the bill as usual. There was some delay she was told, due to technical breakdown of their system.

"Would madam care to wait in the lounge with a coffee until her bill could processed?" Georgio asked.

"If I must," was her reply. "Be quick or I shall be late elsewhere." Georgio instructed staff to take their time. This was said as explicit instruction. They always obeyed.

MacKenzie arrived within the half-hour, along with the policewoman. He carried his official identification and was ready to perform his duty.

The car was left at the front entrance. Running up the steps, through revolving door, they were met by Georgio. "She is in the lounge with coffee," he said.

Moments later, MacKenzie confronted Frau Mayer, showing his official police badge. "I must ask you to accompany us, Frau Meyer. There are questions to be answered."

"By whom?" she demanded.

"By the Bruges Police Department today. My colleague will accompany you. Your luggage is to remain here".

The three were escorted out of the building by Georgio, with other staff watching from the sidelines. MacKenzie raised his hand in silent thanks to everyone. Sighs of great relief were soon heard throughout the business community as news spread of Frau Meyer's detention.

Choices: A Novella

Chapter One: Celebration

"Yes, of course, it's cause for celebration and jubilation! Our long lost grandson has been found." Melanie Cozens spoke joyfully to the press reporter standing before her.

As chief controller of our Exploratory Unit, it had been my decision to personally reveal the good news to the family. Our four-man TV crew had been tracking an indigenous tribe in the Brazilian rainforest, in preparation for a new documentary. There they came across a bronzed, bearded, individual who spoke English. He appeared dazed by the unexpected arrival. Guided by two natives bearing heavy packs of our equipment, the TV team had travelled into the forests through tracks in the dense terrain to arrive at this clearing. Silently dumping the packs, the guides had quickly disappeared.

The leader came forward with a group of young men, all pointing their arrows in defence of our invasion. Our team were ready for opposition and had come prepared. Having no wish to up the ante, the four held their ground. With open arms and hands held high, they made no attempt to move, waiting to see how they would be received. One team member, Bruce Meade, was an experienced veteran of such ventures, and used to ancient dialect. He stood forward and greeted their tribe leader, as he thought.

Jeremy Goodfellow (for that was his English name) walked slowly towards him and then held out his hand in a very polite gesture. There was garbled conversation between the two while explanations were made of who the team were and why they had come.

It transpired that Jeremy had lived amongst this Amazonian tribe for several years, having been found near death and starvation when lost in the dense surrounding forest. He had been taken back to their ancients as a prisoner but had since become a revered leader himself. He had integrated completely and was content never to leave their simplistic lifestyle.

Once the four had brought forth their gifts to be presented to the elders, Jeremy led them forward through muddy tracks to the reservation in all its simplicity. There, he explained to the young defenders that these were friendly invaders who came bearing gifts, wanting to understand how they lived in this remote location. There was nothing to fear, he explained, and it was right to offer food and drink to hungry strangers in payment of gifts received.

The women then brought forth lumps of strange fare piled on leaves which they shyly offered. Jeremy acknowledged that, although unusual, they were to accept graciously and partake of sustenance. The team, all anxious to please, timidly bit into the offerings and were surprised to find, although somewhat bitter, whatever contained within rice was palatable and easy to swallow. The liquid they were given was almost certainly water based, but quenched thirst and they were profuse with their thanks.

The gifts, lain before the tribal elders, included a selection of large modern tools, a number of woven blankets, and pretty mirrors which the women would love.

Jeremy took one and held it to his face, grimacing at the reflection.

He now conversed in halting English and wanted to hear news from the outside world. The TV team were anxious to get cameras up and working to record everything but were sternly told this was unacceptable for the moment.

It would be necessary to ask permission first. This early encounter was a getting to know you" occasion and should not be exploited.

So, they held back and waited to be taken to shelter for the nights ahead.

In such a remote location, there wasn't reception to text messages. They would need report back later. For now, they hadn't been attacked and were protected by Jeremy Goodfellow.

The TV crew spent the next two weeks with the tribe, filming their daily treks to hunt and cultivate using just basic implements. The women folk and young girls were kept securely in the background, within the living quarters, cooking and tending the youngest. Jeremy had secured a "wifelet" for himself, and already had one tiny son. He had no intention of returning to his former family and life. He was asked a number of times if he wished to message on film, but insisted this was now his place on earth and he was busy educating the young ones into better solutions as they matured.

As the time came to depart, the team felt sad. They had their project in the bag, but they were disappointed to leave Jeremy behind. He had shown himself to be a natural leader, respected by each and every one. He continued to help them develop as individuals, but the time was fast approaching when such tribes would be wiped out by climate changes incurring deforestation, and the ever-present poachers and raiders.

Jeremy did not want to hear what he was being told. So, the four said their farewells, leaving the tribe to their way of life and beliefs, while taking back to the UK reels of film focusing on the work of Jeremy Goodfellow. This time willing young guides accompanied them on the return route to the outside world.

Chapter Two: Freedom
© 2023 Beryl Doig

During two weeks of filming, I, Jay Hunt, as the photographer, worked with Jeremy Goodfellow, wanting to bring to life his own story. I made notes each night of his life journey, so I am able to relay much of it. Having been without English-speaking company for a number of years, it took him time to remember speech and how to communicate in English. He gradually became more comfortable in our company and began to open up.

It transpired that from his childhood, Jeremy had ambitions to explore other cultures and countries, especially those contrasting with his own comfortable upbringing and education. As soon as he was eighteen, he announced to his family that rather than go to University he wanted time out to travel far and wide.

With funds and maps, he left the UK for adventure abroad. He travelled to Asia and Africa for three years, stopping at various points for months at a time and getting to know the locals. He said how he liked the feeling of freedom, and the opportunity to understand other people's points of view and culture.

By the time he was twenty-two, he had found the USA and hitch-hiked its length and breadth, living the life of a travelling hobo. Finally, he reached Brazil with all it had to offer and fell in love with its diversity. He worked in various outlets, but mostly in kitchens learning about cuisine. It was on one of his summer breaks that he took off for the rainforests. He thought it would be interesting to test himself in the wilderness, relying on his ingenuity to survive.

This is where he nearly died. The heavy rains had washed away routes he thought existed, and he became very unwell while totally drenched for days on end, and unable to forage for sustenance. He made himself some sort of shelter as he moved along, but each time another rainstorm hit, he was almost washed away. It was pure good fortune that he was found by a group of young hunters from his tribe. They thought they had found a body in the forest, but Jeremy was still alive, dressed in tattered soaked old clothes and unconscious. They constructed a carrying stretcher and lifted his inert body on to it, carrying it carefully back to their homestead as a prize find.

It took several weeks of simple care for him to realise what was happening, but slowly pieces of his life came together. In his gentle voice and manners the elders realised he was no threat; rather, a lone traveller without anything other than himself to offer.

Jeremy was unable to look after himself for many months, and by that time he knew he owed his life to his rescuers. He wanted to repay them for this second chance and started to do small jobs around the centre. He had sufficient skills to be useful and gently, slowly, he was gaining their respect. His image grew, and the elders valued the time and effort he gave to any asking for help. Within two years, the image was raised, and he was presented with the cape of knowledge, which meant he was regarded as a wise man.

By the time we arrived on the scene, Jeremy was a valued member of the tribe and revered for his qualities. He told us time and again that this was his now home and he had absolutely no wish to return to civilisation. When I asked about his parents and family, he replied that they had by now said their farewells from his absence of long years, and he would not go back on that. We even asked him if he wished to send them a message.

"No, not now. It is too late and I am a different man," he began, "and I no longer remember how to live in sophisticated society and have no further wish to. My life is here with my partner and son. This is where I belong."

So, it was with heavy heart that I, and others, said farewell. We all tried to understand Jeremy and appreciate his integrity, but I knew how difficult it would be for his birth family to let go. The films we made would help, but nothing now would bring their lost son home. For him, his freedom was everything.

Chapter Three: Reality

Back in the UK, it would take time for the film reels to be edited and ready for public screening. Jeremy Goodfellow's family received an early telephone call from the controller of the Exploratory Unit informing them of the project. He explained how the TV team had met up with Jeremy and the filming that had taken place.

For his parents, the news was hard to hear. They had mourned for long years the loss of their intrepid son. For them he was a precious memory from the past, for they had always understood his need to explore, accepting he would never stay close at home.

It was different for his surviving grandmother, Melanie Cozens. Jeremy had been her favourite grandson and when he was small they had spent many happy hours together reading exciting stories of derring-do. She had encouraged his interest in wider issues and was a staunch believer of letting children go out into the world, always believing they would return, wiser and stronger. When she heard Jeremy had been located, she was over the moon and considered her views vindicated. She joyfully contacted his parents, wanting to hear details. She couldn't wait to see him on film and expected them to be as thrilled as she.

Actually, they were not of the same mind. Jeremy had been lost for years and their grief remained painful and deep. They felt cheated that he had stayed out of touch with never a thought for his waiting family. His father had always been generous with money, furnishing all his needs for travel. They had loved and let him go but felt cheated by his lack of gratitude or response. His father was particularly resentful; angry that his beloved son had cared so little and stayed away for so long, not understanding how those at home longed for a word. It was disrespectful, particularly to his own mother, he declared.

Melanie tried to intervene, to no avail. "Don't you long to see him on film?" she asked.

"No, that would indeed be painful, and we understand he gave no message for us. He has been lost for too long for us to find consolation," replied her daughter, Henrietta. "Mother, I don't feel strong enough to live through all the pain yet again. Jeremy has made his choice, and he obviously doesn't feel close enough to include us in his world. We are part of his past, not present. I will probably look at the film, but nothing more. I need peace and release."

Melanie was shocked. "But he now has a wife and we know there is a little boy. That is another generation of our family. Surely that makes a difference?"

Henrietta shook her shoulders, sadness throughout her body. "Not for me. Why would I want to see a wild Brazilian woman and child who would never know civilisation?"

Melanie was astonished by this. Could her daughter really be so biased? She considered time was needed and believed that when they viewed the film and saw Jeremy in his revered position, they would soften.

Several weeks later, Jay Hunt, the photographer, came to visit, bringing with him the edited version of their project. He genuinely wanted closure for these people. He had bonded with Jeremy during the weeks they filmed and respected his decision to stay away, but his heart was saddened by the situation. He understood how these people must be feeling now, and he wanted to pour balm over troubled waters.

He received courtesy during his visit, but there was an underlying unease. Of the three, Jeremy's grandmother, Melanie Cozens, was the most outgoing and wanted as many details as he could relate. Bernard and Henrietta Goodfellow were austere in manner, perhaps trying to control their emotion. The screen was set up in the lounge and they all sat waiting.

The film opened up with credits and overhead views of the Amazonian rainforests, before panning down to the arrival area..The voiceover gave explanations of the project before beginning to show the set-up. It took minutes of overview before Jeremy came on the screen. He was shown in full shot, a tall, bronzed, fully-bearded individual in full tribal dress, holding the shield of his office. There was pride, strength, and determination in his stance. He was interviewed by the TV team and gave a creditable performance.

His parents just stared, as if they were unable to relate to him. Melanie jumped from her seat as if she wanted to hug him off the screen.

"Move away, Mother!" shouted Henrietta.

Melanie quickly returned to her seat as the film continued. No-one spoke another word throughout. As the credits rolled at the end, Bernard stood up and shook the photographer by the hand.

"We are indebted to you and the team for the way you have handled the filming. It has been enlightening to see, and at least our son is alive and making a valuable contribution to others". Then he sat down, weeping silently.

His wife and mother-in-law were consoling one another, with sobs of relief or sorrow. He wasn't sure which.

Drinks and food were offered afterward. They were promised photographs of Jeremy from the film, but that it would take a few more weeks. Jay thanked each individually and hugged Henrietta, holding her close as if he were leaving an imprint of her son. He packed away the gear, said farewell and with that his visit ended.

It was if a bomb had hit their home. Silence hung in the air, as if Jeremy's voice were still amongst them. His mother, crushed once again by his absence; emerging consolation from his father, and from his grandmother a feeling of pride that Jeremy had reached a level of valued living she could only dream of.

"Do you think we should make contact now?" Melanie asked them later.

"Absolutely not," replied Henrietta. "This for me is now a closed book. I have used up all my love and energy. I have nothing more to give or receive".

Bernard sadly nodded. "I don't think we would be of use to him now" was all he said.

"This is my grandson and great-grandson" responded Melanie. "How would you feel if I flew out to him? I would love to visit, but perhaps I would need his permission?"

"Well, that is for you to decide. We are both remaining here, and at your advanced age I can't see the wisdom of it," replied her daughter.

Melanie was wise enough to leave the matter for the future, but in her heart, she knew she would try to see Jeremy and his little one sometime if time and her energy permitted.

Image credit: 12019
Pixabay

Blue Moon

I took the chance of early retirement with full benefits as soon as it was offered.

Who'd have thought it: Hannah Darnley, senior geography teacher, retiring at the ripe old age of fifty-two! Well, after many years of teaching, combined with running the family home and caring for elderly parents, I think I've earned it, don't you? With only myself to please after losing both mum and dad, I'd joined a couple local groups with similar interests to mine. It was in the Art painting class that I met Geoffrey Hughes. We clicked and soon became friends. As a middle-aged divorced dad with two grown sons, he was also branching out and meeting new people.

After class one evening over coffee, we were discussing our Wish Lists. I'd always dreamed of seeing volcanoes, but never had found time to travel. Iceland is another country I've wanted to see, with its hot springs and barren landscapes. It has its volcanoes, with walks to experience the heat and molten lava.

"So why not book yourself a long-distance holiday if that's your dream?" Geoffrey asked. "Indonesia is perfectly possible. I don't think Krakatoa is likely to erupt again anytime soon!"

Later, I kept replaying his words. Maybe I should book myself on a trip to Iceland first.

I fancied Reykjavik and beyond, and online it's easy to book. Although expensive, it's not beyond my reach. Would I like a travel companion? Should I ask Geoffrey if he would be interested? I ponder on the implication; then decide to broach the subject when we next meet.

Geoffrey looked interested when I told him. "Would you like me to come, Hannah? I think it would be an adventure for us both. I'd be delighted to accompany you!"

I felt a thrill of pleasure at his enthusiasm. "Leave it with me, Geoffrey. I'll see what's available and cost it out. I know it's an expensive country."

With thoughts of Krakatoa's 1883 eruption, and how blue moons became a phenomenon due to the smoke and dust, I checked the date when our next seasonal blue moon is due: 22nd August 2021. So soon! I thought how wonderful to be somewhere remote to see it unless travel restrictions intervene. I made enquiries. A package, staying in Reykjavik, with a tour to volcanic areas, would be expensive: more than £2,500-for each of us. For me, that's fine, but for

Geoffrey? I needed to relay the news. Geoffrey wasn't as surprised as I expected.

"Don't concern yourself, Hannah. I think the cost is well worth the experience. Let's book it. I take it we would each have a room where we stay - if you feel the same?"

"Of course, Geoffrey. That's how the costs were applied. I'm told we should expect to pay extra for food and drinks. They aren't included. That's the way it is there.

"Also, we should address everyone by first name, as family names are convoluted. Everyone shakes hands on greeting normally. Maybe now we just elbow tap!

"If there's time, it's possible to visit one of the islands and stay in Mongolian yurts. Traustholtsholmi Island is owned privately by a man named Hakon, who hosts tourists in high season. That would certainly be an added experience, but I don't know more." Enthused, we each did our own research into Iceland and its history.

I was keen to have a big shop for top layers and waterproofs. Looking at reviews, it was showing a land of epic landscapes, where volcanoes reach high into the midnight sun and glaciers glint in the moonlight. Very picturesque, but probably very cold!

Suddenly, inside I felt young again. Here I was in my fifties, preparing to travel with a nice male companion into the unknown. A romance wasn't on my radar, but what was Geoffrey expecting now that he was free? I just hoped that our friendship would be strengthened.

I went ahead with the booking. Our passports were checked. Covid restrictions were changing weekly, but as we were both vaccinated, we just needed to follow whatever became necessary. The Travel Specialists arranging our trip had the tickets prepared. Geoffrey's lecture commitments were complete, and I was free as a bird and excited.

Finally, the big day arrived. With everything in place, we reached Gatwick check-in at the agreed time. The flight to Reykjavik was uneventful and we both relaxed companionably. Within hours we were in Iceland's capital, which we learned was home to just 217,000 residents. We also learned that Reykjavik is run on geothermal power and is home to two museums which trace Iceland's Viking history.

As the flight door opened, I breathed deeply the cold air before descending the steps. My heart fluttering, I wanted to absorb every moment. Behind me, Geoffrey's mobile was already busy filming. Transport dropped us off at the hotel and soon we were shown to comfortable, if small, rooms.

We chose some down time before meeting up to sample local Viking food at a nearby eatery. We'd agreed to be open-minded about our first meal. Widely eaten lamb was on offer, as was the seafood platter, served with local rye bread. Ice cream, a specialty, looked too tempting to refuse. We ate slowly, savouring the moment, while toasting each other with a recommended beer.

"Geoffrey, I'm so happy you agreed to join me on this adventure. I feel in heaven having arrived here in Reykjavik. My dream is happening, isn't it?"

Geoffrey beamed broadly. "This is big for me, too, Hannah. I think we will be making memories here."

Over the next few days, with so much to see, we walked throughout the capital. We took in both museums and visited the Perlan landmark situated on top of Oskjuhlio Hill with its planetarium, observation deck and restaurant. Then we explored farther afield, visiting hot springs and geysers, and watching intrepid tourists walk on lava fields, hot enough to start melting footwear. Geoffrey drew a line at that venture! He filmed everything instead.

Our booked tour took us on a journey to see the Gullfoss Falls, the famed multi-sectioned waterfall, then to another 200ft waterfall, the Seljalandfoss. Magnificent – with beautiful unspoiled nature and scenery everywhere.. Volcanoes abounded, alongside massive glaciers, protected within the two national parks: Vatnajokull and Snaefellsjokull.

We were in awe of the dramatic landscape. We drank in each new experience by day, then relished our evenings, reliving it all over interesting menus. Nightly, we gazed into the skies at the late-setting sun. Then, on 22nd August, the latest full Blue Moon beamed down its blessings as we stood close together in perfect harmony. My heart was full with the beauty of the moment as I made silent wishes.

"This has been a wonderful time for me, Hannah. I can't thank you enough for suggesting it. I've been stuck in a rut for too long. I see that now. Life is for living, and here I have come alive again, all thanks to you and your dreams."

"Oh, Geoffrey, what a lovely tribute. This trip would be nothing without your company. I've loved every new experience. We're good together, aren't we?"

Our return to the UK brought us back to reality, but the memories stayed alive as our relationship developed. The more time we spent together, the more I valued Geoffrey.

As a retiree, I can please myself while Geoffrey still has his lecturing commitments. Now, though, he always includes me when making other plans. People we know see us as a couple, and I realize this is what I really hope for in the long-term.

Silhouetted Moonlight

A silhouette in silver, shadows caught in time.

The moonlight paints its pictures,

In the darkness of the night.

I watch from my window, my camera is primed,

As gently moving shadows drift before my eyes.

These moments are to treasure, to capture, to restore,

As photographic memories of nature at my door.

Poem For The Greater Good

For the greater good they gave their lives.

For the greater good they fought and died.

In stinking trenches, from bomb filled skies,

On sodden soils amongst the flies.

Every soul of warfare's battles,

Gave their all for the sake of others.

We salute the millions who were lost,

Through one hundred years of awful cost.

Those killed, injured, or maimed for life,

Deserve recognition of the hard won strife.

Their memory in our hearts we keep,

As we learn to work for long-term peace.

The Ticking Clock

Tick tock, tick tock, sounds the clock,

Rhythmic moments of time.

It may be a calming sound,

But it also brings to mind

Each second past is lost forever.

For precious moments of our lives,

Action needs be now or never.

Or time may stop before our eyes.

Books
© 2023 Beryl Doig

Books of all sizes

Standing in line

Ready for reading

Time after time.

Old friends, new friends,

Authors of years

Bring laughter or sadness

Wonder or tears

Books are a mainstay

When life becomes glum

They present us with stories

Of what has been done.

We learn of adventurers

We see how our world spins

We marvel at creations

We learn how to win.

You are never alone

With a book in your hand

As you walk through the pages

You live in that land.

Missing

© 2023 Beryl Doig

"Challenges expose strengths and weaknesses. Each new day is a blank page - twenty-four hours to be faced or to be rejected."

Sally Meade read the solemn words through her blur of tears: "How can I go forward?" she muttered, stifling deep sobs. Faced with the unbelievably difficult fact that her beloved husband, Ben, might never return, she had lost all her inner strength.

They had been married for twenty happy years, so she thought. Yes, there had been ups and downs, just as in every marriage, but together they had been strong, and Ben was always by her side.

Yet, a weekend ago Ben had completely disappeared, leaving no trace. No word, no message, no scribbled note. Nothing to indicate he wouldn't return home as usual.

Ben loved fishing; it was his main way of relaxing. Whenever he had a free Saturday, he would join a group of like-minded mates and go off to the nearest Kent fishing lake.

At first, Sally wasn't worried. It was late, but maybe they had stopped off for a meal or a drink to celebrate a wonderful catch. By the following morning, she became seriously concerned. No car in the driveway, no message on the landline or her mobile. No sign of Ben. She began by phoning his fishing friends. In turn, each said, "No, Ben didn't join us this weekend and, no, he didn't send any message."

She waited the whole day before contacting the police, asking for help. They took the car details and its registration and asked for a recent photograph of her husband. They tried reassurance. "Maybe Mr. Meade needed time out, or possibly had a memory lapse? It has been only one weekend." The PC paused briefly before asking, "Are there any marital problems?"

"No, none that I know of," Sally immediately replied, "however, my husband has been stressed recently. His scientific research in the laboratory is intense and very specific, and he isn't at liberty to discuss details." She knew something major was in the pipeline, and that Ben had felt the weight of responsibility. Had he cracked under the strain? She wondered if it was a possibility. She didn't want to think about what might be happening.

Waiting anxiously at home was a nightmare. Another week passed. His disappearance had been broadcast on local TV and the papers were showing the photograph the laboratory used for personnel badges. No leads or reported sightings. Nothing so far.

Sally needed to return to her work at the solicitor's but couldn't face leaving the house unattended. Her near neighbour, Jan, was a good friend and support, and offered to keep watch. Sally's parents were on hand whenever she asked, but her low moods didn't sit well with them. They wanted her to 'step up' and act positively.

"You trust Ben, so must believe this is just a blip. He will need you to be there for him. You know how important his research work is. He is probably holed up somewhere, taking a breather," her father suggested; her mother stood anxiously by, nodding her agreement.

Sally wanted to swat them both in her present state. *Couldn't they see this was so much more critical?*

She was afraid – very afraid – for Ben's state of mind. If only she knew where he might have gone. The police were pursuing enquiries but were not yet asking for public help. She felt lost and empty.

Left alone, Sally turned Ben's desk inside out. They'd shared the study space at home, and she hoped for a clue somewhere. So far, nothing new; just many papers of scientific interest with lots of his scribbled jottings. She was fairly sure Ben didn't have a secret life or love. He just wasn't that kind of guy in her eyes. He was too single-minded. It was much more likely that he had discovered a mishap in the lab. Or even had spiked himself in error, she thought. That would really have freaked him out. He had often said it was a possibility.

The long days turned into weeks, with Sally becoming a ghostly presence wherever she went. She had been granted leave of absence when it became apparent she was no longer capable or reliable at the office. Her friends continued to visit, bringing gifts of food or flowers, but no one could provide her with any comfort. The police had drawn a blank and had extended their search to wider areas. Ben's passport was still at home, so he hadn't left the country. His bank cards hadn't been used and Sally confirmed there had been no banking activity. By now she had convinced herself that Ben had ended his life in some lonely corner. Her instinct told her he had infected himself accidentally and couldn't face the consequences. She had no tears left and anger was taking their place.

Her life became a routine on autopilot. The press frequently asked for updates. She shook her head so many times, saying she had nothing to add. The story became yesterday's news, both in the press and on TV. Ben Meade's name was no longer on everyone's lips.

Then, after a drenching autumn rainstorm with swollen streams and flooding, Ben's car was found wedged between rocky outcrops up in rural Cumbria. It was battered and broken with little inside to show what had occurred. No sign of Ben or his body anywhere nearby. It was apparent he had hidden himself away, not wanting to be found.

By now Sally had reconciled to the inevitable. She didn't believe he was still out there somewhere. Ben had signed his own death warrant, likely due to some incident he felt was his responsibility. Her husband had gone out on his own, in his own way, leaving her to pick up the pieces, with only memories for company. She waited for her grief to slowly ease.

Then lockdown replaced normality. It wasn't until the Covid-19 vaccine trials were announced that Sally Meade understood the extent of Ben's involvement in research. She accepted that his legacy was a worthy one and slowly it softened her loss as she was joined by so many others.

Patricia Donoghue
(a.k.a. G. B. Carmichael)

Photo Credit: Patricia Donoghue collection
Used with permission

The Empty Chair

Danny sat at the table in Shades Bar. Old habits die hard and he sat, back against the wall facing the door, just like every other visit there since 1975 when he got out of hospital. He was sixty-five now; he'd barely begun to shave back then. A fresh-faced lad still wet behind the ears and not long out of training. He let the wave of memories wash over him.

1969 Edinburgh.

Jack Fraser's Da was yelling out the window at us as we skipped down the steps of his house, two at a time. "Yis look like a pair eh lassies wi yon long curly locks. It'll be lads gein' yis the wolf whistles wi yous done up in they get ups."

We laughed.

"It's the fashion, ya auld dinosaur," Jack called over his shoulder to his da. It was just banter, filled with love. It's what we Scots do!

We hopped aboard a forty-two bus and headed down to Porty, that's better known to outlanders as Portobello.

"

There was a dance at the town hall. We were sixteen years-old; we knew it all and were invincible, as only the young believe.

We jumped off the bus as it slowed to a stop outside the Police station and shot across the road. There was a fair queue and coming from the Musselburgh Road end of the High Street, a large group of lads all loud and brash, like peacocks. If we didn't get to the queue first, we might not get in.

Reaching the foyer to get our tickets, we noticed the recruitment table set up in the corner. The banner declared they were signing up for the Coldstream Guards. Not the oldest regiment in Scotland but the longest continuous serving regiment of the line, in the British Army. They hail from a wee place on the border, not too far from Edinburgh.

The big guy behind the desk was sporting a very impressive moustache, not a trendy Pancho Villa, but impressive none the less. He called, "Over here, lads. Come and have a wee chat."

Half an hour later, we excused ourselves as we'd eyeballed two fine lassies that we'd met here afore, and we didnae want to miss our chance. However, the old soldier had given us a lot to think about. He'd never know it, but he changed our lives that night, it wasn't only that that did, but it was part of it. Our fates had been rewritten.

Jack and I danced and blethered with Mernie and Bridie all through the evening till the last dance was called. It was a Ladies Excuse Me, where a lad can learn if a lassie really likes you or no.

We were heading back to the girls when we saw them heading straight for us.

"Are ye dancin'?" they asked.

"Are ye asking?" we replied, laughing. From that moment, Mernie and Jack, and Bridie and I were going steady. We spent all our time together except for Saturday afternoons, for then we were at Easter Road at the football or climbing aboard a coach to the away pitch.

Twelve months later, I asked Bridie to marry me. She said yes!

I was so excited I could barely contain myself and couldn't wait to tell Jack. He was late to work, that day of all days. I was burstin'.

As soon as he walked in, I raced over. "You'll never guess what? I asked Bridie to marry me and she said yes!"

He burst out laughing as he dug into his trouser pocked and pulled out a small jeweller's box. He flicked the lid up and revealed a diamond ring. He stopped laughing like a loon and said, "As I walked Mernie home last night, we stopped to look in the jeweller's window. I asked which one she liked. She pointed to this, and I said to her, If I buy it for you tomorrow, will you marry me? She said yes once she stopped leaping up and down and greetin'."

Over the next six months or so, as we planned our joint wedding, lots of things changed. Not all for the good, either. The foundry where we worked was closing and there was nothing nearby like it. All our plans to travel and marry and buy a house were disappearing like sand through our fingers.

Then one night Bridie and I were out for a walk and had jumped the bus up to Princes Street. There was a large crowd gathered at the National War Memorial in the gardens. The Pipes & Drums of the Royal Scots and the Coldstream Guards were playing to commemorate some old battle honours won in the Crimea or somewhere. As they played, I recalled the night at the dance and the old soldier. It brought an idea into play.

Next day in my lunch hour, I went to the recruiting office in Shandwick Place and had a remarkably interesting chat with the captain there. He gave me lots of pamphlets and interesting bits and pieces of information.

That night after my dinner, I was set to meet up with Jack. Hibbs were playing the Heart of Midlothian. It was a real town derby.

In the Artisan bar after celebrating a cracking game, I shared my plans with Jack. If Bridie was game, I was signing up. We sat there for a good two hours; Jack was up for it, too.

Our welding and engineering background was wanted in the army, and the pay was a sight more than the dole or working in the co-op. We left each other at St. Ninians church in Marionville Road.

He headed down Lochend Drive and as I headed on down the road, I shouted, "Jack, I'll meet you and Mernie in the George Hotel Bar at the top of Bath Street on Friday night at seven after I pick Bridie up, okay?"

"Aye, we'll see you there."

I'll not bore you with the minutiae of the following months; both Bridie and Mernie supported our decision to sign up as soon as the foundry shut. Both families had grandfathers and fathers who had served. Some had died on active service, and we were all proud of our service history.

We shared our wedding day, marrying on Aug 28th in St. Ninian of Triduana Parish church. It was a simple affair with close family and friends. The joint families put on a great spread in the church hall, and they'd decorated it with garlands and fresh flowers from both family's allotments. It was a beautiful sunny day, and we couldn't have been happier.

We signed up a fortnight later, did our training and were on the Passing Out Parade on Jack's eighteenth birthday, I'd celebrated mine a couple of months prior. We were warriors now, or so we thought.

Our first posting was to Windsor to join the battalion. In early '73, we were allocated our married quarters. Two smashing wee houses next door to each other, the girls were fair thrilled at having such a big home and a garden too. Life was grand.

At Christmas, Jack announced that Mernie was expecting, and not to be left behind, on New Year's Eve, Bridie passed Mernie the box and me the stick showing that we too were going to be parents. Our bairns were due on Sept 23rd and 29th, the following year.

On Feb 5th we received orders. We were being deployed to Northern Ireland. The girls were devastated.

We were trained soldiers, we told them. Strong, fearless, invincible warriors, and in the way of the young and hopeful, we calmed their whispering fears.

In March, we left barracks in trucks. Next stop, Belfast.

It was to be a harrowing experience. We were such newbies; many there were hardened from time with Mad Mitch in Aden. The troubles were escalating, no thanks to politicians at the time. We lost a few in the first weeks there.

In June, we had five days R&R. We flew home and enjoyed the time together. The girls' anxiety was increasing with the impending birth of our bairns. Scans had shown we were expecting a wee lassie and Jack a laddie. We decorated our nurseries together. Blue in Jack's and lemon in ours. We could for moments forget the horrors that awaited us.

We flew from Brize Norton into Aldergrove Air Force Station. Then, it was full on.

The troubles were fierce and there was a lot of political stuff going on, too, that wasn't helping reduce the tensions. It was a tinder pot.

On Sept. 10th Jack was called in to see the Commanding Officer. Just minutes later, clutching a three-day pass and wearing a grin set to break his jaw, he was heading to catch a helicopter lift back to Blighty, Mernie had endured a fast onset of labour and delivered their son, hale and hearty, at 4 a.m. that morning.

Two days later, it was my turn. Jack and I had a day's overlap of leave and enjoyed time with our wives and new-born wains. They were both ugly wee bundles of red wrinkled faces, though we'd never admit to the thought. The wee tykes had stolen our hearts, and I don't mind admitting it. I cried like a bairn when I had to kiss them goodbye.

Bridie had Jacqueline in her arms and Mernie held Liam tight as we got in the taxi taking us to the station. As we made our goodbyes, Mernie whispered to me, "Keep a watch on Jack. I've a bad feeling this time."

I promised we'd be fine, and I'd look out for him.

A couple of months later, we were on duty down in Crossmaglen. Bandit country, they called it. As we pulled out of the suburbs onto the Newry Road, a large van came through towards us. It came hard and fast and in the middle of the road.

Our driver, wee Shuggie, slewed to avoid collision and we tipped at a precarious angle as the verge sloped sharply. We heard Shuggie say, "Oh, shit!" then bang and darkness.

A culvert milk churn bomb was exactly placed for us to hit, just as the van drivers had anticipated as they ran us off the road.

I have fragmented images in my head, none good. I woke up in Musgrave Park hospital. I'd lost a leg and sustained a serious head injury as well as fragments of shrapnel imbedded in my skull and back. They couldn't be removed.

I'd been in a coma for four days; Bridie was at my bedside.

She'd aged. Her eyes were swollen and red from crying. I managed to croak out, "I'll be fine love, dinnae fret." She laid her head on my hand and wept.

"How's Jack?" I asked a little later. She sobbed even harder then, and I don't know to this day if it was compassion for her distress, or fear that stopped me from pressing her for an answer. It turned out that Jack was in Stoke Mandeville hospital back in Blighty; I'd be joining him there as soon as they were happy that my head wound had stabilised.

I was helicoptered over in the first week of November 1975.

Jack was very poorly. He'd lost both legs and an arm to the elbow on his left side. He was fighting hard to live; He'd be okay if he could survive the infections in the first months. We had never given up on anything, and we sure as hell wouldn't start now,

In the August nine months later, he was in his wheelchair next to me, arm wrestling. We'd spent the morning hearing about our prosthetic parts and how they'd be our next challenge. The banter was fierce, and we had a bet to see who'd be walking first.

Just then, our Commanding Officer and the Families Officer appeared at the ward desk. They were followed by Bridie with Liam and Jacqueline in a double buggy and the regiment's Padre bringing up the rear. Bridie looked awful!

They called us out to the doctor's office and the door was closed. That's when we learnt that Mernie had taken her life.

She'd dropped baby Liam into Bridie as usual in the morning when she would then go to work, but she hadn't gone to work. Bridie found her at about three p.m. when she failed to collect the bairn.

Her note to Bridie said she was sorry, but she couldn't be the wife Jack needed now. She was ashamed of her cowardice, and they'd all be better off without her. I have no idea what she wrote to Jack, but that letter came nearer to killing him than the IED in Ireland ever had.

We finally were discharged early in the following year, me in the January and Jack in the March.

The Army, the British Legion and our combined families all helped to find a house big enough for all of us; Jack and Liam would live with us. They had a job to find one that could be modified to deal with all our needs. The one they found was amazing. On St. John's Lane on the front between Porty and Joppa. It had been a small nursing home for blind veterans; now it would be a home that Jack and I could get around in. A lift had been installed, so nowhere was inaccessible.

The front garden was awesome, walled in but with fine views of the Forth. You could see the ships coming into Leith docks, and at night it was like a navy velvet blanket covered in sparkling jewels of assorted colours as the ship's lights twinkled in the dark evening light. A large garage at the back had direct access to the kitchen and it had been adapted to accommodate our chairs, as had the brilliant big car we'd got with our disability pension.

Every year after, on November 15th, Jack and I would go alone to the War Memorial, then down to Shades Bar in Easter Road. It was owned by Eddie Turnbull, a Hibbs hero, and it was where we went after the game on a Saturday.

We still went to the match; the club gave us lifetime season tickets.

But November was when we let ourselves remember that day, the day the terrorists killed off the lives we'd had planned out. It wasn't about Mernie or us. That day was about Shuggie, Neil, and Rockie, who all died that day. We'd drink to them, get drunk for them. Eddie would always send us home in a cab, no fuss, no foul. We did that every year for thirty years.

Then in 2004, Jack was taken ill with yet another urine infection, or so we'd thought. Within twenty-four hours, it was sepsis, and he was gone. The doctor said his heart gave out.

I think he just lost the will to fight. Liam was with him, as were we all, and he went knowing Liam and Jackie were engaged.

So here I am, fifteen years on in our pub. It's not Eddie's bar now; he's long gone now too. It's not what it was, and I won't be back again.

The IRA have finally felled me too, the shrapnel in my skull is pressing ever harder on my brain stem, the medics say I've maybe six months.

So, I came this last time to tell Jack and the lads to get them in 'up there' ready for me.

Next year, well, there'll be another empty chair.

Image credit: ArtTower
From Pixabay

The Dancer

© 2023 Patricia Donoghue, a.k.a. G. B. Carmichael

The latter years of WW2

She stood *en avant*, then rose up onto her toes, *en pointe*, then raised her arms and scissor jumped. The *pas de Basque* was a step too far and she crumpled in a heap in front of the long studio mirror. She sat for a little while, then throwing off her self-pitying mood, she rose from the floor as elegantly as her 80 year-old frame would allow.

1914

She left the studio and made her way upstairs to her private quarters. The view from her salon offered a stunning view of the *Champs Elysée*. Her apartment was in a building set between *Rue du Colisèe* and *Rue la Boètie*. The honey cream coloured stone with its beautifully crafted balustrades of their balconies gave the look exactly as had been required. Elegance, class, and wealth. It was as stunning inside as it was out. The delicate artistry of French chic was on show in all its finery here. The view from the window down the boulevard of the *Champs Elysée* was just wonderful.

Later in her life, she would say she hated it. She had lost her love of the view having twice watched the German invaders goosestep their way down under the *Arc de Triomphe*. Twice it had heralded the end of the Paris that she loved, and the creation a Paris she no longer could call home.

*   *   *   *   *

Elyse Benoit had, at the height of her career, drawn crowds night after night, month after month, to sold out theatres. She was a *prima donna*, the toast of Paris, Berlin, Vienna, London, and Rome. And one spring at the peak of her career, she was toasted by the rich and famous of New York.

Elyse had returned after a gruelling six-month run and was exhausted, relishing the thought of taking the autumn and winter as an extended holiday. She would, of course, keep up her daily training but refuse any contractual dates until the spring. She had only bought her beautiful apartment late in the previous year. In total, she'd had barely three months in what she referred to as her forever home.

It consisted of two floors; they were the top two floors of the building. She had paid for alterations to accommodate a large dance studio with changing and shower facilities on the lower floor along with a storage room and well-equipped kitchen. The top floor held her private quarters. There was a smaller kitchen, two double bedrooms, a salon with dining area and her master bedroom with *en suite* bathroom and dressing room. Both her bedroom and salon were at the front above the studio.

The view looking right from the terrace outside her bedroom or salon, was the gift that changed throughout the day and night. Always giving something different. A change of pace, the refracted light through the raindrops, the elegance of it in the sunlight, and at sunset, it was different again. She loved it. You could look all the way down the street to the *Arc de Triomphe*. She had loved it from the moment she had first stepped out onto her terrace.

After such a gruelling tour, for now, she just wanted to relax and enjoy being home.

The declaration, on August 3rd, by Germany, stole that wish away.

She survived the *Grand Guerre* in her apartment and had aided where she could the glorious cause against the Kaiser's forces. She delivered messages, rode her bicycle around the streets reporting positions and movements.

Attended dinners with the high officers of the Vichy coven and listened carefully to their loosened tongues. For the duration, much of her energy and the bulk of her wealth went to the cause. She would give everything if need be, to keep France free of the Kaiser's boot.

At Easter in 1939, many of her friends had begun whispering about the new regime and their proclamations regarding ethnic groups in Germany, in particular the Jewish community.

The word was, to "get out if you could." Some of her closest family and friends had already left for America, Canada, and England. The news from the offices of the *Republique Francaise* was less than encouraging.

The French forces had been put on alert. On the morning of May 10th the following year, Elyse had risen and as was her custom, had turned on her radiogram. She'd sank into her chair in shock as she'd listened to the news broadcaster declaring Germany had invaded Belgium, the Netherlands, Luxembourg and had crossed the French border. *Herr* Hitler's troops were heading swiftly towards Paris.

"The dogs of war have been let slip again," she thought. *"We beat them before, we shall again,"* and she prayed it would be so.

In the days immediately after this announcement, the streets filled with a stream of refugees running ahead of the advancing troops. They told all who would listen of the atrocities and barbarism of the Germans and their attacks on innocent civilians. Elyse was horrified yet resolved she would not join the mass exodus.

From her apartment, the crowds seemed like an ever-flowing river of people and their treasures, the belongings of those who were abandoning her beloved Paris to the Hitlerites.

She saw carts with baths and pianos atop of great shipping trunks. *"As if these things were of any real use in their exodus,"* she thought. It reminded Elyse of her ancestors. These people were fleeing their destruction, just not from the Egyptians this time. But the waves that were held back for her forebears would soon, in the form of a flood of grey uniforms, wash over them all. And their destruction this time would, again be Biblical.

Elyse knew of one friend who had been part of the government, before the traitor Marshal Petain had capitulated.

He was a patriot; on that she would stake her life. And of course, if she were wrong, she would like as not forfeit that life.

She approached him after services the following Saturday morning. He stood with others who all greeted her. Pleasantries were exchanged and speculations on the current situation aired between them all. Finally, all but Elyse and David Crèmieu remained.

They spoke of unimportant things as people dispersed around them until Elyse leaned in to take her leave and kiss his cheeks, she whispered, "I am staying to fight again. How may I aid our country?"

David took her hand. Smiling, he leant to kiss the delicate hand, saying softly in reply, "*Moi aussi*, I'll be in touch." He smiled again, turned, and went to join another group gathered at the café tables opposite the synagogue.

Many of her students no longer attended the dance classes. Some had left in the flight for safety; others, children not of the Jewish faith, had been withdrawn by anxious or bigoted parents who wanted no attention brought by association with the woman. A woman whom they had once adored, a woman whose friendship for which they had vied.

Those people did not want to be caught in the crossfire when the hunters found their prey. The slightest suggestion of empathy or aid for the people of the yellow star could get you killed.

People were afraid. Neighbours, friends, business associates, even family members turned on those with whom they had broken bread, people whose houses they had once visited. It all meant nothing. In the clutch of feral fear, humans turn bestial. Survival is all.

And who could blame them? Humans are a herd species, and in a herd, ostracization means death. Man is not an island, no matter what he might think. And herd animals follow the strongest of them. Right then, it was Hitler's forces that looked like the winning side. The side whose followers would survive.

At first, Elyse was asked to look after some boxes put in the back of her storeroom next to the studio. A little later they approached with the request to move her wall of mirrors forward. They wanted to create a void; a space big enough for a person to lie down. It took them two days, but once finished, even she. could see no indication of the alteration, nor the opening device to access the space.

After that, there came a stream of allied and French soldiers, sailors, and pilots. There were a few resistance fighters, too, who needed to disappear out of reach of the Germans. They would stay in her home for a day or two before being spirited away to freedom – or to an appointment with death that had just been delayed.

Sometimes, as she did her daily workout, she was self-conscious, she wondered what the men hidden behind the glass thought of this now-elderly woman. Her body was not the firm nymph like form she once had been. Did they think her sad and ridiculous? She hoped not.

She would have been astonished if she were to have learnt they thought her a heroine, a brave soldier of freedom.

Some children still attended classes. When she was teaching, the men and sometimes women she hid had to lie in that long narrow space. Silent and unmoving as death.

The appearance of normality had to be preserved for their safety. For the sake of the children, too. They needed something, something to anchor them. Her lessons were their only connection to a time when they were not afraid.

It was a cold November day; she had a class and she had two British airmen in her home. One was unwell. The trek to Paris through occupied France, sleeping in woods and walking through winter wind and rain had taken its toll on this young flier. He was full of a very unpleasant cold.

She dare not have him in the void, coughing and spluttering his way to their combined firing squad. She had insisted he stay in one of her bedrooms. There was no reason to suppose it would be unsafe for the duration of the class.

The children arrived; she was surprised to see one of the older boys had returned after a long absence.

Phillipe had been a very promising pupil but had stopped attending when the troops came. He said he had driven his parents mad with his pleading and begging to be allowed to return. How could he be "as good as Vaslav Nijinski if he did not train?"

Elyse patted the boy's shoulder and smiled. "Wise words, Philippe," she said before calling the group to order. At that moment, the boy asked to be excused to use the bathroom.

The session fairly flew by and soon the aging *prima donna* was bidding her pupils good-bye.

Weeks passed in the usual fashion, or what now was accepted as the usual. Men and women arrived in the darkness and left in the darkness. Children came in daylight and left in daylight. The two different worlds inhabited by the two different women that was Elyse, one for the light and one for the dark.

It was a week before Christmas. David had sent a message with the grocer who delivered it to her. Their group was discovered or betrayed; the point was moot. The note said she had to get out.

She could never, would never, abandon her beloved France.

She wore the costume for Swan Lake: she heard their boots on the stairs. The doors to her studio were locked and her music played on the gramophone. It was racked up to full volume. She just about heard their demand to open the door and the threat that they would open fire if she did not comply.

The music was reaching the crescendo when the guns opened fire. She'd never danced more poignantly, nor felt the music stir her soul. Not like this; this moment was exquisite.

When they came through the doors and entered her studio, she was on the floor, in the final position that Anna Pavlova had made iconic. The beautiful costume that she had created herself was of the purest white silk bodice and underskirt, with a white feather overskirt. Her grey hair was up in a chignon and on her head a band of feathers.

All were now tainted by the scarlet of her blood and the miasma of poison, hatred, and bigotry.

Philippe, at first a little unsure, clicked the heels of his new boots, proud in his brown shirt. He stood to attention, saluting *"Heil, Hitler!"* in the uniform of the Hitler Youth. He then turned to go and did not spare a glance at the old woman on the floor.

Image credit: ArtSpark
Pixabay

The Hibernian

The Gift

The letter had arrived last month. Her great-aunt over in Canada, with whom she had only loosely kept in touch, had died, and had left her a bequest in her will. Jeannie was on her way to a local solicitor, who was acting as proxy for her aunt in Calgary.

Two hours later she emerged from Stollen and Cash in utter confusion. Her aunt had left her everything… There was a caveat, however. To claim it all, she must travel to her aunt's home as there were things her aunt had organised to be collected in person.

One angry boss and two weeks later, Jeannie stepped out of the cab beside a beautiful two-story house in the leafy suburb of Alberta's largest city. It was a quaint house with white picket fence and spacious wraparound porch (a secret desire of Jeannie's). The dark rose-coloured door was surrounded with a well-trained wisteria, wrapped like a bower over the frame.

Inside was a lovely light space with solid wood furniture, the walls washed in a soft shade of yellow. It made you want to curl up and grab one of the many books which filled the large bookcase along one wall.

On the huge dining table stood an envelope addressed to her, along with a small package. As she read the letter, she didn't know whether to laugh or cry. Poor Aunt Tilly, she obviously had begun to suffer some form of dementia. The letter was a flight of fancy in anyone's book.

Jeannie opened the box: inside lay a beautiful chain with an intricate design and hanging at the end, a ring. It was such a very unusual design; the marcasite really made it something special. The facets of the dark emerald held the surprises of this delightful prism.

She slipped the chain over her riot of titian hair, a gift from her Hibernian ancestors, along with sharp blue eyes the shade of quality sapphires. The other inheritance from her ancestors was *the GIFT*. She occasionally had insights of the future, "So much for that; I didn't see this coming," she thought aloud. Oddly enough, Aunt Tilly was supposed to have had the gift too.

Jeannie found the kitchen, made herself some tea and curled up in one of the comfy sofas to reread the letter, it really was mind boggling.

In a nutshell, her aunt's letter said that the ring would take her to any moment in time. She had but to slip it on and repeat the phrase written in the ancient Gaelic, a language that predates the Boudicca uprising in England and the Pictish invasion of Alba.

The instructions for use were simple, however the ethical directions were more complex: *"bring nothing back from the past to enhance your material wealth and take only organic things into the past with which to do good."*

She looked at the clock and was astonished to discover she'd spent almost two hours running scenarios through her head to circumvent these instructions. She laughed out loud, "as if I could really time travel… insane!"

After she'd unpacked her case and made herself some dinner, Jeannie was surprised by a knock at the door. Wearing loose palazzo pants and an oversized jumper she opened the door to find a rather serious and dishevelled looking man whose sudden smile changed the whole impression of him instantly. In a thick Irish brogue, he laughingly said, "Well you look just like yer auntie for sure, so you do."

Jeannie was mortified, she was twenty-seven, her aunt was ninety-eight when she'd passed. This rogue was her age, so how could he determine such a personal assessment in the few moments since she opened the door. He had no idea how much danger he was in, for at home Jeannie's temper and sharp tongue was infamous within her circle.

He smiled again. "Ah now sure, don't take on so, me darlin,' that aunt of yours was a glorious Celtic beauty in her youth. Did you never see the pictures of her? Well, are you going to stand there bristling all night or are you about to show you know how Irish hospitality works?"

"What do you want and who are you?" Jeannie spluttered; she was furious at the cheek of him.

"Ah, now I see why we've gotten off on the wrong foot here, and I am sorry for that. I am Liam, good friend of your aunt's. She asked that I came over tonight, she thought you'd be needing some help to get your head round her gift." He dared a sidelong glance at Jeannie, she didn't seem any calmer now.

"And how and what do you know of her gift?" Jeannie growled; her hands closed into a tight fist.

"Let's sit down and I'll tell you, lassie, though I doubt that you'll be believing me tonight."

Hours later she sat in shocked disbelief at his story.

Liam had spun her a yarn of a 17th century battle and how Tilly had made her first journey through time to the edge of the battlefield by the River Boyne near Drogheda. How he, Liam, had lain seriously injured and although he'd crawled to a place of cover, he was losing blood fast. He knew he'd be food for the wolves soon enough. Tilly had appeared from nowhere, though at the time he thought her a figment of his dying mind. She had swiftly bound his wound and he'd passed out as she tried to get him to his feet. He said, when he'd come to, he was lying on the same couch Jeannie was perched upon.

No matter which way she asked the questions, Liam stood firm on the details of his story of their many time travel exploits over eighty-two years. His heritage was from the fairy folk, hence his still young appearance and his longevity. She heard herself ask, "did she bring others back?"

"No, I was the only one. I was her soulmate, as she was mine, but that wasn't why. The fates allowed me to time travel with her because the ring keeper must have a skilled warrior as her guardian on her travels. I was Tilly's, and my life - like hers - is almost done, I shall live only long enough to deliver you to your warrior. Well now, lassie, I'll away and leave you to get some sleep. I'll be seeing you soon. Good night."

Still a little distracted by her own thoughts, she muttered "Goodnight" and he was gone before she realised she had no idea how to contact him.

Jeannie had a long soak in Tilly's huge roll top bath and pondered the events of the last few hours. She didn't believe it was possible to time travel, but how could she challenge Liam's reality if she didn't try the ring and the chant. She picked up the letter and box, the words she was meant to repeat, if she donned the ring, were in Gaelic, she'd no idea how to pronounce the strange phrase.

I gcas ina bhfuil ag I eastail, tigherna a chosaint dom, agus a chonneail, me ar ais go dti mo ait chui. Tilly had written the English translation beneath it, "Where ere I'm needed, Lord protect me and keep me safe, return me to my proper place."

She read them over and over again; each time the cadence and rhythm felt more familiar in her head. Ah well, she thought, here goes nothing. She grabbed her pen and pad and wrote a note. I'm following in Tilly's footsteps; she wanted Liam to see this, and she also took out her phone and selected the camcorder setting.

She set it on the bedside cabinet and videoed herself.

Removing the ring from the box, she smiled at the camera and said "tally-ho" and repeated the chant aloud, feeling very foolish for the split second before everything went into a tailspin.

When she regained consciousness, she was shocked to see Liam sitting beside her as a sixteenth century warrior, beside him stood an Adonis of a man in the uniform of a Roman centurion. Liam introduced the centurion as *Gracus Aurelius*, your guardian. Jeannie fainted.

Image credit: R-region
Pixabay

Out of the Darkness a Heroine Rises

Who will nourish me, protect me?

and love me, as I need to be loved,

whispered the broken warrior crone.

From the great ethereal space of darkness,

Roared a silent, "No-One."

She lowered her head, and communed

With her inner spirit.

And did, as ever, raised her chin.

in defiance of the silence.

She picked up her sword, smiled,

Straitened her spine, stood tall,

And **ROARED** back into the ether,

I WILL!

Image credit: Karabo_Spain
Pixabay

Time Suspended

Mdme Cecilia Allard.

The woman stood aside as her husband broke the lock. The door had been found when they'd decided to take out a built-in bookcase at the end of the corridor on the top floor of their newly acquired cottage. It was really old, but so beautifully maintained. They only wanted to install some central heating, new kitchen units; the bathroom was staying as was except for some minor restoration work.

They both loved the place; they'd holidayed in the area four or five times and always admired the homes.

Then out of the blue, her husband had decided on a total change of career. What had once just been his hobby, was to be his new career path. The history of World War I had held Steve's interest since school, and there was a place in his new idea for Josie to be employed too, but only part time, allowing her to pursue her hobby, writing. They had discussed the options and possibilities many times before finally they had agreed to make a life changing move.

Steve had finally made the move after seeing the advert on the TocH website. The museum in Popperinghe required a couple as custodian/caretakers. She would run the small but very busy café in what was once the kitchen where the food was prepared for these men enjoying a few days respite from the horrors of the front line in World War I. It was a place where the normal mores of everyday life still continued. The difference here, rank held no sway inside the building on *Rue de Hospital*, inside their doors, all men were equal. TocH, its chapel and Padre "Tubby" Philip Clayton were familiar to all soldiers on the Somme, and indeed all over the western front. Now it's a living museum of remembrance, and Josie and Steve would be the caretakers as of the coming September. They had, however, decided to buy a place of their own for when they retired or TocH no longer required their services. So, they sold up in the UK and had bought and moved into their delightful cottage here on the Ypres salient just fifteen minutes from their new post.

Steve had called her away from her job whitewashing the old stone walls of the kitchen. The sanded and waxed oak kitchen units had a honeyed sheen and stood out gently against the bright white of the newly painted walls.

Josie arrived beside her husband as the small padlock fell away and he'd given the door a push. The door hadn't moved, so he followed with a forceful shoulder check, again the door held. "Third time lucky, old girl" laughed Steve as he gave one final and hard assault with his hip and shoulder on this stubborn and strangely hidden door.

The door finally gave way, with a crack it flew open. What they saw, was a place where time stood still.

They were agog, inside was a room, yes. Covered in cobwebs and dust, but it was a perfect vignette of a life long gone. They noticed an envelope atop the Bible on the nightstand. On it, in an elegant and beautiful hand was written: "*a qui donc trouve cela,*" Josie read aloud, to whom so ever finds this is what it said in French.

Let's take this downstairs to read in a better light as we may need the PC for colloquial translations. Steve agreed and they descended the narrow staircase.

With the early afternoon sun streaming into the kitchen and armed with a fresh pot of coffee, Josie began to read.

Thirty minutes later they sat drying their eyes and in quiet contemplation, neither could yet find their voice. The voice of the woman who wrote the letter still rung in their ears.

"A toi qui lis ca," to you who reads this. *(a toey key lisa)*

I hope that many years have passed between my writing this and your reading of it.

My beautiful son joined the French army in 1914, despite his father's denying him permission to do so, and my prayers and pleading that he did not go to fight.

He fought hard and with honour in many of what are now famous battles in the war to "End all wars." But, in 1918 on April 26th, he was killed; his body was never returned to us. This is our memorial to my beautiful, vibrant, passionate, and loving son. I know that I am dying and his father, my husband, died of a broken heart in 1924. That he could not bury his son and have a place to visit was placated in the short time, but in the end, Francois' death broke my husband's heart and mine too. The good Lord has made me wait for my reunion with Gilbert and Francois, but it will be soon.

I have arranged for the door to be sealed then hidden behind the bookcase. It is as sacred a place as any place among the stones in the consecrated ground of the church.

I therefore pray, and beseech you now, having found my son's room that you treat it for what it is and give honour to a brave soldier of France and a loved and mourned son of mine.

Signed,

Mdme. Cecilia Allard

Jose was first to speak, "His surname means noble, how apt," as she wiped another tear away.

"What shall we do now? I feel like we just opened a tomb like that Carter guy in Egypt. Do you remember? He died soon after. They said he was cursed for opening a sacred burial place."

"Oh Steve, Mdme. Allard hasn't cursed anyone finding it, she asks only that we treat it for what it is and be respectful." She looked at him and smiled, a sad rueful smile, but a smile.

"Okay, but what do we *DO*?"

"Let's sleep on it and discuss it more as we absorb and accept what we have found and how we feel about it all. What do you think?"

Steve looked at Josie and said, "Yes, let's give ourselves a little time. Shall we walk into the village and ask old Jaques Dupont what he knows about the history of the house?"

"Good idea," she replied.

Josie made some food; they cleared up and showered then headed into the village, where they spent a very pleasant but uninformative evening in the local bar with a few locals. No-one recalled the name Allard.

After hours of discussion and a good night's sleep they were agreed.

They contacted the Museum de la Guerre in the Cloth Hall in Ypres and arranged to donate Francois Allard's medal, Bible, and a few sepia photographs. They first obtained a copy of the medal, Bible and pictures of Francois proudly posing in his uniform and ones of him with his parents; these they placed in his room along with Mdme. Allard's original letter and one from them. Their letter said that on August 28th. 2018, they had discovered the room. Had read the mother's letter and replaced the original Bible, medal and a few photos which were placed in the Bible. Enclosed with their note was the receipt from the *directeur de muse*, for the items belonging to Second Lieutenant Allard.

They expressed their wish that any future discovery of the room would be as respectful.

Time would continue to stand still beyond the bookcase.

The Break

The break happened quietly, without fuss or drama, just a bump from a felled giant fir. But, like the boxer with the glass jaw, the biggest can be felled, and it doesn't take much effort if hit directly on the weak and fragile fault. This unassuming tree had done exactly that at four a.m., on the Wednesday morning. Two days later, the barrier would be gone and the tree one hundred miles to the south.

Jorgen Sigfridsson was the dam's manager, a short, fat, lazy man who rarely descended the long winding stairs or travelled in the cage lift to the galleries below.

These were the places below the water level, where close inspections should be made and logged regularly. Instead, he left this laborious work to his juniors, who - under his tutelage - had not been properly instructed or assigned the job. Consequently, they only viewed these areas occasionally and then only in passing.

Leif Eriksson was snoozing in the office chair on Level 20, about thirty meters below water level on the near side, when he heard a distinct cracking sound.

He immediately called to the office of Mr. Sigfridsson,

"Sir, I think there's a problem."

"What kind of problem?" replied his boss distractedly. Mr. Sigfridsson was watching X-rated videos on his laptop and barely listening.

"Sir, I heard a loud crack."

"Settlement noises or your vivid imaginings. There's no warning lights on is there?"

Leif was buckling, "No, sir, but it was loud."

Almost like an absent-minded professor his boss then said, "OK, so go and look, and don't call me back unless there's something to report."

Leif was beginning to feel embarrassed at his panicked call, but he had heard the crack, so he set off to walk the eight hundred meters of gallery on this level. An hour later, having traversed the full width of the structure, almost a mile of metal walkways and concrete, he was back at his post. Feeling decidedly stupid, "*I have behaved like a spooked rookie,*" he chided himself.

Hence, later, much later when he heard another louder crack, he didn't log that nor call his boss. He didn't want to be seen as gullible or scared — though he knew in his heart he was.

He was very relieved when his shift ended. It was the longest twelve-hour shift experience in his six months on the job. He signed out of the daily log and headed for the cage lift that would carry him topside. Arriving at the viewing platform and admin offices he blinked in the bright sunshine.

It had been twenty-nine hours since the fir tree had so gently nudged the dam.

Ragnar Havard signed in to work at 0845 hrs. As he was taking over from Leif, they chatted, "Anything I need to know?" Ragnar asked.

Leif momentarily considered telling Ragnar about the cracking sounds but bottled it, "Nope, all good my friend. Are you coming to the bar tonight, Ragnar?"

Ragnar didn't particularly like Leif, but crews who worked the dam had to rely on each other, so he replied, "Yes, OK, I'll see you there, but it will be later I've errands to run first."

Leif waved as he went through the door saying, "Don't be too late, you'll miss all the fun."

Ragnar headed to the cage and descended to his post on Level 20. He did cursory checks on switches, and he included some metallurgical tests on the girders and walkways. He must remember to look at damp and condensation levels.

All in all, there were quite few tasks, and he was busy for the first couple of hours. Everything seemed as it should be except for a moisture reading: it was up by 0.5. He called his boss, "Mr. Sigfridsson, the moisture level is up half of a point."

"Okay, check it again," Jorgen looked at his watch, it was 1339 hrs, "check it again at 1600 hrs and let me know the results, okay?"

"Yes, sir." The line clicked and went dead; Sigfridsson had hung up!

At 1541 hrs Ragnar was walking the gallery heading back to his post to report again to his boss. He'd finally finished the check on the whole eight hundred meters when he heard an almighty noise, a noise that made his sphincter clench and his blood chill. He knew, his gut knew, long seconds before his brain acknowledged and processed it into words.

He took off like a rocket heading for the midway cage to access topside. He threw himself into the cage, his heart almost exploding from his chest. He slammed the button that would take him from this tomb. He knew if he didn't get out fast, this would be his grave.

So, so slowly it seemed that the cage climbed: 19, 18, 17… up it went, he was sure his heart would burst it was beating so fast… 9, 8, 7…

"Come on… come on!" He grabbed the phone, he didn't wait to identify who answered, he just blurted out, "Tell the boss I'm coming up. Get everyone off the dam." He looked up… 4, 3… then in that moment, the same moment he heard Sigfridsson say, "Don't be a damned idiot."

He heard the other sound; the unmistakeable sound of rushing water, crashing concrete and twisting steel. The cage went dark. Power was gone. He then heard a strange snapping sound. Just as his mind identified it, the gate bucked before beginning its furious freefall descent. Ragnar screamed, but no-one heard.

The newspapers, TV, all the media were full of the horrifying toll this disaster had visited upon the area. A village lower down the fjord was destroyed and hundreds were missing.

Almost one hundred miles away, a logger hauled a huge fir from the water. He'd never know it was this tree that was the catalyst to the disaster. He went about his work: he had many crosses to make for the burials upriver.

Image credit: lilandie
Pixabay

The Few
© 2021 Patricia Donoghue, a.k.a. G. B. Carmichael

High in the sky, into the blue,

Up went the few,

holding each breath they drew,

and flew,

Then breathed again, or not

For some were lost, shot

Down in flames, so hot

it flayed their skin from bone,

dying up there all alone, No,

had our mates, SO,

we died as we lived, forever,

together,

we few, who flew,

who drew the line.

That none may cross,

Whatever the loss.

We knew,

We few,

Who flew, we must do

For you,

We could not fail,

and so.

You, Salute

The Few,

Who flew,

Those Lions who,

Were flying crew.

Allan Tipping

Being Frank

"Pickles you horrible little man, where are you?"

"Over here, Sergeant," came the reply from a very particular soldier.

Frank Pickles was surrounded by his kit, trying to get a polish on each part of it. He was on jankers for jumping from one whitewashed stone to the other, all in front of the Sergeant's Mess. It could have been the chair held in one hand, with a vase of flowers on it, or the fact he had his cap on the ground hoping for a tip, that upset the Sergeant so!

"Pickles, you are to report to the commanding officer, at the double." Frank jumped up running to the door. "Pickles, put your clothes on!" shouted the Sergeant.

At the sound of 'come in', Frank opened the door, marched in, and came to attention, saluting his Colonel.

"Sit down Pickles. Smoke if you wish," said the Colonel.

This concerned Frank, he was expecting a bollocking.

"Right, Pickles, let me be honest with you. I have no idea what it must be like being Frank Pickles. For me, the war is deadly serious and your stunts clash with that fact. Your

Sergeant has told me that each time we go into action you act like a professional soldier and that you don't lack courage. Now I am going to make a proposition to you."

"Is that in the articles of war, sir?" Frank asked.

"Please, Pickles, what I have to say is very serious and could be dangerous. I need you to understand what I'm saying and at least give me a fighting chance to believe you have understood." Frank nodded.

"Right. Pickles, what is said in this room is secret and must never be divulged."

"I give my word," Frank acknowledged.

"Do you, Pickles?"

This had now got Frank's interest, overruling his boredom at army matters. Either the Colonel had got lucky in finding the way to speak to him or was alarmingly far more intelligent than his rank indicated.

"Yes, I do, sir," replied Frank.

"Good. Now I need to confirm two incidents were of your making. Remember, there will be no action taken on whatever you say." Frank was expressionless, unsure of what the Colonel was talking about.

"Firstly, did you, Frank Pickles, dress up as an American soldier and mention to a team of men from the Irish Regiment repairing downed phone lines, that you thought that there was a group of Germans dressed as MPs? Then did you contact the Military Police, still disguised as an American, and tell them that a group of Germans, dressed as Royal Irish, were interfering with our communications?"

"Yes. That little prank was mine, sir."

"Little prank, indeed! Three MPs needed medical help after that! Now to make sure it was you, what name did you give to the MPs?"

"Let me think... Oh, yes, that will be Oppenheimer, sir."

The Colonel stubbed out his cigarette and immediately lit another. "Okay, Pickles, now the big one: did you contact this base by phone and inform my clerk that General Montgomery was on a secure line and wished to speak to me?"

"Yes, sir. That was one of my better ones."

"Montgomery told me that he wished to witness and encourage my men in their P.T. He told me that he would be there at 3 p.m. and the men, and officers, should be on parade in their P.T. kit. I have spoken with the General before and would have sworn it was him speaking."

"I know, sir. It felt odd being at attention with my flappy shorts on."

"Go on, Pickles. Why did you do it"!

"Well, it started out of boredom, so I set myself challenges to amuse myself."

"I have to admit that these pranks must have taken some planning and a lot of skill to pull off."

"Thank you, sir."

"So why the silly chair trick outside of the Sergeant's mess?"

"The complicated pranks are the challenge, but sometimes I can be a bit of a prat."

"Why have you never joined the concert party and put on a show?"

"I suppose I could have done an act; I can mimic anyone. I even do a reasonable imitation of you, sir."

"I think I see now, Pickles. It's a power thing: you have created a situation that is under your control. And if people see your ability to copy peoples' voices, you lose that concealed control."

"Yes, sir, but a load of burly Gunners stomping around in frocks attempting to sing dull songs is hardly entertainment… Can I ask a question, sir?"

"Go ahead, I'll do my best to answer it," the Colonel replied.

"How did you come to suspect me, sir? I tried very hard to make sure I was not suspected."

"Do you remember when you came into my office with one of your very polite requests? You asked if it was possible to wear your American helmet as it was more comfortable."

"I should be shot at dawn for that mistake, sir!"

"There are quite a few NCO's who would agree with you," the Colonel said in seriousness.

After pausing for effect, the Colonel continued, "Now I shall come to the point. Things are hotting up in this war and we are likely to be much more offensive; no jokes Pickles. General Montgomery is going to meet with our allies to prepare combined attacks. It would be nice if the Germans didn't know this, so Monty needs a double."

"The answer is yes, sir. The thought of putting one over the German army appeals to me."

"Steady, Pickles... There have already been attempts on Monty' s life, so this is no cake walk."

"I have risked my life every time we stand to, it would be nice to do it under my terms."

"Are you positive, Frank?" It was the first time the Colonel had ever called Pickles by his Christian name. Addressing an underling by their Christian name was reserved for special situations and this was one of them.

"Yes, sir. I really am."

"Right. I shall sign your transfer to a new regiment."

"Which one will that be, sir?"

"Pickles, you are going to join Military Intelligence."

"Isn't that a contradiction in terms, sir?"

"You may go now and the best of luck to you," said the Colonel as a dismissal.

Pickles stood up crisply, saluted, and turned to face the door. Then, in one of his many voices, he called out: "Corporal, come in here and escort Pickles back to his barracks."

Bigfoot
© 2023 Allan Tipping

Austin and Payton were born within a week of each other and having parents who were best of friends spent a lot of time with each other. Both families had small farms in Kentucky and lived quiet God-fearing lives.

It was soon very obvious that the young ones loved each other very much. When they were together, they sat face to face laughing and confiding with each other.

The parents were delighted: not only were their children always happy but they both totally embraced their rural life.

As time moved on, Austin's parents were especially perplexed by their sons easy going and perhaps overly good attitude towards life. The only time he was happier than doing chores on the farm was when he was with Payton. He never even had the terrible two's and went to church with a smile, where he and Payton sat attentively. Austin's Dad was almost braced for all this to come tumbling down when school was started. He knew of folks whose children had turned into little monsters once the peer pressure of school began to bite.

Well, school began and the love between the two of them seemed to grow. Payton could run and was soon representing the school at track and field. Austin was a big lad, very strong because of all the work he did on the farm and found he enjoyed playing American football. Slightly out of line for a very polite church boy, Austin settled at playing the position of linebacker. That was not the offence position but very much defence. He was never rude or aggressive but on the pitch, this was a game and he embraced the physical clash.

Time moved on and very little changed. Austin did get bigger and much stronger, whereas Payton was developing into a very attractive young lady. The two were as close as ever and tongues were beginning to wag. One silly man actually spread a rumour that they were physically connected at the hip. Austin's dad went into a major rage and bounced this chaps butt about, quite a lot. Even Austin acted out of character when the opposing team's tight end made some unsavoury comment; the legal hit when it came was so hard that stretchers were needed.

It was some sad news which kind of brought this to a head: Austin's grandmother died. She had reached a fine old age and died peacefully in her sleep. It was a sad time because Austin and Payton had hiked up to her remote farm many times and had always been made welcome. The will was read to the family, where certain items were left to relations, but the farm was left to Austin.

The family as a whole approved of this move. Austin took it very seriously and for many hours sat talking with Payton in the old barn. It was a Friday after school that Austin dressed in his Sunday best and quietly slipped out the house. He had gone to see Payton's dad.

This was the hardest thing he had ever done as so much hinged on the outcome. He explained that they had always loved each other and that a country life was all they could have wished for. Austin explained that they had a farm, and both wished to run it together and would it be OK if they were to marry when they reached eighteen, which was in two years.

Payton's mother cried, possibly for about a week. Payton's dad shook Austin's hand and said he would be proud to welcome him into the family. The look on Austin's face obviously asked a question, which was answered by Payton's dad.

"We knew you two would marry and the way you have both behaved is beyond reproach and we are proud of you both."

One down two to go. Payton, now in her Sunday best, walked back to Austin's home to speak with his parents. There were tears from mum but also a sterner look from Austin's dad.

"Look, son, you both have done so well in a situation that could have got out of control. There is no way in which I can fault either of you, but will you take some advice with my blessing?" The young couple nodded in unison. "In the next two years, work hard at school and finish it well but work like you have never worked before to get the farm ready. Talk to other farmers to create a plan that will work. Don't be shy asking for help; all your family and friends will willingly help you. Lastly, you both wear belts, tighten them and don't borrow money."

With that he shook his son's hand and hugged Payton, for a long time; coffee had been made before the embrace ended.

Round three, the pastor.

John, the pastor, sat very quietly listening to the young couple explain their hopes and dreams. He smiled at the young couple and simply said, "that seems like a plan."

The months went by and many family visits were made to the remote farm. During the first visit, Payton found an envelope, addressed to Austin, on the small table next to the fire place. Austin opened it, only to find another envelope inside. That was also for Austin, and it simply said, "Austin please only open this when you first hear loud knocks or calls from the woods."

The months passed quickly and the farm was ready for the newlyweds to take possession. The wedding was a simple service followed by hog roast and dance. Needless to say, Payton danced the first dance with grace and beauty; Austin did some moves which made a passing resemblance to a man putting out a fire with his foot.

The young couple were so happy. they worked together and the farm was soon well established. Austin kept growing and became a man, very tall and strong. Payton surpassed the beauty of her wedding day when she told Austin they were going to have a baby.

It was one autumn evening whilst sitting on the porch, watching the light slowly fade, that they heard a loud knock coming from the wood. This knock was followed by an obvious call, very close to a scream.

Payton dashed inside and came out with the envelope from his grandma. Austin opened it and read the letter out so Payton could hear.

"Austin, Payton, I am sure you married and starting your new life as farmers. You have my blessing. Now I am going to give you a bit of advice. You will have heard the knocking and screams so please take great care. You have a creature to deal with which lives in the forest and visits here quite often. Do not be worried as He and I came to an unspoken agreement which hopefully you will follow.

"There is a tree stump in the wood, where the fence line meets the trees. Here I leave shiny stones and apples, as well as other bits and bobs. I give the stump a thump with a log and leave. That night, if he is around, he will return the knock and leave objects like a bone or feather. I also will not allow hunting in the woods and make no attempt to trap or photograph him. In return, he leaves all my stock alone, in fact I suspect he also keeps other predators away. You are a large man now Austin, but I saw him once and he is over nine feet tall, with shoulders like my bull. It is my belief he will be waiting to see if the new owners are going to keep the same policy. That is why I left the farm to you; I think you are more than able and will do this. He and I were sort of friends.

All my love

Grandma.

The next evening Austin and Payton found the tree stump and left some apples and a shiny stone. Austin made a loud knock and the two left. Austin was curious but overcame the urge to hang back and see what happened. Just as the light left and the cool of night began, they heard the knock coming from the wood.

A few weeks later Austin was fishing in the creek, his favourite food being catfish. He caught one but felt he was being watched. With out looking around him he recast and caught another. He packed up and, being ready to leave, he raised one hand as a greeting and left the fish on the bank.

Payton had her baby girl and had passed gracefully into motherhood. Austin found the whole birthing quite beyond him and was on the porch trying to master smoking a pipe.

A few weeks later he noticed a movement in the trees and then this huge being stepped out and stood motionless. Austin quietly called for Payton, asking her to bring the baby. The young couple stood together on the porch and Austin held up the new baby as if to show the neighbours. There was another movement in the trees and another huge being came forward, this time carrying a child. The male then took his baby and held it high, Grandma's agreement still stood. The two beings then took their young one back into the woods, leaving Austin and Payton on the porch.

"What shall we call them," Payton said, "Bigfoot is unfriendly and even rude."

In The Heat of the Night

© 2023 Allan Tipping

"This is madness!" Jane shouted to all four walls of her tiny flat. One week ago, she was desperately trying to keep warm. There was actually frost on the inside of her windows. Now she was lying on a towel, on her bed, desperately trying to sleep in the 40-degree heat. Nothing worked, the power went down three days ago, water was just a trickle and by the sounds coming in through her open window all hell was kicking off.

Jane was not a person of sour thoughts, nor was she afraid to look after herself. She had for quite a time been worried about the breakdown of society and had prepared to some degree. She had all she needed for several weeks, even bottled water, for which she was really grateful. She had even brought some books on how to survive from the wild.

That brought a smile to her face. At about four the previous morning she had ventured out to a patch of rough land near her home and picked a carrier bag full of a silver leafed plants.

The smile became a laugh as she looked at her naked body covered in these silver leaves. The book had said that these leaves could cool the skin and they had, a bit!

Jane was very slim and the first image she thought of was a picture of Eve, with her fig leaf, or maybe a woodland elf sleeping with just the leaves of the forest floor to keep her warm. The exceptional circumstance she was living through had not bubbled up into fear, at least not for her herself. She did worry about her aging parents especially as the mobile phones were the first thing to go down.

The night dragged on, without any wind to cool anything down but the urban existence she now lived in had become quieter. Those poor souls walking the streets, searching for anything which help them, had even given up on that. They were not desperate enough to start raiding people's homes; there was still a vestige of human dignity left, but maybe not for much longer.

So there, 'in the heat of the night,' she made a plan. Her initial optimism that the government would get the measure of this emergency had come to nothing. She had held her ground, but now it seemed a prudent thing to run. There was only one place she wanted to go and that was to her childhood home, especially as she hadn't heard from them for over a week and was becoming increasingly worried for them. She did also have a brother; he was strong and quite capable of looking after himself. If she were going to go it would have to be now: people were off the streets and would be for a few more hours. Plenty of time to leave the city and get into the countryside.

For the next half an hour, Jane pondered over the road map, creating a route home that avoided as many towns as possible. It would take longer, and more petrol, but hopefully would avoid people.

Yet again her planning was made possible by the preparations she had done; her pride and joy was a 250cc Honda motorcycle. It was serviced and tanked up, ready to go. There was even a can of petrol to take with her. She hoped it was still safely locked up in the garage that went with the flat.

Before she dressed Jane used one of the bottles of water to wash herself down, some of the silver leaves had migrated and were getting itchy.

She had a set of saddle bags that she filled with the items she felt would be most beneficial. She did slip in a few things that were very special, but most of the flat's contents meant nothing to her and she left them without a further thought.

Jane opened the garage door and to her relief found the bike safe and ready to move. A few moments with some bungie cords and it was all strapped on, she was set in her mind and eager to be off.

The bike started first kick and, keeping the revs to a minimum, she pulled away.

Quiet and steady was the way to be, not giving away her position to those who would love to get her petrol. *"Good old Honda,"* she thought; *"Speed kills. Ride a Honda and live"* was the slogan aimed exactly at her bike. There was a good moon and no traffic, so Jane did not bother with lights. There was a thrill in being alone in the dark with the engine vibrating gently through its frame. She had confidence in this bike and that confidence steadied any of the concerns for her safety. She was a good rider and knew full well that even though she only had 250cc at her disposal, she was light and the bike could move quickly if pushed.

The first glimmer of daylight found her on a lane, between two of the towns she wished to avoid. She was moving north and would have to for many miles yet before she could head east and home. It was on this lane she saw her first human, a young chap with an enormous rucksack. Jane gave a wave as she passed him and was greeted with a smile in return. *"I bet he has walked all night,"* Jane thought, *"and is now going to find a place to hide up during the day."*

As the miles kept mounting up, a worrying though kept nagging at her. She had seen only one soul and he seemed perfectly friendly! Had her mind got the better of her and sent her off on a crazy tangent? But if all were sorting itself out, she would at least have seen her family.

Jane was feeling very confident by now. Her concerns had not materialised and she was recognising some of the countryside. She was spending most of her time now wondering what welcome she would get. Her parents would be happy, of course, but what were they living like? Was the countryside not having the same problems the city was having?

She had spent too much time thinking and not enough studying the road ahead, so she was cross with herself when an armed man stepped out in front of her. She had no choice but to pull over. The man moved courteously towards her when she recognised him. "Nick, you arse, what's the meaning of frightening the life out of me?"

"Is that really you, Jane? How on earth did you get through to us here?" Three other men now showed themselves, all armed. "It's OK, lads I know who this is and she has good reason for being here."

"Nick, are my parents OK and what in heavens name is happening here that warrants guns?"

"I have heard no news of your parents to answer your first question. It seems like it's every man for himself to answer the second. There have been raiding parties searching for food, tools, and petrol. We are here to protect this border and there are others on other routes into this area."

"It was getting very bad in the cities as well. Nothing worked and the shops had run out of food," Jane responded.

"It's the same here: no electricity or water, but worst of all we have no idea what's happened. All communications are down. You had better be getting on because it's not that safe here and your parents will need help."

"Thanks, Nick, and look after yourself." With that, Jane kicked the bike back into life and was on her way.

She was very close now. Every tree seemed to welcome her back. Every mile felt so slow, it almost felt that to leave the bike and run would be quicker. Then came the corner. She knew that her parents' home was just around that tight bend. She pulled into the garden, quickly got off, and rested the bike on the side stand. All she wanted to do was rush to the door but held back for a second to lovingly pat the bikes petrol tank.

The door opened a bit and a well-known voice shouted out, "State your business!"

Jane sobbed out the words, "It's me, Dad." The next minute she was being spun around and being kissed by a man who's age and fragility was forgotten in his joy.

"Come in, come in and see Mother," her father said as she was tugged towards the now open door. The house was unchanged. It was almost as if her adult life had never happened. There was her mother, arms wide open, and her brother, smiling at her as he unloaded the shot gun and stood it in the corner.

The world could do its worst now. There were no gaps, no tugging in a direction. They would see this out together.

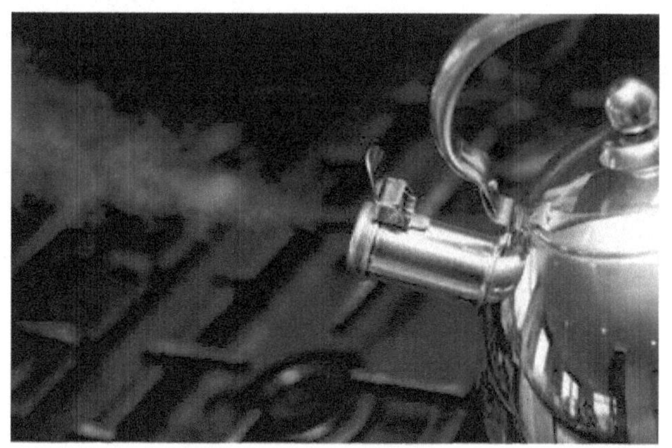

Image credit: KenBoyd
Pixabay

The Singing Kettle
© 2023 Allan Tipping

Don pulled the bike over at the only cafe they had found all morning. It was very quaint, nothing like the service cafes he was more use to. Still, a tea is a tea, and a warm room would be much appreciated on a nippy spring morning.

The well-practised dismount routine went ahead. Don's girlfriend got off first and fidgeted with her clothing. Tight jeans and an old Triumph do tend to create a formidable wedgie. She then removed her helmet and tried to do something with her wind tussled hair. Don then dismounted and put the motorbike on its centre stand; he then took the large chain from off his shoulders and secured the bike. Off came the sunglasses and the helmet, Don not bothering with his hair, which was longer than Bev's and a lot more unruly.

They made a for a different sort of customer as they walked under the swinging sign of a large copper kettle. Don knew that their appearance might seem a bit shocking. He didn't dress as an old-school biker, more what they call now a greaser. His leather jacket had over it a denim cut-off with Triumph painted on its back. There were no club colours as

Don did not like riding with large groups. He liked to do things his way.

As the door opened, it made a little bell tinkle and a small old chap walked into the cafe from what must have been the kitchen. He had round horn-rimmed glasses on his completely bald head and a pristine white apron tied round his waist. He stopped dead in his tracks when he saw the two of them. Bev would have been a foot taller than him and Don at least two feet taller. But if the proprietor showed any shock it was soon replaced with a welcoming smile.

"Come and sit here, close to the fire. You must be quite cold," the proprietor said.

"Thanks a lot," smiled Don, "do you mind if we put our gloves near the fire to warm up?"

"Course not. Now what can I get you?"

"Any chance of two bacon sandwiches and two mugs of tea?" Don asked.

"That will be no problem, I'll just pass that order on to 'she-who-must-be-obeyed' in the kitchen." With that, the little chap nipped through the kitchen door.

Don pushed his feet out to get them closer to the fire and gave a large comforting sigh, "I like it here Bev."

The two bikers were looking at the pictures which covered nearly all the wall space when their food arrived. The proprietor could be described as a small man, while his wife could not be classed as small. She was taller than Bev and quite a bit heavier. She was a woman who showed both strength and calm in abundance. 'She-who-must-be-obeyed,' seemed very fitting! They were left alone to enjoy their food and enjoy it they did. Don was chewing on the thick slices of crusty bread with ample quantities of bacon.

It was between swallowing the last chunk of bread and washing it down with tea when Don saw a small old photograph hanging close to the fireplace.

"Look at that old bike," Don said, "it's a really old Royal Enfield, girder forks and plunger back suspension. It's hard to tell because the old black and white photo has gone a brownish tinge, but I'm sure I've seen that bike on another old photo."

Don was now getting agitated, pacing back and forth and constantly coming back to the picture.

"It's only an old photo of a bike, Don," Bev said as she started to become concerned. Don was mostly a calm chap but could work himself up, angry he could become hard work.

The old boy came in to clear the plates away and Don spun round to face him.

Bev touched his hand and whispered, "Steady..."

"I'm sorry I seem to have a bit of a funk on and its over that picture," Don said, desperately trying to steady himself. "Do you know any history of that bike?" Don almost pleaded.

"Yes, I do actually. Believe it or not, I was in the army during the last war and that bike was part of our detachment. It was on that bike that I had my first and unfortunately my last ride on the back of a motorbike."

Don was now riveted to the spot and quietly asked, "What regiment were you in?"

"I was in the Royal Artillery. Not being built like a soldier, I was attached to communications," came the reply.

Don was now looking positively pale as he asked the next question, "Were you in North Africa?" Don sat down; he was shaken but still keen to ask more of the old man.

"Yes, I was, for a short while."

"I'm sorry to come across so pushy," Don said, "but I have a picture just like that at home, only this one had my dad sitting on the bike. I have so little of the story of my dad's life and I'm sorry if I'm coming across a bit too intense."

"So, you are wondering if I knew your dad. It might be good if you could describe him for me," said the proprietor.

"He would have been about 18 to 19, slim, of medium height. He had blond hair with side parting and also had a pipe in his mouth almost permanently."

The old fella closed his eyes and fell silent. Suddenly, he looked up and said, "Would his name be Cecil by any chance"?

Don put his hand on the table to steady himself. "Yes that was Dad's name."

The older chap, sensing Dons distress, told him all he knew of Cecil. "I only knew him for a couple of weeks, which was unfortunate as we seemed to get on well. As you can imagine being such a small man, I use to have the mickey taken out of me quite a lot. Knowing Cecil made quite a difference. He was a boxer. you know, and a good one. Anyway, just before his unit was deployed, he took me on a spin and that picture was of the bike. It's quite probable that I took the picture of your dad on his camera. He was a good man, but after his deployment we lost contact. Now I have question, is Cecil still with us?"

Calm now, Don answered the question, "Sorry, no. Dad died quite young – a heart attack of all things. I was young and didn't think to ask much about his life. It's too late now."

"I am sorry to hear that," the old chap said, "you should be proud of him."

Don's mood switched so quickly; sadness changed to a smile. "Do you know what? You had a spin on my dad's old bike. How about spin on his son's bike?"

The old chap squared his shoulders and turned to 'she-who-must-be-obeyed,' "Wife, fetch my coat and gloves, I'm going to be out with the lads for a while." He may have been small, but he didn't lack courage!

We Meet Again

© 2023 Allan Tipping

There is something wrong with going into a city, even to see a specialist! It does not matter if it's by road, air or train, there are masses of people all crushed together or are just stuck waiting. It is madness and yet people choose to go through this day in and day out.

John had just got over a serious bout of angst having paid for a ticket and yet had to stand the whole journey. The ticket office were without sympathy when a ticket refund was asked for. In fact, they became quite sadistic when they laughed and pointed out that he had missed his connection. John had an hour to kill.

He found the right platform, eventually. This must be what it's like for one of his ferrets down a large rabbit warren. Up and down, and around and around; it was enough to make your head spin.

He did find an old chap busking in a tunnel; hat a life! No sunlight, just thousands of people not giving a damn. He did play well and seemed friendly, enough for John to ask for a request: "Horse With No Name," by America. The chap knew it and played it for him. John thanked him and dropped a few pounds in in his hat. It was then time to leave the only sanity he had found in hours and make his way to platform six.

As expected, the platform was full of people waiting; all the benches were taken except one. That was right at the end of the platform and stuck out in the elements. Air that stank of fumes was at least preferable to playing sardines with the very glum fellow passengers. John could not understand why they were there if they hated it so much. So, with a conversation with someone looking most unlikely, he made his way to the end of the platform and began the waiting game.

He was enjoying a little bit of reminiscing, the black coffee from his flask, a home rolled cigarette, and singing quietly to himself; "I've been through the desert on horse with no name," when an odd thing happened. Walking boldly up to him was a young lady, and not any young lady. She was so like the girls he knew in the sixties; it was uncanny. Blue jeans and a duffel coat and a smile that could melt your heart.

"Have you a light, please?" she asked.

"Of course," John replied.

"And maybe a cigarette to go with it?" she smiled back to him.

"There's the tin, and there is some coffee in the flask if you like." John smiled as she deftly rolled a smoke, lit it with his lighter and blew out a long stream of smoke as she poured out her drink.

"Well, then. It's nice to meet you. My name is John."

"Blue," replied the young lass.

That caught John completely by surprise. He had once known a young girl of that name; in fact, he had a crush on her. That would have been in '69 or '70 when John was seventeen. John was now I his late sixties and as good as his memory would allow, this girl was the spitting image of her.

"I knew a girl called Blue once," John replied.

"Yes I know," she said smiling at him.

This was becoming a bit surreal and beyond John's comfort zone. He decided that whatever was happening was very nice, much too nice to be troubled with oddities.

"So, what brings you to this urban spot, Blue? Are you waiting for a train too?" this was Johns attempt at making conversation. It sounded a bit of a limp question given the huge question that John really wanted to ask, "Are you the

Blue I once knew all those years ago?" John wanted to know, but was worried the answer might break the spell and Blue would just vanish.

"I come here quite often, just hanging out, waiting for the right moment."

"Is this the right moment?" John replied.

"No, not yet, but it will be soon," was the equally mysterious reply.

"Was it you who asked for that America song a few minutes ago?" Blue asked.

"Why, yes," John replied, "it was always one of my favourites."

"Mine, too. I remember it played by the campfire up on Durlston Moor. Anton was always there singing into the night." Blue's eyes went even softer and distant as she responded to John and John went very silent.

After what seemed an age, John sighed and said, "They were the best of years, weren't they?"

"Yes," Blue said.

In that one word, John felt all the loss of happiness a few bad decisions made. This was becoming a bit morose so in an attempt to lighten this, 'brief encounter' he said, "Well at least we had that summer. I have never forgotten it."

There was another brief silence before John got up the courage to speak again.

"Blue, I have to ask this and I wish I had the courage to ask this all the way back then. Are you waiting for me?"

"I've always been waiting for you, John, but now is not the time. Go quickly. Your train is coming."

"I moved away at the end of one summer, against what my heart said. I shan't do it again, not now."

"You must go, John. The time is not now. please have faith in me."

John's dulling eyes filled with tears as he gave her his tobacco tin and lighter, and with a strength he did not know he had, smiled, "Till it's time, then." He went to embrace her, but he was all by himself.

When he arrived back at his cottage, there was a reluctance to open the doo. He knew what he would find. There would be no dog to greet him, and it would be dark.

He left his case by the door and wandered into his garden: at least there would be colour there.

He wandered around just touching the flower heads admiring their shape and form. When he first had a garden to work in, he use to value every seed and plant; each one had that grain of life within it, each one special.

It was no use putting it off. He had to go inside and reclaim his home. It didn't really need a fire, but a fire is comforting and John was in need of comfort. With a brew made and a crackling fire, John sat in his chair and just looked around him. He was quite happy how his working life went; he even thought Blue would have been happy to share in it. His emotional life was a mess and best left in some dark corner. John hadn't really been happy anywhere else since the early seventies. It was there he took a masterclass in 'not fitting in.'

The days slid one to another and the seasons passed. John always kept Blue close to him, in thought anyway. There were times when he lost hope and believed he had a bout of madness brought on by some strong drugs in the sixties flashing back on him, but those thoughts soon passed.

It was early one spring and John was sitting on his bench; the days of rolling a cigarette had passed. His fingers were now painful and full of arthritis, so it had to be a fag from a packet. He was just about to light it when he heard the tenderest of words, "We meet again."

There was Blue in front of him, smiling and with a face filled with beauty.

John said, "Is it time, Blue?"

Her gentle reply was "Yes."

Without a second thought he held out his hand so she could help him up. The moment their fingers touched, John saw his hands change. The lumps and bumps the arthritis had created faded away; the liver spots on the backs of his hands were no more. He stood up, nearly lunging forward as his legs had the power of youth back.

As he stood, so very close to Blue, the sights of his life began to fade and in their place was a camp fire and smiling faces.

The singer put his guitar down, looked up and smiled, "John, Blue, where have you been."

"Went off track a bit, Anton, but we're back now."

Image credit: Amaynut
Pixabay

One Summer Long Ago
© 2023 Allan Tipping

The storyteller sat in the corner of the village inn, minding his own business and drinking his ale. His peace was shattered by a slightly drunk young man demanding a story.

"I will recite you a story as long as my glass stays full. Now, what do you want to hear?"

An old man who had sat for at least an hour in silent contemplation, looked up and said, "Tell of Payne."

The storyteller closed his eyes and when he looked up to start the story, he seemed different. It was as if the story to come was going to stretch him and jangle parts of his soul that were best left misunderstood.

"One summer long ago, a stupid king made an arrangement with a secret organisation, who, if the arrangement was in their best interests would send an assassin. The one sent was called Payne, their most feared member. Payne accomplished his task but made a demand on the king, that he was not to harm those in Payne's company. The king not only killed the lord and lady but did so in the most brutal way, a sneer to the underlings' demands. I call him stupid because he considered himself to be following some divine right to rule. Stupid because he massively underestimated the man who was not only Templar, healer and hermit but also possessed. I for one do not want to think of what possessed him.

"The Duke of Northumberland was making ready to leave his castle and join with the other dukes and barons at the hunt arranged by the king. That night, he held a leaving feast, where he could indulge himself in eating, drinking and entertainments. Northumberland found the antics of his jesters, perhaps more so than his guests, hugely funny.

That night the great hall rang with laughter, especially when the new jester did his turn. A large cartwheel was brought into the hall and wooden torches placed around its rim; the light flickered as the wheel was spun. The noble guests watched and when it stopped there was a hooded man, standing tall and mysterious in front of them.

The man raised his hands to remove his habit and when it dropped to the floor, there stood a hunched clown. His face was painted into a mask of stupidity, his back was bent and deformed, his clothes were mismatched styles of every colour imaginable. The duke laughed until his sides hurt at the crazy contrast in front of him.

The jester's act was defiantly novel. He told stories about the rich and famous and at the punchline he farted and through some powders into the flaming torches. When the wheel stopped spinning, the jester told another story, ending with a totally different fart. Soon the hall was filled with spinning lights and different coloured powders. The last story was about the Mother Superior and the tremendous blast that ended that story left the duke falling from his chair gasping for air, trying desperately to get his laughter under control, so he could breathe. The poor duke had only just regained his chair to fall again at the sight of the jester scratching his arse.

When the duke had gained his composure he asked one simple question, "I wish to reward you for the fun you have brought here tonight. What would you wish?"

The jester replied, "I would wish to perform in front of the king."

Northumberland's response was immediate. "So be it. You will leave with us on the morrow."

At that, the jester threw some more powders onto the blazing wheel and in the blinding flash and detonation vanished.

Now the hunt had gone well, and the guests entered the royal hunting lodge, both jolly and grovelling. Each wanted to praise the king on his hunting abilities more than the others. Any sane man would have been sickened at these lickspittles, but the king was neither sane nor moral in any way.

During the feast, the duke was hoping that the new jester would please the king. As he was finishing yet another glass of wine, imagining the praise to be heaped on him by the king, the floor was cleared to make ready for the entertainments.

The king's jesters were very good and had the hall laughing out loud. When they were finished, the king announced that it was now time for the Duke of Northumberland's wandering jester.

The king said that the jester "comes very highly praised, so we shall see."

The duke had a sudden fear that the king might be put out if his jester made the king's own seem a bit lame. The wheel and its torches were brought in, and the hall sat in readiness. There was a flash of light and the heavily cowled tall figure stood before them. Again, he let this robe fall to the ground and there was the hunched, ridiculously colourful, and grinning clown. That drew a cheer from the hall and a smile from the king.

Now the clown had done his homework and knew the people that the king disliked, so the first joke was about the king's cousin, a pompous high-born woman whose dislike for the king was quite well known. The fart that ended that story screeched around the hall and powders were thrown into the spinning wheel. All the guests were watching the king and burst into laughter as soon as the king did.

The act progressed like this and the clergy were at the butt of many of the stories, ending with one noble bishop. The clown jumped around the room doing an impression of a horse farting at full gallop. As the jester went past the wheel, he threw a large handful of powder into the flames. It erupted in blue flames and a huge detonation. The clown now stood alone in the quiet great hall; all the others there were asleep.

Slowly, the clown moved towards the king. With each step, his back straightened and his height grew. The clown became Payne and with each step the room darkened and chilled. Fear now walked before Payne as he moved towards his kill. Payne looked long and hard at the sleeping king and then pushed something, looking like plant stamens into the king's mouth. He then blew a powder up the king's nose and the king stirred.

The king was smiling when he came to, until he saw Payne standing before him.

"You!" he shouted, "where are my guards?"

"Asleep," came the reply. That simple word, asleep, was full of the horror of the grave. The voice that said it hissed and rasped the sound, in a way you would imagine a snake to sound like, if one could talk.

The king forced himself deep into his chair and with a shrill "What do you want?" began to cry.

"I have already got what I came for. You are going to die within a week. My last task here is to explain to you how that will happen. You have taken into your mouth stamens from a very rare flower, along with the pollen and fungal spores. The fungus will spread to every part of your body and with each cell they crush, you will scream in pain. You have millions of cells in just your hand. You will be kept alive for a while because they will want to save you, but they won't be able to."

The king, now grey and trembling, pleaded with Payne, "There is a fortune hidden in this hunting lodge/ If you agree to end my life quickly I will tell you its location."

Payne moved close to the king and held up one finger as he spoke, "When I touch you sleep will happen. When you awaken, you will be able to see and hear everything, but you won't be able to speak. Even your screams will be silent. Something for you to ponder as your life is ripped away. You were a hindrance on my path, like a nettle that has tilted in the way. I would choose to walk around the nettle rather than bash it aside. I want you to understand how insignificant you really are and the size of the hell you are destined for."

So, with one touch of Payne's finger this story ended.

With the story finished, there was no loud cheering or praise in any way; those listening were numb and silent. The storyteller rose to his full height, put on his cloak, and pulled its cowl almost over his face. He then drifted slowly to the door and disappeared into the dark night.

Martin Radford

Image credit: 495796
Pixabay

The Outfit

Peter groaned as he twisted painfully to his left. Adjusting his position allowed him to reach forward and firmly grip the wide metal grill that constrained the air conditioning duct. He winced as a sharp edge sank into the soft flesh of his palm. Ignoring the discomfort, he wrapped his fingers tighter and pulled himself forward. The freelancer was careful to raise his rubber-soled shoes so they did not inadvertently squeak, giving his location away to any unseen individuals below.

With his randomly camouflaged face held a couple of inches away from the grid, Peter softly pulled on the magnetically held flap of the large pocket on his skin-tight one piece. Blood dripped from the open wound on his right hand. It pooled quickly on the heavily waterproofed material before sliding into winding rivulets inside the open pocket.

While he reached into the pocket and pulled out a small pair of powerful optics, Peter thought in reflection on an earlier conversation today.

I knew I should have listened to Connie. He offered me a pair of fingerless gloves while mumbling something like, "Give yourself a little more protection. Pete."

It did, I admit, surprise me. Because it was way out of character when he genuinely looked concerned.

But No. As usual, I had to be a 'macho man,' ignoring the rare advice given by my boss.

Peter Taylor wiped away a little blood from a protective plastic cap before exposing the actual lens. Awkwardly raising the matte black device to his eye, he rocked a small pair of soft protrusions at the top. An almost silent whirring noise purred from within as the magnification adjusted, allowing him to concentrate on the chained man, sitting cross-legged in the centre of a circular, tarmacked courtyard.

Touching a microphone extended from an earpiece inserted into his right ear, he swallowed before quietly announcing, "Target in sight."

Almost instantaneously, a tense female voice hissed the single word, "Check."

A gruff second voice also responded to the radio transmission, "Okay, Becky, make your way to your identified vantage point — and make it sharpish. Abdul Sharma will be here in a few hours."

"Roger, on my way," Becky acknowledged.

"And, Pete, don't forget: no heroics this time, please. Becky is more than capable."

"You'd better tell Jacko as well. As I recall, he was the one who randomly yelled, 'Tequila.' That half-witted terrorist didn't know whether to shoot Becky or invite her to a bar for a drink." Pete heard David Jackson inanely chuckling into his communication device.

"Okay, you comedians, open mic night will have to be rescheduled for another time. We need to keep our eyes and ears sharp and open." Connor Brightman smoothly shifted his team's focus back to the job at hand.

From his precarious vantage inside Hotel Spaz, allegedly, the tallest building in Pratella, northern Chile. Peter could see a vague cloud of dust moving like a magic carpet, floating above the single-story shanty buildings that haphazardly bordered the poor-quality road which ended at the undocumented prison next door.

The crunch of tyres on gravel brought his attention to focus on the forecourt next door. A group of previously out-of-sight armed men materialised to greet the unknown visitor.

Inside the Bentley motor, a smartly dressed driver cracked his neck before he exited the vehicle. Admiring custodians couldn't fail to notice his muscled torso, as he loped to the opposite side to assist his passenger. The rear door of the sleek prestige car opened, causing involuntary gasps, as a shapely pair of stockinged legs extended into the sun outside. The surrounding guards gripped their Soviet-made AKM rifles and pointed them unwavering towards the smartly dressed female about to exit the vehicle.

Rebecca Sontig took a deep breath and pulled herself out of the sumptuous luxury of the air-conditioned Bentley. The warmth of the moist air made her gasp, but she kept her composure and marched straight towards the nearest man wearing an officious-looking uniform.

She heard a distinct click as they disengaged multiple assault rifle safety catches.

"Who is in charge here?" she asked, ignoring the impudent stare from the swarthy man standing in front.

The man spat into the dirt. "What do you mean, woman, and who are you?" His countenance was arrogant and contemptuous.

"I would like to ask you the same question." She paused and pursed her voluptuous lips. "I think your employer, Abdul Sharma, would like to know the name of the peasant who *dared* ask me who I am. My name is Casella Bantu, and I deal with Mister Sharma's security issues."

The scruffy man bared a set of rotting teeth, before replying in a slightly deferential voice. "I am sorry, madam. We have no instructions to say that you were going to be visiting our establishment. We are ignorant of higher levels of authority here at Pratella. We just receive anyone sent to be homed here for a while, and then pass them on when required."

Becky looked the man up and down and wrinkled her nose. "Take me to the prisoner. I want to ask him questions in private, and make sure you wash before talking to me again." She twisted towards the car and gave the driver a come-hither signal.

Staring at the guards, unconsciously daring them to make a derogatory comment, Rebecca Sontig followed the lead guard, forming a small convoy of mixed races, heading silently towards the heavily reinforced steel gates.

"Team members have gained access," Conrad whispered over the comms circuit.

"Oh, come on, Connie. Who is on the lookout here? Even though I am crammed into a metal sweatbox. I can still see what's going on around me, you mincing doughnut."

"Maintain radio silence, Taylor," replied Conrad without a trace of emotion in his gravelly voice.

Concentrating on the courtyard, waiting for his team members to show themselves, Pete took a little time before realising he should have made another sarcastic riposte. He missed the opportunity as his friend's voice whispered sharply into his ear.

"You crack me up, Pete. If only our sponsors realised how unprofessional we can be!"

Peter imagined his friend lifting two fingers in salute to his microphone. "I try to please," he chuckled. "Righty oh. Toodle pip. The boss is off to work — don't wait up…"

Pete, feeling amused, watched as another vehicle created its unique carpet of dust, travelling towards the prison. A tatty old Foden lorry skidded to a halt on the gravel, triggering the guards to tumble out of the door for the second time today, their guns covering every side of the wreck. A dark-skinned man, casually dressed in jeans and a hoodie confidently stepped down from the cab.

"Well?" he called in a commanding voice, reaching out to no one in particular.

Each of the gaolers looked confused, looking at one another to see if anyone knew who the hell this guy is. The random head-flicking eventually landed on the lead guard. The man did not have an excellent education but there was no way he would be making the same mistake he had previously made.

Offering a hand in friendship, he uttered a timid greeting. "Good morning, sir. Nice to meet you. How may we help?"

Pete watched in amusement as more guards left the confines of the prison to observe the antics outside. Moving his focus to the prisoner in the courtyard, he saw Becky reach into her adequate cleavage to withdraw an extendable pair of chain cutters.

"Hmm, the entertainment outside obviously, outweighs the joys of watching over the prickly lady inside," He thought. He was amused watching her effortlessly snap the captive's chains one by one.

As soon as the final padlock fell away. Becky raised an arm as a signal, and half dragged the ex-prisoner towards the rear wall.

The front of the prison was becoming quite crowded. Inquisitive locals had wandered down the basic road to mingle with the confused guards. The newly arrived stranger had announced his name was Abdul Sharma, their employer and benefactor. He had instructed the lead guard to organise his men and get them ready to unload the lorry. The first items to appear from under the canvas appeared to be various lengths of rusted scaffolding.

Abdul Sharma took a step backwards, sweeping his arms outwards in an encompassing gesture, then commanded, "Leave your guns in a pile on the other side of my lorry. Of course, I want any obstacles placed out of the way of my important employees. I do not want any accidents." He smiled graciously.

"When you carry my construction components to the front of the prison. I do not want to see a single man without an item in his arms."

He heard the gentle thrum of a helicopter somewhere in the distance. *"Time to wrap this up,"* he thought. "I want you to all stand in a line holding the item you carried. I am extremely proud of my staff and would like to show my competitors what they are missing."

He reached inside his jacket and extracted a mobile phone.

He pointed to a gaggle of residents standing to one side. "Tell you what. To make this a photo to remember, why don't you stand behind the guards, and any children sit cross-legged in front."

The onlooking crowd obliged, milling across the gravel towards the proud-looking employees. A fair amount of jostling disturbed the laden men, who were already tired of holding random pieces of heavy steel.

The man calling himself Abdul Sharma turned towards the lorry and began ascending a dangerous-looking ladder, to stand on the top of the cab. "Just getting the optimal position," he explained.

Conrad could see a dark shape silently and rapidly approaching the rear of the two-storey building.

From his vantage position, Pete could watch the almost silent H130 stealth helicopter twist sideways as it came over the rear wall of the prison. The instant it changed its motion to become static and hover, it released a steel knotted cable to fall towards Becky and the men below.

The leader of the outfit, who was currently posing as Abdul Sharma, noticed a few of the guards had been randomly twisting their heads left and right, unsure where the surrounding dust clouds had risen from with the lack of any apparent wind.

"Okay, everyone. Hold your positions, I will count down from three."

Smiling prison staff noticed as the count reached one, Abdul mysteriously dropped through an opening in the cab's roof. As confused men watched, the lorry roared away, heading in the direction it had initially arrived from. A shout from within the building alerted them that the prisoner had somehow escaped. Pandemonium ensued with no one able to decide what to do.

Peter Randolph wriggled backwards to escape the confines of the airway and return to the comfort of his plush hotel room. Peter sighed. "Last to leave as usual. Still, on a pleasant note. The real Abdul Sharma is going to have a really shitty day when he reaches Pratella Prison…"

The Red Box

Another Barbie doll flew across the room to join a mountain of old teddies. The cherry on top was a usually smartly dressed male doll, now transformed into 'One-legged Ken,' with his trousers pulled down over his arms and head.

When asked about his questionable fashion statement just a few moments ago, four-year-old Stacy told Mum, "The perve was peering out of the cockpit of his Power Ranger monster truck. He was staring at me when I woke up." She frowned innocently and looked at her mother, Tania, to elicit a bond of female solidarity.

Tania had refrained from explaining that Ken could not hide the stare, as he had not yet gained the ability to move his moulded eyes in any other direction. Tania simply nodded and wiggled her eyebrows to affirm her daughter's claim of her personal space being invaded.

"Changing the subject sweetheart, is there any reason for the dolls piling up beside your bed?"

"I can't find it…" Stacy pouted while simultaneously putting her palm against her forehead. Tania sighed as she recognised her daughter mimicking herself when frustrated with life.

"I'll try to help if you could give me a teensy-weensy clue about what we are looking for." The young woman knelt down next to her daughter and gave her a reassuring smile.

"Thank you, Mummy." Stacy reached towards Tania's extended hand and gripped her wedding ring. Tania closed her fist lightly over her little girl's fingers "My pleasure Stace, that's what mummies are for."

"I'm looking for the golden chain that Daddy gave me before he went away." She looked questionably towards her mother.

"Have you looked in the chest of drawers?" Tania asked her youngest daughter in an attempt to be helpful.

The young girl stood up and walked confidently beside a handmade piece of MDF furniture, painted gloss white. Accessorised with her own pink handprint on top, which Daddy had insisted made the drawers uniquely hers.

"I've pulled out each drawer, and personally looked in each one of them," Stacy said, sounding very mature for her age.

Tania raised an eyebrow in mild shock, *"Where the hell had her four-year-old daughter learnt to phrase a sentence like that?"* She shook her head lightly to focus on the here and now. "I've just had an idea pickle; did you know every chest of drawers has a secret hiding place."

Stacy placed her hands on her hips and looked at her mother as if she had just grown an extra head. "Duh, you are trying to treat me like a child. I can see that the only openings are the drawers." The pout began to emerge once more.

"Where has my baby girl gone? I will have to ensure I'm alone next time I have a reality show binge. She's growing up way too fast," she thought to herself and sighed.

Tania rocked backwards slightly, enabling herself to rise from her knees and stand beside the wooden drawers. She bent over and pointed to the furniture of interest.

"Okay, I admit you have probably made a superb search of the drawers themselves. But what about the secret compartment?" Before her daughter could protest that they had already confirmed there was no hidden area, she gripped the chest and lifted it onto the bed in one swift movement.

Before she could turn and see whether the missing necklace had been exposed after falling out of the back of a drawer onto the floor, she heard an especially loud inward breath and her daughter emotionally murmured one questioning word — "Mummy?"

Tania looked down at the floor, ready to say, "*I told you so.*" She took a deep breath.

Lying on the carpet smothered in dust was a small red box.

It looked like a box that someone would receive with jewellery inside. On the top was a small tag originally held by Sellotape which looked flaky and dry.

Before Stacy could pick it up, Tania rudely snatched it from the floor and held it tight against her beating heart. Ignoring the box, Stacy got back onto the floor and wiped her tiny hand across the carpet. "Well, you were wrong Mummy; the necklace wasn't under here."

Now becoming curious about the box instead, she looked wide-eyed at her mother's face. "Why are you crying Mummy?"

Hot salty tears flowed in a torrent across her cheek and the base of her nose. Tania wiped them away as best she could with the sleeve of her cardigan. Trying to gather her composure, she gave a final sniff and looked into her daughter's eyes.

"Well, I thought it had got lost, Daddy said he was going to leave me a birthday present before he went away with the other soldiers. He had an argument that night with some other men and – "

She choked with the memory of when she had found a policeman on her doorstep late at night that there had been a fracas, and he had been stabbed in the heart by an unknown man.

Her hand shook as she slipped off the box lid and saw nestling on top of a small velvet cloth was the eternity ring she had pleaded for.

Another small note lay inside.

Tenderly she extracted the piece of paper from its hiding place and began to sob uncontrollably.

The note fell from her shaking hands. On it was written only a few words in her husband's handwriting... "If you are reading this — I could not have made it back in time, to remove this note before I gave you your gift. Look after our daughter, Tan."

"Love you forever — forever by my side. Until we meet again, my darling."

Tania wiped the tears from her face and scooped up her daughter into her strong arms. "Silly, silly, Mummy, eh? It's just a bit of paper that reminded me of your dad and how much he loved us."

She spotted something behind Stacy in the wall mirror that faced the wardrobe. Hanging slightly down from the top was a locket that no doubt still had the rest of the chain attached. Lifting the child into the air near the side of the wooden piece of furniture, Tania grunted with the effort. "Hey up, pee-wee, guess what I found?"

Stacy squealed with joy as she grabbed the missing item of jewellery, raising it triumphantly in a cupped fist. "Look Mummy! Daddy must have been playing hide and seek." The child tenderly put a small hand on her mother's cheek. "He didn't reckon on our girl power though, did he, eh, Mum?"

A fresh flow of tears began falling in crystal rivulets down Tania's cheek once more. She sniffed and smiled, "Yup, it's gonna take more than a missing necklace to bring us down. Now where have you hidden Ken's missing leg?"

The Lonely Road
© 2023 Martin Radford

Mack watched as the milkman's float buzzed intermittently along the narrow street.

First stopping at Mrs. Dixon at Number Three, Ted Butler loped towards the rear of the boxy vehicle. Taken with a practised swoop, he had one bottle of sterilised in one hand and a particularly fruity bottle of crushed orange and grapefruit with the other.

He confidently stepped over the abandoned bike lying on the gravel path. The angled handlebars nearly caught his apron as it swung with the rhythm of hips. Placing each bottle carefully into the aluminium crate at the corner of the doorstep, he stooped down to retrieve a tube of rolled paper from the empty bottle waiting for collection. Unfurling the note and reading the contents, he grinned as he looked furtively around, trying to determine whether any nearby curtains were twitching.

No one. Not one moved.

Ted stood tall as he whacked the copper knocker against the solid wooden door. Out of the corner of his eye, he saw

Sally Dixon briefly peer through partly angled slats of the blind in the living room. Just as quickly, she disappeared.

Hearing the rustle of door chains being removed. Ted stood back and twisted the peak of his cap to a jaunty angle. He waited for the door to open enough for him to slip inside. The door then slammed shut as a girlie-giggle wafted outside.

Mack's refocused attention was drawn towards Number Six as Richard Hill lightly kissed his wife, Jean, goodbye. She stood smiling in her velvet red dressing gown wrapped tightly around her, trying to pretend that she couldn't feel the prickle of the cold against her skin as she watched Richard saunter down to the kerb.

Richard climbed into his black Peugeot 206. Ignoring his shivering wife, he deliberately waited for the window heater to demist before pulling away. Jean waved him off, waiting until he was out of sight before wiping an errant salty tear from her blackened left eye.

On either side of the road, refuse waste operators violently drag individually numbered green wheelie bins. Each man looks briefly inside at the contents to ensure council-defined parameters have been adhered to before emptying them.

Luckily for the inhabitants, today was not the day when nonconforming trash bins would be abandoned where they stand, leaving the poor owners to guide them gently back to their property, shaking their heads in disbelief at the cruel decision made by the operative concerned.

A feeling flowed through Mack the milkman, momentarily diffusing his view of life as it passed him by. He ignored the intrusion.

An old Ford Fiesta pulled up outside Number Twenty-four. A young man exited the car and leaned against the passenger door, possibly waiting for somebody or something to appear. The young man flicked his hand backwards and an errant hank of ebony hair fell into place on his greasy coiffure. Reaching into a pocket in his Levi's jeans, he extracted a small silver box. Releasing the retaining catch, he caught a cigarette between his puffy lips, igniting it with a lighter that had mysteriously appeared in his other hand. As the youth slowly inhaled the grey-blue smoke, his lips curled slightly in the corners.

A very mature-looking female had just appeared on the front doorstep of Number Twenty-Six. The curvature of her torso was obviously the focus of his attention. The young man leapt forward as he noticed that she was about to step onto an abandoned aluminium drink can. His intuition had been correct as she lost her balance and fell forward into the safety of his arms. However, something had changed about the woman's appearance. On the grass at the side of the footpath lay a rich auburn hairpiece. Her shiny pate was a testament to its missing cloak of hair follicles.

Mack saw the look of horror on the woman's face as she saw the errant wig imitating a fancy nest that had fallen from a tree. She patted herself on her head to prove to herself it was no longer where it should be. In a chivalrous act, the man drew her closer and wordlessly placed his lips on hers in a display of lust and love. Mack saw them mouthing each other words of endearment before happily climbing into his vehicle.

The forgotten hairpiece was soon under investigation by an inquisitive seagull. Satisfied with his find, the bird snatched it in his beak and flew onto a nearby roof, adding it to a half-built nest. Its mate stood nearby watching the natural events take place in their world of togetherness.

Mack again felt the strange sensation spreading within. Something was radiating towards him from somewhere near the bowels of the earth. He heard randomly spaced waves of pressure pulsing against his structure. At first, he could not understand what was happening until he realised they were soundwaves. They were just a lot slower than the audible voices and other noises he heard from the surface world around him. He concentrated on each pulse, carefully arranging them into a formula that could be identified as a speech pattern. His inner being listened to the words contained within.

"The feeling you are receiving and do not fully understand. It is not external but is being generated by yourself."

"This is a simple lament — to the ailing of the lonely road..."

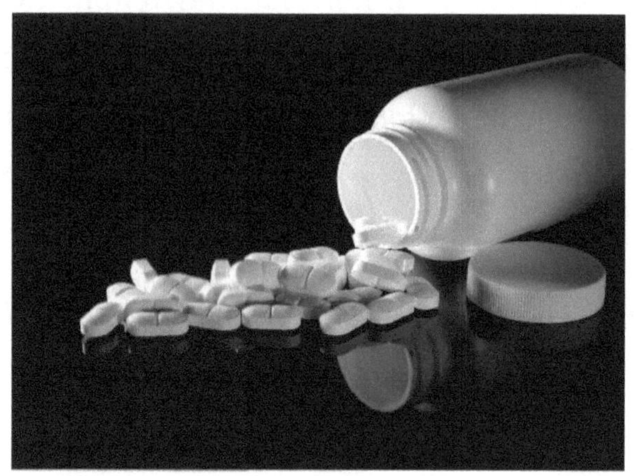

Image credit: Sprinter_Lucio
Pixabay

The Bittersweet Music of Life
© 2023 Martin Radford

Today *was* going to be Tilly's birthday but she had left George far behind in another time and place.

It all happened after a short bout with cancer, where every blow, had been completely below the belt. Her tenacity had managed to make the predicted seven remaining days stretch into a whole month of focus and forethought. In disbelief, they watched what was unfolding in the inevitable destruction of both of their lives.

Six months previously, she had been active, happy, and still deeply in love with her husband of thirty-seven years.

They had originally met in downtown Austin, where she would sing professionally in whichever venue had deigned to hire her amazing voice. Tilly had an unusual vocal range of five octaves, similar to Mariah Carey. So, the odds of her becoming an instant success should have been weighing heavily in her favour. The trouble was, she had not been born in the U-S of A. Wolverhampton, England, didn't resonate with any leading producer or discerning artist working in Austin, which had a reputation for being one of the top ten cities in America for all genres of music.

When she arrived for the first time at Austin-Bergstrom Airport, her new agent, Robert Heston, the third, had met her at the international gate of the Barbara Jordan Terminal. His well-tended walrus moustache instantly put her on her guard. The slow Texas drawl didn't instil confidence in either his ability or personality. Tilly later admitted her concerns to friends, of when she had first seen the heavily tanned man, dressed smartly in a brown checked business suit.

George himself had been an in-demand, session musician. Well-known for his ability to play a range of instruments, he was always in employment, often taking the part of four or more absent professionals. Studio producers definitely enjoyed value for money in those times. Naturally, Robert Heston, the third, had insisted that Tilly's demo tape, should be, as he put it, "bare bones."

Therefore, George had been the obvious choice to be brought in to work with the studio's meandering and confusing ethos of "keep 'em keen, don't spend any money, be a hero to the mean." With rapid appreciation of each other's chemistries, the two artists found themselves coalescing into one special entity. Even the guys in the control room appreciated that they were witnessing something special and devoted an extra two hours of studio time free.

After the success of their demo tape, they would spend most of their time professionally in the same studio. Robert Heston was happy. They were making him money as well as ensuring cheap studio time. It was a win-win situation as far as he was concerned.

It soon became obvious to not only each other and anyone observing their undivided devotion to their craft couldn't fail to miss the growth of personal interaction either.

Sealing the knot after a short trip to Las Vegas cemented the fact they were destined to spend the rest of their lives together. They purchased a small two-bedroom condo in historic Clarksville, ,where together they had built a home.

Naturally, they tried for children. However, Tilly had discovered after multiple examinations that she had medical issues, sadly preventing her ability to bear children. They also discovered they would not be eligible to adopt, as they had not yet applied for permanent citizenship in the United States. On work visas, they felt they would be fulfilled if they could still be around children in some capacity.

A solution of sorts was part-time teaching posts at a local private school. Tilly would spend as much time as she could tutoring promising five to eleven-year-old individuals or multiple pupils within a choir. The establishment was quite progressive and possessed, amongst other things, a media recording studio within the sprawling premises.

George was instantly in his element, with his intimate knowledge and experiences. He was able to help older children navigate their way around the technology and instruments involved.

Eventually, they had accumulated enough money to buy a large cottage in rural Somerset back in the United Kingdom. They also were able to transfer their activities to a UK branch of the American private school. The rest of their spare time would be spent in the studio they had built in the converted barn outside,

As the years passed by, their love for each other continued to grow. They would sit next to each other in the library, where they would write lyrics for their expanding portfolio. Self-publishing from their premises, they made a fortune and bypassed the middlemen.

Eventually, retirement beckoned. Sewing and embroidery became Tilly's escape from normal housework. George took to spending all of his time in the garden, nurturing fruit, and vegetables, then sitting in the garden shed, composing, and playing new songs weekly. The new material would eventually make its way indoors, where he and his wife would record his creations together for posterity's sake.

Their happiness snapped in two when Tilly received a devastating phone call from the doctor's surgery after a routine check-up, where she told the GP that she had been feeling out of sorts lately. The last thing they had expected to hear was how aggressive the cancer was likely to be.

Tilly's death was a certainty in a short amount of precious time. There was no wake; only George and a few close friends attended her funeral. After George had informed everyone, he wanted to mourn at home on his own.

Walking through the house, he stopped temporarily in the lounge where the palliative care workers had provided a comfortable air-cushioned bed for her final days. Beside the bed, he picked up a dark-coloured bottle and thrust it into his trouser pocket. Then, gently touching the soft pillow, where his wife had recently passed away, he breathed in deeply, fighting back a sob from somewhere deep in his soul.

Taking off his grey suit jacket, he draped it carefully on the bed. George then picked his favourite waxed jacket off the hook by the back door that led to the garden outside. Putting the jacket on, he slowly walked to his garden shed, looking around.

He felt a grim smile creep onto his face as he found himself admiring the neat rows of runner beans. Each plant had twisted around the support of several bamboo poles tied together and firmly pushed into the supporting soil. The shed door was never locked; he pushed it softly, watching it swing open silently on its well-oiled hinges. Familiar tools and airtight jam jars full of seeds greeted George. His eyes wandered lazily around the interior and sighed.

There had been a time when they had been so happy. Tilly would sit indoors, tinkering with her sewing machine and materials, while he was transported to another world, listening to the wind blowing cold outside. Their worlds were separate, but they were always emotionally together.

Suddenly feeling very alone, George remembered the bottle in his pocket and shook a handful of the capsules onto the wooden table next to his old armchair. He popped one onto his tongue and dry-swallowed it down. Tilly had taken them in her final days, no longer able to manage the pain wracking her frail body. She called them her "little friends."

Filling a kettle from the standpipe he had fitted himself; he twisted the valve on the gas bottle, lit the gas ring, and put the kettle on top. He then put his old mug on the table and spooned in coffee and powdered milk, reaching up to grasp a packet of ant powder from a sturdy shelf.

Tearing open the box, he walked over to the kettle and lifted the top off. The bereft man gave the box a little shake, before pouring a considerable amount of the pepper-like powder into the water. George then turned up the gas to its highest setting and sat back down in his chair.

Feeling the effects of the morphine beginning to take hold, he scooped up the rest of the tablets and popped them into his mouth. At the same time, the phosgene gas was pumping out of the kettle, filling the air with its deadly fumes. As he popped another handful of drugs into his mouth, George knew he would never wake up to feel his tortured lungs tearing themselves apart.

As George began to hallucinate, the kettle began to boil, the monotonous whistle growing in intensity.

All the dying man heard as he approached death was his wife singing in a choral duet with the kettle.

And then the silence came...

Image credit: StarGladeAdvantage
Pixabay

A Mandatory U-Turn

© 2023 Martin Radford

"Hubble bubble, toil and trouble," Morag cackled as she threw another struggling toad into the bubbling cauldron. With a swift swing of her wooden spoon, she discouraged a previously introduced ingredient to quit clinging to the pot's rim.

"This is NOT going to work!" she grumbled in frustration.

She wobbled slightly as she tried to display her anger by attempting to stamp a foot, an awkward task at the best of times while wearing high heels.

A happy-looking frog had finally managed to surmount the rim of the large cauldron. Turning back towards the animated fluid, he leapt into the air, achieving a double mid-air twist before splashing back into the water below. Surfacing a few seconds later, he lazily rolled onto his back and swam through the bubbles to join a pair of frolicking sheep eyes, enjoying the mild warmth surrounding them.

"Damn, and blast this government! This — is a step too far!" the green-haired witch screamed.

Morag and the rest of her coven had all received a red envelope sealed with an official-looking green frog's head the previous afternoon. She had taken the letter from the post cat and eagerly wandered back inside her hovel to tear it open with a long, red-painted nail. She then extracted the enclosed parchment and removed the creases with the flat of her hand on the old wooden table. Popping on her wire-framed reading glasses, she flicked her eyes over the content:

Dear Madam,

We wish you unwell from all of us here at the headquarters of 'Twitches for Witches.'

It has come to our attention that the British government has been pushing for even greater austerity measures. In clause 102, section 5, it states: 'After recommendations from governmental scientists, we can confirm that we must now take extreme measures to reduce energy consumption.'

Forthwith, combined with any other 'with's' that may have been accidentally withdrawn, we declare that heating any liquid above 40 degrees Centigrade will therefore be deemed illegal and really selfish, according to our newly created official 'Snowflake Department.'

Therefore, ANYONE that is found to have broken this edict (and this includes any females purporting to be witches), will be put on a plane and banished to Rwanda.

"What the flipping heck is this country coming to?" Morag screamed. She felt an insistent tapping on her shoulder. Turning to face the interruption, the witch came face to face with a tall handsome skeleton.

"Oh, hello, Slim. I didn't hear you creeping up behind me. What can I do for you?"

Slim popped a couple of large glass marbles into his eye sockets before answering the witch standing before him. He also had a copy of the same letter in one bony claw and was attempting to read, what he described as the small print at the bottom of the page.

"Sorry about this Morag, but I dropped my marbles onto a stone floor yesterday." He placed what she assumed was a forefinger onto the left circular piece of glass acting as a lens. He gave a little poke and one green clear dobber popped out with a muted plop, falling into his other hand already formed into a cup.

"Look, my faux eyeball appears to have a crack..." He held the orb between two fingers and offered it to Morag for confirmation of the suspected damage. "It's a god-damned disaster. If I could make a guess. I'm hoping for the answer to our dilemma. Could it maybe be somewhere within the small print?"

Morag twisted the eyeball between her fingers. "Well, unless the magic words are 'Made in China', I would have to say — Nope, I can't see any other writing within the marble, let alone on the document itself. I admit the crack, I suppose, would be distracting if you were riding a broom or something..." she pondered.

Without a word, Slim took the alleged faulty eyeball back and re-installed it into its socket. He tried to look serious, but the best he could manage was a blank look, so he simply sighed.

"Look, we need to take on the British Government on this. It will affect your and my livelihood. Admittedly, mine is going through a bit of a dead patch — at the moment." Slim punched the air, awaiting laughter responding to his intentional pun, "But we need to stand together in principle — eh?"

Slim waited a couple of seconds for a response from Morag. Seeing that the witch was not ready to commit to any opinion just yet, he realised that she still had no idea what he was blabbering about.

They were both disturbed from continuing their thought-provoking conversation as a large bang from somewhere on the roof caught their attention. Morag pointed an accusing wagging finger towards the ceiling.

"If that is you, Tiffany Green, might I suggest you use the landing pad in front of the house the next time you decide to visit?" The sound of squawks and screeches interrupted any reply that Tiffany was likely to attempt.

"Scritch and Scratch have just entered the vulture mating season, and they will not be best pleased if you have disturbed them." Slim and Morag waited for confirmation that the person on the roof had heard her warning.

A hole appeared in the ceiling, revealing a brazen young witch with mauve hair covered in feathers. They watched as she floated down through the gap on a pillar of green smoke. Her fingers wiggled up and down, allowing her to land near the non-bubbling cauldron. Tiffany stood fascinated whilst she watched the adventurous frog perched on the rim, now attempting a double backflip with panache.

"Bravo," she said in a deceptively deep voice. The frog responded with a shy nod in reaction to the unbidden compliment. Tiffany flicked a chunk of her coloured hair, shading her right eye and revealing a pirate patch decorated with a winking yellow smiley. The emoticon slowly opened one closed eye, revealing a ghastly red pupil staring evilly at Slim and Morag.

Morag and Slim leaned slightly forward and stared back with gusto.

Tiffany raised an eyebrow, intrigued by their reaction. She caught her reflection on the blade of an exceptionally sharp knife hanging from a piece of leather cord. Momentarily, her lips parted as she recognised the reason for their freshly adopted attitude. She cackled in amusement as she flicked the hair back over the pirate patch, obscuring the glare of the smiley. "Don't mind him. He is sulking because I am fresh out of boiled-rat for his breakfast, and he had to put up with Special K instead."

Tiffany noticed the questioning look from Morag and tilted her head coquettishly to one side. "C'mon, it's not that bad a choice. A girl has to keep an eye on her figure, you know." She smoothly changed the subject. "Anyway, what is all this about a reprisal from the masses?"

Slim looked guiltily at Morag's pursed lips about to ask the pointed question about his forgotten discretion. He needn't have bothered.

"Yay, have you organised some trouble, Slim? Will there be uncomfortable government officials with sticky, starched collars present?"

Morag gripped and pulled up her long skirt, revealing a hairy pair of legs, as she began to jig excitedly on the spot.

Slim flashed his teeth, "Those are good questions and the answer is most assuredly a big fat yes to both!" He tried unsuccessfully to emulate Morag's dancing style, only managing to achieve a good impression of Mike Oldfield's 'Tubular Bells,' as he rattled his hollow bones against each other. The skeleton finally abandoned the attempt when he noticed a group of rats headbanging in the corner of the room.

Morag and Slim looked across towards Tiffany, who was whistling a jolly little tune as she tickled the tummy of the appreciative frog on the cauldron rim.

Tiffany looked up, "Ahh, you have both finished re-enacting Saturday Night Plague, I see. Are we going to create some mischief now? I just heard a couple of squadrons of our comrades land outside a few moments ago."

Morag rushed towards the fireplace and lifted down her favourite sporty broom. She headed straight towards the doorway, followed closely behind by Tiffany and Slim.

Close to two hundred broom engines were being noisily revved by their owners. Tiffany whistled, and her broom immediately flew down from the roof. She lifted her skirt and sat astride before tapping the broom to initiate readiness for take-off.

Morag climbed on her own steed and waited for Slim to occupy the rear seat. She looked back towards the skeleton, her eyebrows shaped into a V. "Just one rule for anyone riding as a pillion on my broom. Don't hold me around the waist if the flight gets a bit bumpy — Tough. Try it just once, buster, and I will knock your block off."

Slim nodded his head in acknowledgement.

With a massive roar, the coven lifted off the ground, leaving behind only a cloud of sparkling dust as proof they had ever existed.

The British public watched the evening news on television, aghast at the spectacle of thousands of flying witches from around the United Kingdom converging on the roof of the Houses of Parliament.

Anchorman Steve Scott described the gathering as looking extremely ugly. Tiffany took particular umbrage with his statement and cursed him with a bloating spell. Which wouldn't have been too bad, apart from the croaking he had developed before hopping back into the outside broadcast van.

Scenes of pandemonium ensued as witches dropped stink bombs and other smelly items onto the heads of screaming members of parliament. A plague of frogs invaded the Hallowed Hall's rest areas. Unspeakable creatures that swam in glasses of members' pints and cocktails were the final straw.

Enough was enough: an immediate vote for a mandatory U-turn regarding Clause 102, section 5 passed in record time.

As the speaker of the house announced the decision to the house, the witches simply disappeared.

Ten short minutes later, somewhere over Brixton town, a skull was seen heading towards the earth. Mysteriously, the rest of the skeleton was never found. However, reports told of a male voice screaming pathetically as it fell.

"Sorry!!!"

Image credit: Gorkhs
Pixabay

A Slit in Time

© 2023 Martin Radford

Melissa yawned slowly and rolled over onto her side. She stretched out her legs and felt the warm rays of the sun completely loosen her tight muscles. She allowed herself to relax even deeper and felt her fifth appendage wrap tenderly around her slender waist.

Something buzzed closely around her ears, disturbing her feeling of self-satisfaction with the world around her. Melissa consciously flicked her ears rapidly, hoping to deter an unplanned stopover from an unwanted guest.

Today had so far been totally perfect. She had managed to couple that Tomcat down the street. He had always leered at her as she had haughtily padded past the dustbin, where he usually spent most of the day asleep on the lid.

She lifted a paw to her head and scratched at her pinna gland, gently passing her paw over her ear to clean the detritus that had collected from the air. It was still a bit sore around that area due to the treatment she endured last month. The fear that she might have cancer of her ceruminous gland was not something Melissa had ever contemplated when she was younger.

The wait for the results seemed to last half a lifetime, and she was sure she had another grey hair appear due to the worry. But the relief of finding it was not life-threatening and could be treated with a course of drops was offset by how uncomfortable she felt during the process. Often Melissa thought it would have been easier and less painful to just accept her condition, it was her ears after all. But now she was through the other side, and that idea now just seemed so silly.

She left home early this morning for a 'spot of hunting' across the road onto the Old Rec.' Pouncing onto unwary rodents kept her entertained for a few hours before she decided to take a quick nap in the sun.

Now fully refreshed, she stood up and stretched in one easy movement.

Melissa felt a strange tingling in her whiskers; they were feeling particularly sensitive at this point in time, more than they usually were, due possibly to the after-effects of the medication. A shudder passed down her spine as she remembered the implications of not continuing the medicinal course. She looked around quickly to try to identify its source. Sometimes Melissa briefly wished she had been born a canine, with their enhanced sense of smell.

But overall—she was happy as she was, and content with a feline coexistence with humans.

Speaking of which, it should now be time for Mrs. Wilkins down the street to be putting out some choice tidbits of meat for Munty, a resident Alsatian living in a kennel outside the property.

Melissa sorted him out at an early age with a quick swipe of a clawed paw at the snout. Now, as soon as the dog spotted her out of the corner of his eye. He would rapidly shuffle backwards into the kennel—letting her have her fill from his bowl until she was replete before he dared emerge again to consume the remains.

Purring contentedly at her visceral thought of the pleasure to come. She put her paws parallel in front, preparing for a final stretch for the short journey to come.

Melissa never had time to feel even a twinge of disappointment, as the rear half of her torso instantly vanished, only to be replaced by a heavy leather boot instead.

Without the balance of her rear half, the corpse of the cat teetered forward, with internal organs ejected from the now unenclosed rib cage.

"Fuck," exclaimed an annoyed female voice.

It was followed by a gloved hand reaching down to wipe the bodily fluids and accompanying detritus from her footwear.

The woman, dressed in black, put her hand on her hips as she surveyed her surroundings, then looked back down at the remains of the cat named Melissa.

She wrinkled her nose at the gruesome sight. "Sorry kitty but time travel can be a bitch. You were just occupying the wrong place at the wrong time." Emma Taylor felt the tight corners of her mouth begin to elevate, as she amusingly appreciated the expression she had just offered the feline cadaver. "Yeah, definitely the wrong time…"

Acknowledgements

I am Vicky Armstrong; I am the chair and one of the authors. I write this on behalf of the Bexhill Writers group.

The BWG was founded forty-five years ago, and we still follow the format established in 1978. We meet once a month to share work 'sparked' by a pre-selected title. We hope you enjoy reading our stories as much as we have enjoyed writing them.

I should like to thank Michael Paul Hurd of Lineage-Independent Publishing for taking us under his wing and turning our very disparate pieces of work into this anthology, "Pebbles on the Beach." Mike also handled the myriad of administrative tasks associated with making this compilation ready for publication in both print and digital formats.

A thank you too, goes to Patricia Donoghue who cajoled and strong-armed us into producing our stories on time and in sufficient quantity – herding cats doesn't come close to describing the process! Well done Pat.

And finally, I should like to thank all the members of the Bexhill Writers Group who contributed to our anthology, three of whom are previously published authors in their own right.

Thanks go to Edna Akim, Beryl Doig, Brian Langley, Pat Reilly, Allan Tipping, Martin Radford, and Patricia Donoghue. Without their willingness to expose their work to public gaze, there would be no book.

www.ingramcontent.com/pod-product-compliance
Lightning Source LLC
Chambersburg PA
CBHW030957190726
48285CB00004BB/1342